SEVEN
HOTEL
STORIES

LEIGH TURNER

Copyright © 2019, 2022 Leigh Turner

The right of Leigh Turner to be identified as the Author of the Work has been asserted by him in accordance with the Copyright, Designs and Patents Act 1988.

Apart from any use permitted under UK copyright law, this publication may only be reproduced, stored, or transmitted, in any form, or by any means, with prior permission in writing of the publishers or, in the case of reprographic production, in accordance with the terms of licences issued by the Copyright Licensing Agency.

All characters in this publication are fictitious and any resemblance to real persons, living or dead, is purely coincidental.

About the Author

LEIGH TURNER IS a writer and former British ambassador to Ukraine and Austria. He grew up in Nigeria, Lesotho, Swaziland and England and attended Cambridge University.

In 1979, Leigh hitch-hiked through 27 states of the continental US. His diplomatic career took him to Vienna, Moscow, Kyiv, Berlin, Hong Kong, Washington D.C., St Helena, Buenos Aires, Beijing, Tokyo, Samarkand, Istanbul and Las Vegas.

In Berlin, Leigh took four years off diplomacy to look after his two children and became a travel writer for *The Financial Times*. You can find the results at his **rleighturner.com** blog. His other books include the Berlin thriller *Blood Summit*, his satirical thriller *Eternal Life* and his Istanbul thriller *Palladium*. Leigh's next project is a diplomatic handbook, *The Hitch-Hiker's Guide to Diplomacy*.

Author's Note

THESE STORIES ARE published in chronological order. The first three take place in a luxury hotel in the historic capital of Tatiana's beautiful but economically not yet fully developed homeland. The fourth, *The White Blouse*, is set in another country in the same region. *Gents* takes place in a resort hotel in Florida; and *Ask for Scarlett* and *The Three Heads* in an Ultra-Platinum branded super-luxury establishment in the remotest, wildest and ruggedest corner of Tatiana's country. None of these locations, for obvious reasons, can be identified.

I apologise for the occasional grammatical errors that creep into Tatiana's narrative voice, particularly in the earlier stories. Tatiana was a keen and brilliant student in her small village far from the historic capital of her beautiful homeland; but her school was, sadly, starved of funds. As the *Hotel Stories* proceed, Tatiana's English improves, although she is hampered by the fact that few of the international staff who work in her hotel chain are native English speakers themselves.

Contents

1. Britches	1
2. The Two Rooms	37
3. The Swedish Woman	55
4. The White Blouse	103
5. Gents	135
6. Ask for Scarlett	167
7. The Three Heads	200

To my parents

SEVEN HOTEL STORIES

1. BRITCHES

03.00

'The music is too loud.'

'I beg your pardon, sir?'

'You are kidding me, right?' The customer in the dressing gown peers at my name badge. 'Tatiana.'

'No, sir, of course I am not kidding you. But I cannot hear you too good.'

The man is narrowing his eyes. I think he is deciding whether it is worth being angry with someone so unimportant as me.

'OK Tatiana. You can't hear me because the music is too loud. Is that correct?'

'Yes, sir.'

'And this is a five-star hotel, right? With five-star prices?'

I do not know what a five-star hotel is or what five-star prices are, but I know that the man in the dressing gown is a customer so I agree with him. 'Yes, sir.'

'And do I pay five-star prices to be woken up by a disco at 3 a.m?'

'No, sir.'

'So will you please get them to turn the music down, or even off? Now?'

'Yes, sir.'

I turn around before he can say anything else and enter

the Dionysus Bar, which we call inside our hotel the BLV, for Basement Luxury Venue. The customer cannot follow me because the door to the BLV is guarded by Nigel, our Duty Security Manager, and two of his famous assistants with legs like tree trunks. In my opinion they have brains like tree trunks also, although no-one says this to them.

I am guessing that the customer in the dressing gown is not invited to the event in the BLV, even though he is coming from a rich western country. This is maybe one reason why he is so upset about the noise.

I also am not an invited guest. I am coming from a poor village far from the historic capital of our beautiful country. But I can enter because I work in the food and beverages team of our hotel. It is my job tonight to welcome guests and make sure they have their first drink within thirty seconds of arriving in the BLV.

The normal service standard for providing guests their drinks when they enter the Dionysus Bar is one minute, because this is a Luxury Venue and all our customers are special.

But tonight, we are serving the drinks a whole thirty seconds faster than normal. This is because tonight's party is a birthday celebration for a customer who is even more special than the others and it is important that we do everything in our power to make him happy.

Before I am entering the BLV, the music is loud enough that I am not being able to hear the customer in the dressing gown. Now I am inside, it is so loud I am touching my ears to see if they are bleeding and I am wondering if perhaps I will never hear any customer, or anything else, ever again.

But the condition of my ears is not important because the request from the customer in the dressing gown to turn the music down, or even off, has put me in a difficult position.

Inside the Dionysus Bar, maybe eighty people are partying. Partying is a new word which I have learned in English since I started working in this hotel three weeks ago. What it means in the Dionysus Bar is that some women wearing small red thong-type underwear, red high-heeled shoes and nothing else are standing on bistro tables moving their bodies in time to the too-loud music.

I am hoping that these bistro tables are fixed to the floor or there may be an accident.

The guest women, who are not standing on the tables, are wearing what I am learning to call designer clothing. This is a funny name because so far as I can see all clothing must be designed by somebody. The women in this designer clothing are standing in groups around other bistro tables and drinking tall thin glasses of a drink called Dom Perignon. I have not tried this drink but have been serving it to the women all night on trays which we have been told we must not drop because they are made of solid silver.

More women, also wearing the so-called designer clothing, are dancing on the floor near the bistro tables. They seem to be smiling at each other, but it is hard to be sure. This is because many of them have strange, tight faces with sharp noses and big lips and it seems that any other expression except a smile may make their skin burst apart with the effort.

The fact it is hard to tell if the women are really smiling is a problem for me because I need to find someone friendly to ask about turning the music down, or even off. So I am pleased when I see leaning against the bar a woman who is definitely smiling. In fact, her mouth is stretched into one of the biggest smiles I have ever seen.

The woman is wearing a long dress of which the top part is sticking closely to her upper body and seems to be made entirely out of silver, as shiny as the trays on which we are serving the drinks. Also, the parts of her upper body to which the silver is sticking closely are generous in the way which many men are liking. This means that at first I am not surprised that she is smiling.

I am also thinking that perhaps I have seen this woman somewhere before.

But when I am getting closer I am seeing that her eyes are not smiling.

In fact, I do not think that I have ever seen eyes so sad as hers.

For a moment, I am staring at the woman in the silver dress, even though this is not the professional behaviour I have been taught when I joined the hotel. I am even thinking that maybe I should ask her why she is so sad, even though this would be inappropriate.

But before I can speak to her, someone grabs me from behind and starts pulling me in the opposite direction.

A man is holding my wrist so hard that it hurts. I do not say anything because I am certain he is one of our guests and it would not be appropriate for me to shout in protest or to punch him in the face, as I might do back in my village. He is pulling me backwards behind him through the crowd as if he does not care if I might trip, or fall.

I try to relax and to focus on my task, which is to turn the music down, or even off. As I am being dragged I examine the people I am passing in case they can help me. Most of the men have more white hair than the women, but their noses are not so sharp and their lips are less stretched. They are dressed in black suits with black or white open-necked shirts and some of them have what look like small white moustaches. But when I look closer I see that they have dabs of white powder under their noses as if they have cut themselves shaving.

It is as if there has been a bad-shaving massacre in the Basement Luxury Venue.

We stop by another bistro table on which a person is dancing.

But this time the dancer is a man.

The man dancing on the bistro table is young and wears black trousers and a white shirt and is holding a bottle of the Dom Perignon drink in one hand. He too has a white moustache and his table is surrounded by a crowd of people who are dancing and shouting up at him and smiling as if he is the most wonderful man they have ever met. Actually, he is dancing well and in time with the music and with a lot of energy and he is shouting back at the people around him.

Of course, I cannot hear what anyone is saying because the music is making me deaf, perhaps for ever. But slowly I begin to understand what the dancing man and the people around him are shouting.

They are shouting 'Louder! Louder!'

I am thinking again that probably these are not people I can ask to turn the music down, or even off.

The man who is holding my wrist begins to say something to the man dancing on the bistro table. At first the man on the table does not notice and goes on shouting 'Louder! Louder!' and I see that his white moustache goes all the way to the end of his nose.

Then suddenly he is bending down and shouting 'Yes! Yes! Yes!' and someone is pushing a chair into the back of my legs and someone else is pushing me up onto the table where I am forced to grab hold of the dancing man's waist to stop myself falling back down to the floor.

Of course, there is not room on this table for one person, let alone two, and I am wondering again how firmly the table is fixed to the ground. But the man is pulling me close to him to make use of what little space there is and I can feel his lips on my ear and I am thinking maybe he is going to kiss me and then I feel his slimy tongue inside my ear and I am feeling sick. Then for a moment the tongue is gone and I hear him speaking in my own language.

'Hey, pretty waitress,' he says. 'It's time for you to...'

Actually, I do not wish to repeat what he says it is time for me to do because I am not used to saying these words or even hearing them. Also, I am thinking that to stand on a bistro table with this man, even without doing the things he is talking about, is inappropriate.

I am also thinking that my chances of turning the music down, or even off, are not looking good; and that the customer in the dressing gown is going to be disappointed.

Because the man who is sticking his tongue in my ear is the owner of the hotel, Mr Minas, and this is his birthday party.

I, on the other hand, am a waitress. I have been working in the hotel for only three weeks. It is not my birthday.

In addition to our hotel, Mr Minas is owning: our country's largest chain of gas stations; our monopoly car-import business; our steel plant; our mobile telephone company; our biggest bank; our oil- and gas-trading company; a university named after himself; and a hospital with world-class doctors named after his father-in-law, our democratic and incorruptible President Abdullatov.

I am owning, the last time I checked, nothing at all. Even the uniform I am wearing is belonging to the hotel and I must pay for this from my first month's wages, when I am receiving them at the end of next week.

The thought that I am not fulfilling the needs of my customer in the dressing gown, and the slimy feeling of the tongue of Mr Minas in my ear, and the fact I am not even owning the clothes I am wearing, make me feel sad.

So when I see the woman in the silver dress looking up at me with her awful eyes I find that my cheeks are wet with tears.

Then things are getting worse.

I am feeling that something is pressing against me and when I am looking down I am seeing that the hands of Mr Minas are on his trousers as if perhaps he is thinking of opening them and taking something out.

At first I am thinking it is not possible that Mr Minas, the owner of our hotel and the son-in-law of our democratic and incorruptible President Abdullatov, will take something out of his trousers while standing on a bistro table in the Basement Luxury Venue. But then I am remembering that he is the owner of our hotel and many other things and already he is sticking his tongue in my ear and telling me to do something I do not wish to do or even think about. So perhaps he is thinking that in his own hotel, at his own party, he can do whatever he wants.

In my panic, I look around the room and see a small woman wearing high heels and the grey suit of a member of the hotel management standing at the entrance to the BLV with her head to one side, as if she is surprised by what she is seeing.

I have never seen this woman before, and I do not get a good look at her now because she is at once turning around and marching out of the BLV.

If I am honest I am a little bit disappointed by this because the way the woman in the high heels was observing the inappropriate scenes in the BLV had made me think that she might do something to help me in my trouble with Mr Minas, or that she might at least manage to turn the music down, or even off.

But I do not have long to be disappointed because the next instant the BLV is plunged into darkness. Also, the music is cut off completely.

All I can hear is the sound of people screaming.

Mr Minas seems as surprised by this as I am because he takes his tongue out of my ear and begins to say something and then we both are falling off the bistro table into thin air.

12.35

THIS IS THE first time that I am trying to serve drinks with only one hand and, if I am honest, it is not easy.

Pierre, the Director of Food and Beverages who until yesterday I have only ever seen from the back of a crowded room, is walking towards me with his straight back and small steps.

'My poor darling,' Pierre says. 'If only we could sue the brute.'

'The brute?'

'Monsieur Minus. They have told me he fell right on top of you. It is only good chance you were not impaled. Monsieur Minus has impaled nearly each one of our waitresses. He will be starting on the waiters next.' Pierre straightens his back a little more. 'Except I hope I have taught them higher standards.'

I stare at him. 'What is impaled?'

'Do not worry, Tatiana. You are safe with us.'

The voice comes from behind me. I turn around and see the same short woman who has been standing by the entrance of the BLV the night before. She is looking at me with her head to one side and her eyes are sparkling as if we are old friends.

'This is Ms N,' Pierre says. 'Our newly-arrived Director of Rooms, who is acting Hotel Manager this week. Also, a trained electrician.'

Pierre gives Ms N's full name; but I have removed it here because I know that Ms N does not like people saying good things about her in public.

'On the contrary,' she says. 'When the power failed in the BLV last evening I alerted the Head of Engineering at once. How could I know what was wrong?'

'The Head of Engineering was in bed,' Pierre is looking at me with his eyebrows raised. 'When he came to the hotel, he found a morsel of metal foil in the principal fuse-box. This had created a short-circuit for the power in the BLV. By the time it is fixed, the party is over. A catastrophe.'

Pierre is smiling in a way I do not understand.

'Pierre tells me that Mr Minas, the owner of our hotel, has broken your arm by falling on top of you.' Ms N is frowning. 'Was this cast applied by the world-class doctors at the President Abdullatov hospital?'

'Yes, Ms N,' I say.

Ms N taps the heavy plaster. 'Mr Minas should not have done this to you.'

'No, Ms N,' I say. I am wondering how a piece of metal foil could get inside one of the hotel fuse boxes, which have fat rubber seals.

'Pierre also tells me that you are a clever and reliable girl,' Ms N says, 'who he would be happy to lend to me to help organise our two big events this evening in the Sapphire Ballroom and the Diamond Ocean.'

'I will be pleased to help, Ms N,' I say. 'Unfortunately, for the next six weeks, I have only one arm.'

'Tatiana, do not worry,' Ms N says. 'For the jobs I need you to do, one arm will be plenty.'

15.00

WORKING FOR MS N is surprising. Up to now I have been thinking that I am busy working in the hotel as a waitress. But I understand now that I have not been busy at all, but simply carrying a few drinks from time to time. I am also beginning to understand that the work and ideas of some special people can make a hotel work much better.

Ms N is one of these people.

The Diamond Ocean is a large function room in our hotel. It is not an ocean and it does not contain any diamonds. But it is painted blue and when it is lit with the crystal lights and chandeliers which fill the ceiling and the walls, some of us in the hotel who have never seen a real ocean or real diamonds are saying that perhaps an ocean or diamonds could be looking something like this.

Right now, the Diamond Ocean is filled with staff from our hotel. They are moving tables, hanging decorations, bringing in rows of warming dishes and setting up serving stations.

'Tonight we have a big challenge.' Ms N seems calm, even though people are coming to her every few seconds to ask for a permission or an instruction. 'It is also, I hope, a big opportunity. The President of China is arriving at our hotel this evening and will be guest of honour at a banquet in the Diamond Ocean hosted by the democratic and incorruptible President Abdullatov.'

'Our democratic and incorruptible President Abdullatov is coming to the hotel?' I know my mouth is open but I cannot help this. 'This is an honour for us.'

'It is indeed an honour.' Ms N's mouth is not open. In fact, she is smiling a small smile. 'The democratic and incorruptible President Abdullatov is hoping that our Chinese friends will buy some of the fabulously rich agricultural land and ultra-modern factories of this country.' Ms N is still smiling. 'The two Presidents will sign a special agreement for the sale at the banquet tonight.'

'But who is owning this land and these factories now?' I say.

Ms N's eyes sparkle. 'Pierre told me you were clever, darling,' she says. 'Of course, it is the democratic and incorruptible President Abdullatov himself, and his family, and his closest friends, who are owning everything in this country including the valuable properties which he is selling to the Chinese tonight. So it is important we make sure that the conditions are one hundred per cent perfect at the signing ceremony.'

Ms N is looking at me with her inquisitive expression and for a moment I am wondering what these one hundred per cent perfect conditions might be. But I do not have much time to think about this because she is leading me through a side door into a long service corridor.

'You see, Tatiana, the Diamond Ocean banquet for the two Presidents is not our biggest challenge tonight.'

I examine the service corridor, which I am seeing for the first time. Here, too, there are many hotel staff rushing in every direction.

'Our biggest challenge,' Ms N says, 'is the Combined Burns Night and St Patrick's Day Ball in the Sapphire Ballroom. To this we are expecting three hundred guests, most of them men from the foreign business community in our city, with their wives, or maybe partners. They have ordered enough alcohol for twice as many people. Also, they are planning a show, which is complicated and can go wrong. It is important that everything runs smoothly in both rooms. I want you to help me with this tonight.'

I look at Ms N. 'Is there not a risk that two big events happening at the same time so close together could interfere with each other?'

'Thank you, Tatiana, that is an excellent point,' Ms N says. 'But we plan to erect sound barriers in the service corridor to ensure there is no risk of our events disturbing one another. This will be good practice for our engineering team. It will allow us to test our facilities at maximum capacity and boost our bottom line.' Ms N smiles. 'In my view, every risk is also an opportunity. I hope we will prove this tonight.'

17.45

I HAVE NEVER before met a man who is wearing a skirt. But for me this is not a problem as I believe people should be allowed to wear whatever they wish. Also, the skirt is showing off the man's legs. These legs are looking healthy and well-shaped and are covered in thick red-coloured hair, like fur.

'The Red Hot Chilli Pipers are playin' at eight while we pipe in the haggis,' the hairy, shapely-legged man is saying to Mr Minas in a strong accent. 'That's the national dish of Scotland.' He winks at me and I see that he has beautiful green eyes. 'Sheep's heart, liver and lungs, you'll love it. Leprechaun Blitz are on at nine. After that it's the raffles and whisky-tasting. At eleven it's all go with the Long-Legged Lovely Lassies and our Super Climax event. Then the disco starts.'

'Long legs? Lassies? Super Climax?' Mr Minas is finding it hard to speak. 'You will have naked girls?'

'Mr Minas!' The man with the hairy, shapely legs strokes his chin. 'Our Combined Burns Night and St Patrick's Day Ball is a classy event. There will be no naked girls. But check this out.' He picks up the hem of his skirt and raises it a little.

I am thinking that the man in the skirt is talking mostly to Mr

Minas and is not paying me too much attention. So, when he raises the hem of his skirt I am taking the opportunity to examine a little bit more of his shapely, hairy legs, since I am expecting that such an opportunity may not come along too often.

'You may think ma' legs are cute,' the man in the skirt is saying to Mr Minas, 'but wait 'til you see –'

Suddenly, the man turns to me. 'Are you tryin' to look under ma' kilt?' He has a beautiful smile, although I am thinking I am perhaps not the first woman he is smiling at today, or the last. 'Because if you're lookin' without askin', it's rude. And if you're askin', you'll have to ask very nicely indeed!'

For a moment, his green eyes look into mine and I think maybe I want to kiss him, although of course this would be inappropriate behaviour.

But before I can worry too much about what is inappropriate, the man has turned back to Mr Minas.

'She's wonderin' whether it's true about the britches, right? Well, it is. But the point of my showing the lovely Tatiana ma' legs is, wait 'til you see the Long-Legged Lovely Lassies. Their legs are nearly as good as mine, but not so hairy. Their kilts are a bit shorter than standard. An' when it comes to britches - I trained 'em myself!' He roars with laughter.

I am not sure what these britches are, or what the man with the hairy, shapely legs thinks I am wondering about them, or why he is laughing. But as he is a hotel guest I smile and make the small panting noise which I know men like to hear when they make a joke, or actually, in many circumstances.

Mr Minas does not seem to recognise me from the night before, perhaps because last night my arm was not in a sling. He is watching the man with the hairy, shapely legs and I am thinking that he also is not sure what is so funny. But when he sees me smile and make the panting noise he starts to laugh so loudly that at first I am thinking he is maybe having a heart attack.

'Britches!' Mr Minas says between his laughing and his panting for air. 'You trained them yourself! Britches!'

'Or not,' the hairy-legged man says, and laughs again.

'No britches!' Mr Minas laughs even louder.

The two men are still laughing when I leave the Sapphire Ballroom. Even if I am not sure why britches are so funny, I am confident that preparations for the Combined Burns Night and St Patrick's Day Ball are under control.

This is the job which Ms N has given me, so I want to succeed in it.

In fact, I am thinking that I should always try to do what Ms N wants. One day, if I work hard, maybe I could be like her.

20.30

If today I am seeing my first man wearing a skirt, now it is seeming nearly normal.

The Combined Burns Night and St Patrick's Day Ball is crowded with men in skirts. Many other men are wearing green trousers and jackets and hats and socks and even shoes, as if perhaps someone is painting them before they come into the room.

Although most of the men are from foreign countries, many of the women who are the wives or perhaps the partners of the men in skirts and men in green are from my own country. Most of the women are young and are able to smile without difficulty. In fact, I am proud to see how beautiful they look. I am also noticing that many of the women are seeming younger than the men they are with, although it is hard to be certain when the men are wearing skirts and green trousers.

Also, the men are enjoying the drinks.

I have seen men drinking before. The men of my country are not afraid of alcohol. But in my country men are mostly drinking vodka, either from the shop or from their friends who are making vodka at home.

The men at the Combined Burns Night and St Patrick's Day Ball are drinking everything. I see them drinking wine, beer and vodka, one after another. In-between, they are drinking something called cocktails, which I have learned means taking from the store-room all the old bottles of strong spirits which no-one is drinking and mixing them together with ice and juice and sugar to hide the taste.

Also, there is a stand where women in tight red and black clothing and straight black hats, who are probably also from my country because they are tall and beautiful, are handing out glasses of a whisky drink called Johnnie Walker. Behind the stand, I see cases of the whisky drink piled up almost to the ceiling.

If I am honest, I am wondering if it will be enough. The men in skirts and green trousers are liking the Johnnie Walker, and perhaps also the women in the tight clothing, very much. Many of them are crowding around the stand and trying to grab as many glasses of the whisky drink as they can.

The women who are the wives or perhaps the partners of the men in skirts and green trousers are mostly grabbing glasses of cocktails at the other end of the room.

One reason the men and women are drinking a lot is that they cannot talk to each other. This is because on stage there are eight young men wearing skirts and playing musical instruments which are so loud I am reminded of the Dionysus Bar the night before. Most of the men are making a kind of music using a bag which they put under their arm and fill by blowing into a pipe. This is amplified by giant loudspeakers to make a noise like an out-of-control jet aircraft crashing into a home for cats.

The noise is so loud I am worrying when I go to visit the banquet for the President of China and our democratic and incorruptible President Abdullatov, which is happening in the Diamond Ocean just a few yards away on the other side of the service tunnel, that I will be able to hear the bags and pipes. But as instructed by Ms N, our engineering staff have built sound barriers down both sides of the tunnel and when I enter the banquet I cannot hear anything.

In fact, the first thing I notice is that the Diamond Ocean is silent except for the clinking of cutlery and glasses.

The second thing I see is that our democratic and incorruptible President Abdullatov is sitting at a table on a raised podium next to a man wearing glasses who I am guessing is the President of China.

Both the men are looking serious.

Maybe this is because they know that only if the banquet goes well will they be able to sign the special agreement to sell to the Chinese the fabulously rich agricultural land and ultra-modern factories which are belonging to President Abdullatov and his family and closest friends.

The agreement itself is sitting on a table at the front of the podium. I know this because I have helped our engineering team to place this table in the exact place which the advisers of the Chinese President and Ms N wanted. The table must be in full view of the hundreds of television cameras from China and from our own country and perhaps from some other countries which are massing at the back of the Diamond Ocean.

So far, I hope they are not filming, because this banquet is perhaps the most boring event I have ever witnessed in my life.

In fact, the whole room except for the podium and the space in front of it is filled with round tables of people eating a sixteen-course Chinese-style banquet prepared by the chef of our democratic and incorruptible President Abdullatov.

To eat this banquet is taking a long time.

I am thinking that everything in the Diamond Ocean is functioning tip-top, and I should return to the Sapphire Ballroom, when I see Ms N walking towards me.

Ms N is not alone. She is accompanied by the sad-eyed woman from the night before.

'Tatiana, how are you?' Ms N says.

'I am well, thank you, Ms N,' I say.

'Tatiana, I have a special request for you,' Ms N says. 'As

you know, Mrs Minas, or Ms Sofia as she prefers to be called, is the daughter of the democratic and incorruptible President Abdullatov. She is also the wife of the owner of our hotel, Mr Minas. Indeed, you may be interested to know that this hotel was a wedding gift from the President to Mr Minas.'

Suddenly I am understanding why I was thinking last night that I have seen the sad-eyed woman before, even though this was actually the first time I am seeing her. It is because she is resembling our democratic and incorruptible President Abdullatov, whose face I am seeing every day in the newspapers and on television and on posters and on statues and also most places I am looking in the Internet.

I am also understanding why Ms Sofia was sad last night to see Mr Minas, her husband and the owner of this hotel, behaving in an inappropriate fashion on the bistro table in the BLV, including with me.

On the other hand, I notice that Ms Sofia is tonight wearing a dress which is making the silver dress which she was wearing last night in the Basement Luxury Venue look dull and ordinary. In fact, tonight's dress seems to consist entirely of diamonds, which are somehow being stuck with invisible glue to those parts of her body which are generous in the way which many men are liking. From what I can see of those parts of her body which are not covered in diamonds, the whole of her body is in very fine shape indeed.

I am thinking that Ms Sofia should be happy that she is married to one of the richest men in our country; that her body is perfect; and even that the events we are organising tonight in the Diamond Ocean and the Sapphire Ballroom will make Mr Minas thousands more dollars.

So at first I am surprised to see that although the mouth of the wife of Mr Minas is still stretched into a huge, tight smile, her eyes are looking as sad as they were last night in the BLV.

Then I think of Mr Minas on the bistro table with his tongue in my ear. I remember his comments about the Long-Legged

Lovely Lassies and whether they would be wearing britches or dancing naked on stage. And I am starting to think that I, too, would be sad if I was married to Mr Minas.

'Ms Sofia is a brilliant woman,' Ms N is saying. 'I have been discussing with her several ways we could improve the running of this hotel, including a water feature in the lobby and a proper sushi restaurant.' Ms N purses her lips, which are not so large as those of Ms Sofia but make her look as if she is thinking about something funny or naughty. 'I am a lucky woman because I have studied at a famous hotel school in Switzerland. But talking to Ms Sofia helps me see that there are options open to hoteliers which are not taught even in the best hotel schools.'

I nod. Although I do not understand what Ms N is talking about, I see that she has her head to one side in the same way which I was seeing last night, before the lights went out in the BLV and I was rescued from the probing tongue of Mr Minas. So I am hoping that perhaps tonight also Ms N has a plan which will make things better.

Ms N turns to me. 'One thing I did learn in my hotel school is that to make any important change you need a strong team. What I have planned tonight may not be easy. But I hope it will be fun. Are you prepared to carry out some difficult instructions for me, Tatiana?'

I look into Ms N's face. Then I look again at Ms Sofia with her sad eyes.

'I want to be on your team, Ms N,' I say.

21.00

THE FIRST PART of my night's work for Ms N is simple. I am to take Ms Sofia to the Platinum Megastar lounge on the 20th floor and serve her one of our hotel's famous Megastar gin and tonic drinks.

I have never been to the Platinum Megastar Lounge before. In fact, I did not even know until today that it was existing. But I now learn that this is where the most honoured guests of our hotel chain are allowed to come and enjoy free drinks and snacks while they look out of the plate-glass windows at the historic capital of our beautiful country.

I quickly realise that for Ms Sofia this is not her first visit to the Platinum Megastar Lounge. In fact, she heads straight towards the bar area, where there is an open bottle of the Dom Perignon drink on ice. There is also some sushi prepared by our hotel's new Japanese chef, who I have not yet met; but Ms Sofia ignores this.

Instead, Ms Sofia takes from a freezer cabinet a bottle of gin made in a country called England, which is puzzling me because according to my history studies in my small village far from the historic capital of our beautiful country, no country called England has existed since 1707.

Ms Sofia clearly is not worried about the existence or non-existence of England because she takes from the shelf a glass of the type which the hotel has trained me to use only for beer and fills it nearly to the brim with the English gin from the freezer, which is so cold that the outside of the glass is covered at once with a thin layer of ice. Ms Sofia then adds to the gin a piece of lemon from a saucer; and pours into the glass a few tea-spoons of tonic water from a yellow bottle. There is so much freezing English gin and so little tonic that I see the tonic freeze into crystals as it is added.

Up to now I am thinking that Ms Sofia has forgotten that I am here. But when she has completed making the gin and tonic drink, she turns towards me and says: 'This is for you, Tatiana.'

I take the glass and watch as Ms Sofia mixes another drink for herself. Then we sit down on the black leather sofas which face the plate-glass windows.

This is a strange place for me to be when three weeks ago I was arriving in the historic capital of our beautiful country from my small village to start my job in the hotel and had never in my life seen a plate-glass window or a gin and tonic drink.

'Cheers,' Ms Sofia says.

'Cheers.' I raise my glass to hers and take a sip of the drink, which is tasting like cold, lemon-flavoured vodka. As I am feeling the freezing liquid descending my throat into my stomach I smile at Ms Sofia but she is still drinking from the glass.

At last Ms Sofia lowers her drink. The first thing I notice is that she has left half a circle of bright-red lipstick on the rim of the glass.

The second thing I notice is that Ms Sofia's eyes are no longer looking so sad as they were in the Diamond Ocean, or even so sad as they were in the BLV the night before. In fact, between her big stretched smiling lips I can see her teeth.

Ms Sofia's teeth are even and smooth and the cutting edges are capped with a red line of lipstick. In fact, it is looking as if Ms Sofia has just finished biting through something which has been bleeding.

Her glass of gin and tonic drink is half empty.

I am thinking that Ms Sofia's stomach must be frozen.

But when Ms Sofia puts her hand on mine, it is as warm as if she has been drinking a mug of our hotel's signature Megastar Hot Chocolate, rather than a giant ice-cold gin and tonic drink.

'Come on, Tatiana,' she says. 'Let's do this.'

22.15

PERHAPS I AM lucky. I do not know. But as a teenager growing up in my small village far from the historic capital of our beautiful country, I am having to drink many things which are maybe not very healthy. This includes our famous fermented mares' milk, a speciality of my rural cousins, which keeps for six months without refrigeration and which is tasting like paraffin mixed with iron filings.

This training in drinking substances of all kinds helps me to keep pace with Ms Sofia as she consumes more gin and tonic drinks, all of which she is mixing herself. The more drinks she is consuming, the less sad her eyes are becoming; and the more she is showing her teeth between her big stretched smiling lips. The tips of these teeth are becoming redder and redder as she is making trips to the ladies' room to refresh her make-up.

Ms Sofia does not seem affected by the alcohol, and I am thinking that perhaps she, too, has grown up in an area of our country where fermented mares' milk is one of the more healthy drinks available to our young people.

In fact, Ms Sofia is giving me some good advice as we are enjoying our gin and tonic drinks. She tells me that if people ask where I am from I should not say the name of our country, which is a new country which not too many people have heard of. Instead I should say I come from Ukraine.

'Our country is famous for its beautiful women, but only inside our country,' Ms Sofia says. 'Ukraine is famous around the world for its beautiful women. If you say you are from Ukraine, people will think you are even more beautiful than you are already.'

'But do I look Ukrainian?' I say.

'People in the old Soviet Union were always moving about and marrying each other,' Ms Sofia says. 'It is nonsense to suggest anyone in any of our countries is one hundred per cent Russian, or Ukrainian, or anything else. Also, there is a famous western song about Ukraine girls knocking you out. You can make a joke about this.'

I listen to Ms Sofia and think that she is wise. I would like to sit for hours with this woman who is the daughter of our democratic and incorruptible president and enjoy gin and tonic drinks with her.

But this is not what Ms N has told me to do.

So at half-past ten precisely, I rise to my feet.

'It is time for us to go downstairs now, Ms Sofia,' I say.

Ms Sofia looks up and shows her bright-red teeth. She is no longer looking sad. She is looking like a happy bear which has just finished eating a large, juicy animal. She rises slowly to her feet and stands up so straight, in her beautiful but in many places nearly non-existent diamond dress, that I am thinking I will fall in love with her myself if she is not already married to Mr Minas.

'I am ready,' she says. 'Thank-you, Tatiana.'

To say that Ms Sofia and myself are not badly affected considering the amount of gin and tonic drinks we have drunk is not the same as saying that we are not affected. It takes several minutes for me to guide Ms Sofia to the lift down from the Platinum Megastar lounge to the banqueting zone. Nor does the fact that my right arm is in plaster make it easier for me to steer Ms Sofia in the correct direction. It is also taking us a few moments to find the correct button in the lift.

It is while we are trying to find the button in the lift that I notice my telephone is ringing. I see that I also have two missed calls.

'Tatiana. How are you?' Ms N is sounding calm, as if she has not called me three times in the past five minutes.

'I am well, Ms N,' I say. 'I am in the lift with Ms Sofia.'

'That is good,' Ms N says, 'because it seems that the President of China has run out of things to say to the democratic and incorruptible President Abdullatov. The signing ceremony has been brought forward by ten minutes. You will need to be quick.'

'Yes, Ms N.' I am thinking that when I saw the man wearing glasses who I was guessing was the President of China with the democratic and incorruptible President Abdullatov two hours ago, they had run out of things to say to each other already. 'And Ms N?'

'Yes, Tatiana?'

'Ms Sofia is showing her teeth.'

'Good,' Ms N says. 'I think that will help.'

At the ground floor, I take Ms Sofia by her hand and lead her towards an unmarked door next to the lift.

Every day hundreds of our valued and special hotel customers are seeing this door, because it is only a few metres from the lobby. But none of them ever goes through it. This is because the door is what we call in the hotel business a SOD or staff-only door. This means it is one of the only doors in the hotel a guest will ever see which is not open; or made of glass; or with a room-number on it.

When we open the SOD Ms Sofia stops walking and puts her hand to her mouth. 'What is this place?'

'This is a service corridor,' I say. 'The staff are using it to move from one part of the hotel to another.'

'It smells horrible.'

'We are close to the kitchens,' I say. 'That is the smell of the haggis which they are having eaten earlier. It is sheep's heart, liver and lungs.'

'Please God, help me to escape from here.' Ms Sofia's face is pale.

We come to a swing door. Ms Sofia is right. I can smell something strange, although actually I am thinking it smells better than the fermented mares' milk which some of my rural cousins are making. When we enter the kitchen the first thing I am seeing is a row of glistening packages on trays, like the warm stomachs or entrails of animals which have only recently been killed.

A tiny oriental woman in a tall white hat, who I am guessing is our new Japanese chef, steps in front of us. In each of her hands she is holding a knife made of bright metal of a kind I have never seen before. I take a step back.

'They do not eat it!' The woman waves a knife at the glistening stomach-type packages. 'They order it. We cook it. My kitchen stinks. And then they do not eat it. What I do with this... product now? Is probably illegal in this country.'

Before I can reply, the tiny woman throws both knives up in the air.

If I am honest I am terrified because I have heard this Japanese chef has a bad temper and can quickly become angry. When she throws the two knives in the air I flinch, and hold onto Ms Sofia with my good hand, and watch as the knives rise, turning in the air, their blades gleaming in the bright kitchen lights.

I do not watch them for long.

There is a whirl in front of me and a thud and I see the little Japanese chef has somehow grabbed the two whirling knives out of the air by the handles and slammed one of them down into a glistening stomach-type package which is sitting on a wooden cutting board by the stove.

The knife stands up by itself on the cutting board. The stomach-type package splits open and out spills what I am guessing is the sheep's heart, liver and lungs about which the man with the hairy, shapely legs was talking earlier.

I hear a noise from Ms Sofia as if she is going to be sick.

'Where is the Super Climax cake?' I say. 'We need it quickly.'

The chef ignores me.

'You know what they serve the two Presidents?' she says. 'So-called sixteen-course Chinese-style banquet from Presidential palace. You hear that? Chinese-style? I do real Chinese banquet in my sleep. I meet that so-called Chinese-style chef, I kill him.' She weighs the other knife in her hand as if thinking how she can use it on the Presidential chef.

I think of Ms N telling me to hurry. 'The cake! Give me the Super Climax cake!'

'The cake? This is next disaster.' The Japanese woman points the knife across the kitchen. 'Is here. Please. Take away.'

Standing in the corner of the kitchen is the biggest food item I have ever seen in the hotel or anywhere else. At first, I am not sure what I am looking at but when I step closer I am seeing that it is indeed a huge cake, standing on a trolley. At the top of the cake in big letters are written the words *Super Climax* with a picture of a bottle of the Dom Perignon drink tilted at an angle with white foam spurting out. Round the bottom of the cake are pictures showing men in skirts and men wearing green trousers holding hands and dancing together.

'This not cooking,' the little Japanese chef says. 'For cooking, Ms N pay attention. She say, "do this, do that". Results fantastic. For this I like to work with Ms N. But for cake, Ms N say only "more cream on top, more cream, more cream". I think Ms N don't care about this cake.'

I see that there is indeed a lot of cream all over the cake except for the special place about which Ms N has told me. But I cannot see the top. The cake is taller than me.

I have a problem.

'How do I move the cake?' I point towards my broken arm, although from a safe distance as the chef is still holding one of her sharp knives. 'Will you help?'

'Am I porter? Am I waiter? Ask your friend.' The chef waves her knife towards Ms Sofia, who is holding onto the wall as if perhaps she is trying to stop it from falling over. 'Ask concierge. Ask bell-boy.'

I am again remembering Ms N telling me to be quick.

Who will help me?

The Sapphire Ballroom is full of noise. On the stage at the Combined Burns Night and St Patrick's Day Ball is a row of women wearing short skirts. I am guessing these are the Long-Legged Lovely Lassies, although so far as I can see, these girls are from my own country as they are tall and beautiful. Their legs are certainly long. In fact, the legs of the Long-Legged Lovely Lassies are so long that, when combined with the short skirts they are wearing, they are hardly wearing skirts at all.

I remember the man with the Scottish skirt and the green eyes and the hairy, shapely legs telling me that under such skirts people may be wearing britches and I look with interest to see what they may be. But I cannot see any britches at all.

Perhaps this is why, although the music where the Long-Legged Lovely Lassies are dancing is so loud that I am being reminded of the Basement Luxury Venue the night before, nearly every man in the room is crowded at the front, watching the dancing.

The stand for the whisky is closed. Behind it rises a neat stack of empty bottles and crates.

Most of the women who are the wives or perhaps the partners of the men in skirts and green trousers are clustered together at the other end of the room clutching glasses of the Dom Perignon drink. Maybe they are talking about the men.

It seems that everyone is having a good time, but in different ways.

I am looking for the man with the green eyes and the hairy, shapely legs. But as I am trying to fight my way towards the stage I feel a hand touch my shoulder.

The man with the green eyes and hairy, shapely legs has found me.

'The lovely Tatiana!' The hand is moving around my waist, so that it is, perhaps accidentally, brushing my breast. 'Ah've bin' lookin' for you! Where's our Super Climax cake?'

I look up at him and despite the perhaps-accidental touching of my breast I am again tempted to kiss him because his eyes are so green and his legs are so hairy and so shapely. Then I remember why I am here, and smile.

The situation is desperate.

Sometimes that is good.

I stretch up towards the man with the hairy, shapely legs and kiss him gently on the lips.

Then I reach under his skirt with my good hand.

I am not sure what I will find under this skirt, but from seeing the Long-Legged Lovely Lassies I have some idea.

I am knowing that this behaviour is inappropriate with a guest in our hotel, or with anyone else. But I need to help Ms N urgently.

Also, the man has beautiful hairy legs and green eyes.

Underneath the skirt, the situation is as I have expected.

'I need your help,' I say.

I kiss him again, and squeeze what I am finding under the

skirt. Then I am telling him the help I need.

For a moment, the man with the hairy, shapely legs is looking distracted, perhaps because he is thinking more about what is going on under his skirt than about my request for help. Then the big red eyebrows are going towards the ceiling.

'Tatiana,' he says. 'I think in the circumstances helpin' you with a cake is the least I can do.'

If I am honest, I am thinking that the man with the hairy, shapely legs has already tonight had one or more drinks. But in a moment, he is shouting orders; and has pulled three other men in skirts from the crowd of men who are watching the Long-Legged Lovely Lassies. All of this new group also have hairy, shapely legs. In fact, I am wondering whether this is because men with hairy, shapely legs are enjoying wearing a skirt more than men with legs which are not so hairy or shapely; or whether it is because wearing a skirt makes a man's legs more hairy and shapely.

I walk with the four men in skirts towards the kitchen. Behind me I am hearing that the music from the giant loudspeakers is changing to a strange, jerky beat. The Long-Legged Lovely Lassies are climbing down from the stage. They begin to follow us towards the kitchen. Many men follow them.

When the four men in skirts are approaching the Super Climax cake on its trolley in the kitchen, the cake is no longer looking so big.

The hairy-legged man with the green eyes pulls at a rope attached to the trolley; and the other three men push. Slowly, the cake begins to move.

'That'll do.' The man with the green eyes and the hairy, shapely legs takes me by my good hand. 'Let's roll.'

As soon as we pull open the door to the Sapphire Ballroom, I hear the strange, jerky music blasting from the giant loudspeakers. At once all the hairy-legged men who are pushing and pulling the cake, including the one who is holding my hand, begin to laugh and dance.

This is a dance I have never seen before.

But all the men in skirts and green trousers in the Sapphire Ballroom seem to know it.

In fact, the men in skirts and green trousers know the dance so well that they can perform it even after drinking so much alcohol that the whisky stand has closed down.

The Long-Legged Lovely Lassies know the dance also, although perhaps this is not surprising as they are professional dancers.

The hairy-legged men in skirts are pushing the cake right across the Sapphire Ballroom, dancing as they push, in time with the strange, jerky music.

Behind the cake every single person in the Combined Burns Night and St Patrick's Day Ball, including the Long-Legged Lovely Lassies and the women who are the wives or perhaps partners of the men in skirts and green trousers, is dancing in a line, each one holding the waist of the person in front and every few beats kicking their legs high in the air.

I, too, am learning this dance as I walk alongside the cake with the man with green eyes and the hairy, shapely legs.

Even Ms Sofia, who is walking by herself and whose face is still white from the smell of the glistening stomach-type objects in the kitchen, is dancing.

This shows in my opinion that this must be one of the easiest dances in the world.

As they are dancing, the people also are beginning to sing.

If I am honest it is hard to hear the words of this song because the strange jerky music from the giant loudspeakers is so loud.

But I think they are singing: '*Let's all do the conga.*'

Of course, I am not able to pull the cake or steer it with one arm in a sling but the man with the green eyes and the hairy, shapely legs is strong and I have told him what to do. So when our giant cake and our line of hundreds of dancing people approaches the door which separates the Sapphire Ballroom from the service corridor, I run ahead and pull it open.

One or two men wearing skirts or green trousers are following me, and help me to pull aside the sound barriers which Ms N has had placed in the corridor to prevent noise from the Combined Burns Night and St Patrick's Day Ball from disturbing the banquet which our democratic and incorruptible President Abdullatov is giving for the President of China.

For a moment, I am afraid. What if I am not having understood correctly the instructions of Ms N?

Or what if Ms N for some reason has asked me to do something which will get me into trouble?

Already, as soon as the sound barriers are pulled to one side, the sound of the conga-song from the giant loudspeakers is filling the corridor.

I turn and see the giant cake, followed by hundreds of singing, dancing men in skirts and green trousers, Long-Legged Lovely Lassies and wives or maybe partners, heading towards me like an express train.

All of these people have, I think, had one or more drinks.

I look at the giant cake.

I look at the doors to the Diamond Ocean.

I think about the instructions which Ms N was giving me earlier today.

I think about Ms N's warm brown eyes, and the way she is cocking her head and pursing her lips when she is asking me to do something.

Then I turn and, with my good arm, throw open the doors to the Diamond Ocean.

What I am seeing is like a photograph, because no-one is moving.

On the stage, at the special table at the front of the podium which we have placed here for this purpose, our democratic and incorruptible President Abdullatov is sitting next to the man wearing glasses who I am guessing is the President of China.

Both of the men have pens in their hands.

As I am entering the room, two young women, who I am guessing are from my country because they are tall and beautiful, are putting in front of each man a bundle of papers.

I am guessing that these bundles are the agreements to sell to China the fabulously rich agricultural land and ultra-modern factories which are belonging to our democratic and incorruptible President Abdullatov and his family and closest friends.

Perhaps this is why our democratic and incorruptible President Abdullatov is looking like a cat which has been given a bucket filled with cream.

The man wearing glasses who I am guessing is the President of China is still looking serious.

The hundreds of television cameras from China and from our own country and perhaps from some other countries which are here to film tonight's ceremony are all zooming in on the moment when the agreement will be signed.

Everything is quiet, like a morning after a fresh snowfall in my small village far from the historic capital of our beautiful country.

But then everything is changing because our Super Climax cake enters the room, together with the jerky beat of the giant loudspeakers from the Sapphire Ballroom and hundreds of men in skirts and green trousers and Long-Legged Lovely Lassies and wives or maybe partners, all singing 'Let's all do the conga', and dancing what I am guessing must be the conga-dance and every few beats kicking their legs high in the air.

Also entering the Diamond Ocean is Ms Sofia, who has stopped dancing but is still looking as pale as a dead person.

Our democratic and incorruptible President Abdullatov and the man wearing glasses who I am guessing is the President of China and the hundreds of TV cameras and the other guests who have been sitting at the tables eating the sixteen-course Chinese-style banquet all turn to look at the Super Climax cake, and at the hundreds of singing and dancing people who have burst into the room.

Actually, I am thinking for a moment that the cameramen and many male guests, despite being important political and business persons attending an official government banquet, are paying particular attention to the Long-Legged Lovely Lassies, who are kicking their legs high up in the air as they perform the conga-dance.

It is not, perhaps, surprising that the arrival of the Super Climax cake and the singing and dancing people who have had one or more drinks is attracting attention from the people in the Diamond Ocean, because before we were coming in they were suffering one of the most boring evenings of their lives.

Now, no-one is looking bored at all.

Meanwhile I, with the help of the four hairy-legged men in skirts, am steering the cake into the spot between the TV cameras and the table on the podium where our democratic and incorruptible President Abdullatov, and the man wearing glasses who I am guessing is the President of China, are sitting with their pens in their hands.

I am noticing that our democratic and incorruptible President Abdullatov is quickly signing his copy of the agreement while the Super Climax cake is approaching. He is looking at the man wearing glasses who I am guessing is the President of China as if hoping that he will sign his copy also.

But the man wearing glasses who I am guessing is the President of China is staring at the Super Climax cake, and at the dancing and singing men in skirts and green trousers and Long-Legged Lovely Lassies, and wives, or maybe partners, as if he has forgotten that he is here to sign an agreement.

As I am seeing this I am placing the Super Climax cake in exactly the right spot, and noticing that the space is just the right size for the cake. I am also noticing that the TV cameras, if they were taking a picture of the cake instead of the Long-Legged Lovely Lassies, would be able to see our democratic and incorruptible President Abdullatov, and the man wearing glasses who I am guessing is the President of China, sitting behind the cake with their pens in their hands.

I also see that Ms N is standing to one side of the TV cameras in a place where not too many people will notice her and where she will not appear in any TV pictures, but where she will see everything which is going on.

Ms N has her head tilted to one side and is smiling her mischievous smile.

The Super Climax cake stops.

The singing and dancing begins to die down. It seems to be hard to do a conga-dance without moving forwards.

The man wearing glasses who I am guessing is the President of China frowns and picks up his pen.

I look at the spot on the cake about which Ms N has told me and where there is not too much cream, and smack it hard, three times, with my good hand.

Nothing happens.

The people at the round tables are beginning to talk to each other. The people who have been doing the conga-dance and singing are calming down and looking as if they might like to go back to the Sapphire Ballroom. The man wearing glasses who I am guessing is the President of China shrugs at our democratic and incorruptible President Abdullatov and smoothes the paper of the document he is about to sign.

I see a movement close to the TV cameras.

Ms N is still smiling as though this is a day like any other. Next to her I see Ms Sofia in her diamond dress, her smile fixed beneath her sad eyes and with no sign of her red-tipped teeth.

I look again at Ms N. She is tapping her arm with her finger. She does it again. Tap, tap, tap. She nods towards me.

I understand.

My broken arm is still in the heavy plaster cast put on by the world-class doctors at the President Abdullatov hospital, here in the historic capital of our beautiful country.

I lean across and thump the cast three times against the Super Climax cake in the spot about which Ms N has told me.

I hit the cake so hard that my broken arm is hurting very much; and I am afraid that the cake might be damaged.

But instead, a different thing happens.

Something begins to break through the top of the cake, from the inside.

At first, I am thinking that this thing breaking through the top of the cake is perhaps a big egg, or a ball.

But I am wrong. It is a human head.

To begin with, I am not certain whose head this is because it is covered in all the extra cream on the top of the Super Climax cake about which the angry Japanese chef was complaining; and the eyes are covered by a leather mask, like a criminal.

But as the head emerges further from the cake I recognise it.

It is the head of Mr Minas, the owner of our hotel and the husband of Ms Sofia, the daughter of our democratic and incorruptible President Abdullatov.

Actually, it is not just his head.

Mr Minas has one arm around a kind of metal pole which is rising with him from the cake. His shoulders are bare, except for some leather straps which are wrapped around his body.

Mr Minas, like his father-in-law, is also smiling like a cat with a bucket of cream. I am surprised by this, because it seems to me he must be able to see that something is wrong. Mr Minas is expecting to come out of this cake in the Sapphire Ballroom as part of the Super Climax event at the Combined Burns Night and St Patrick's Day Ball, perhaps with the Long-Legged Lovely Lassies dancing on the stage.

Instead, Mr Minas is coming out of the cake in the Diamond Ocean in front of his father-in-law and the man wearing glasses, who I am guessing is the President of China, and hundreds of TV cameras from China and our own country and perhaps other countries.

He is also coming out of the cake in front of his wife, Ms Sofia, whose mouth I now see is open once again and showing teeth whose tips are bright red.

So I am surprised that Mr Minas is still smiling like the cat I am mentioning earlier.

But then I realise that with his leather mask, and the masses of cream and decorations which Ms N ordered especially for the top of the cake and which are now covering his head and shoulders, Mr Minas cannot see too much. In fact, the small, cruel-looking eye slits in his mask are filled with cream. Also, the giant loudspeakers from the Sapphire Ballroom are filling the Diamond Ocean with the conga-music.

I am expecting that Mr Minas will use his hands to wipe his eyes so that he can see better.

Then I see the reason why he is not doing this.

I am seeing a woman also rising out of the remains of the shattered cake.

The woman is… I do not know the words to explain what the woman is doing. In fact, I do not think it is appropriate to describe what all the guests of our democratic and incorruptible President Abdullatov, and the man wearing glasses who I am guessing is the President of China, and the hundreds of TV cameras are seeing as Mr Minas and the woman are rising from the cake except to say that perhaps it is helping explain why he is looking like the cat I keep talking about.

For a long time, it seems everyone in the Diamond Ocean is frozen except for Mr Minas and the woman. Then I see that the mouth of Ms Sofia is opening wider and wider in a grim smile of delight, the tips of her teeth shining redder than ever.

Mr Minas lifts up his head and shouts out in English: 'Welcome to my hotel!' He laughs as if he is perhaps the happiest man alive.

He reaches up and scratches under his nose, as if something there is itching. And then he tears off his mask.

'WHAT DO YOU think of our new hotel owner?' Ms N lays her newspaper on the table in the lobby lounge.

'I am thinking that she is happier now than she was before,' I say. 'Before, her mouth was always smiling. Now, her eyes are smiling also.'

Ms N takes a sip of her cappuccino drink. Her brown eyes are moving as she is checking what is happening in the lobby bar and the entrance of our hotel.

'I guess she likes it that the Dionysus Bar is in profit, now we no longer hold private parties every week which no-one pays for,' she says. 'I guess she likes it that our guest satisfaction scores are rising and we are getting more repeat visitors now the hotel is quiet at night. I guess she likes it that the hotel is making money.'

'The staff satisfaction scores have improved also.'

'Yes. The female staff like not having to worry about being impaled.' Ms N looks towards Pierre, who is walking across the lobby with his quick, small steps. 'The male staff, too.'

'Also, you are improving the hotel,' I say.

'I hope so,' Ms N says. 'Ms Sofia has agreed that we should install a water feature in the lobby. She has also agreed that if we invest in a new sushi restaurant it will give our Japanese chef, Kyoko, something useful to do with her ultra-sharp Chroma knives.'

I remember the Japanese chef seizing the whirling bright metal knives out of the air and stabbing the glistening stomach-type package on her chopping board and the sheep's heart, liver and lungs spilling out.

'Is Ms Sofia a good hotel owner?' I say.

'The key thing is that an owner should not obstruct the running of the hotel,' Ms N says. 'Ms Sofia tells me that when she is sure the hotel is profitable she might sell it to a friend of hers. His name is Mr Dolgov.' She shrugs. 'I hope he will not interfere, but you can never be certain about this.'

'The world-class doctors at the President Abdullatov hospital say that my cast can be removed in two weeks,' I say.

'Yes.' Ms N tilts her head to one side. 'How do people feel about the fact that the Chinese will not be buying most of your country after all?'

I sip my own cappuccino drink. Although I am off-duty and

am wearing a smart new felt jacket in the style and colours of my country, I feel strange to be sitting in our lobby lounge with Ms N and talking about politics.

'It is not most of our country,' I say at last. 'It is only some of our fabulously rich agricultural land and ultra-modern factories which are belonging to our democratic and incorruptible President Abdullatov and his family and closest friends. If I am honest, I am not sure that most people are caring too much whether this land and these factories are owned by the family of our democratic and incorruptible President Abdullatov, or by the Chinese.'

'No,' Ms N says. 'I can see that. But I think President Abdullatov cares.'

'Yes,' I say. 'That must be why he is allowing or perhaps encouraging our independent and transparent European-style justice system to sentence Mr Minas to twenty years of hard labour in the salt mines in the mountainous south of our country for...' I pick up the newspaper which Ms N has been reading. 'Drug trafficking, tax evasion, provision of sexual services, stealing of state assets, illegal importation of vehicles, illegal currency transactions, use of substandard hospital drugs, illegal re-sale of mobile phone licences, issuing of fake university degrees, fraudulent trading of oil and gas and failure to meet kitchen hygiene regulations.'

'Kyoko is angry about the kitchen hygiene accusation,' Ms N says, 'which seems to me obviously made-up. But surely your independent and transparent European-style justice system cannot be influenced by President Abdullatov or anyone else?'

I look at Ms N and shake my head. Although she is very clever, sometimes I am thinking she understands nothing about our country.

'You did a splendid job that night, Tatiana,' Ms N continues. 'But tell me: how did you persuade the brawny gentlemen in kilts to help you move the cake?'

'It was not easy – ' I begin. But then a thought occurs to me.

'I wanted to ask you,' I say, 'why so many of the men in skirts have such hairy, shapely legs.' I blush as I say this, because I am thinking of the man with the green eyes.

'I don't know,' Ms N says. 'What do you think?'

'Well. I am thinking it must either be because men with hairy, shapely legs are enjoying wearing a skirt more than men with legs which are not so hairy or shapely; or because wearing a skirt makes a man's legs more hairy and shapely. One or the other.'

'Tatiana.' Ms N smiles. 'I think it is the first of these. And I think you will go far.'

'Thank you,' I say; and sip my cappuccino drink. I think how bad our hotel was, the first time I am ever seeing Ms N, when I am standing on a bistro table with Mr Minas sticking his tongue in my ear and me being upset that I could not see any way to turn the music down, or even off, and knowing that I could not help the hotel guest who was waiting in his dressing gown outside the Dionysus Bar.

I am thinking how good the hotel is, now that Ms N has removed Mr Minas; and how, soon, it will be even better.

Ms N is good at solving problems. One day, I would like to be like her.

2. THE TWO ROOMS

12.34

'I'M NOT MOVING, Tatiana. That's final.'

Mr Burke is a tall, dark-haired man in a designer denim jacket with subtle stubble and a deep, melodious voice. He is achingly good-looking and he knows it.

'Unfortunately, you are booked to move out at 10 a.m. today. All our rooms are full this evening.'

'I want to speak to the General Manager.' That lovely voice again. I wish he would use it to say something else.

'Yes, sir. I am afraid the General Manager is not available right now. But if you would like to speak to the Hotel Manager I will be happy to arrange that.' I smile my thousand-watt smile.

'Whoever. But I'm not moving out of my room.'

'I am calling the Hotel Manager now.' I wish I could tell Mr Burke about the imminent arrival of our morally irreproachable Prime Minister Kaya and the fact that even if Mr Burke were not being awkward, the hotel would already be one room overbooked. But of course, I cannot tell him any of this.

'So… I don't see this manager you promised. I don't pay five-star rates to wait for a receptionist.'

Mr Burke sticks his hands in his pockets and turns his back on me, leaning the elbows of the denim jacket on the counter and looking out at the lobby. It's a fine lobby, with a thirty-metre water feature and a sushi bar with a Michelin star. But I know he is turned his back to indicate his disgust with me and the service I am providing.

In fact, he is trying to humiliate me.

But this is OK. I am trained to stay calm.

I keep smiling at his back and look around for any other customers who need help. The first thing I see is two men in dark suits moving towards the counter. The second thing is the Hotel Manager gliding into view from the Business Centre on the other side of the lobby.

The two dark suits are nearly at the counter. They are walking stiffly, as though the fabric of the suits is too rigid to be able to move properly. I turn towards them and try out the smile again.

'Yes, sir, how may I help you?'

'It must be pork,' the first man says. 'Tonight. Anything else is not acceptable.'

This problem is an easy one for me because I have explained it to customers many times.

'I understand your preference,' I say brightly. 'But unfortunately, the Ministry of Agriculture has banned all pork products following the health scare last month. There is no pork available in the country. If our hotel were to import or serve pork products, we would be breaking the law.'

The second man looks at me as if I am an idiot. In fact, he looks at me with such contempt that I wonder if I am, in fact, an idiot and have simply never noticed up to now.

'You do not understand. Your hotel is arranging a banquet tonight for the birthday of our patron, Mr Dolgov. For this we are paying you eight hundred dollars a cover, excluding the drinks, which will include Chateau Petrus and Dom Perignon, all sourced from your cellars. Mr Dolgov agreed personally with the hotel owner, his friend Ms Sofia, that we would hold this event here. Ms Sofia assured Mr Dolgov that this would be the best birthday of his life. Yet you are now telling me that the pork for the main dish, which we ordered at Mr Dolgov's express request two months ago, is not available. You will find some pork.'

Behind the two men in suits I see that the Hotel Manager, whose name is Ms N, is heading for Mr Burke. Ms N is from a large European country which is rich in talent but which has not yet provided a General Manager for any hotel in our chain, and everyone is expecting she will be promoted to GM any moment. She started off working Reception like me. She still helps out sometimes when things are busy. She is short, even in the high heels she always wears in the hotel, and she always has an inquisitive expression, as if she is figuring out how to solve some problem. Maybe she always is. That is her job, solving problems. Ms N is the best problem-solver in the world.

I want to be like her.

Ms N has identified Mr Burke as an unhappy customer. She walks up to him and stops close enough to engage but not so close she has to peer up at him. She has amped up the inquisitive look with a hint of a smile, so that she looks as if she is fascinated to meet him. I see he has clocked that she is a person of power. Already he has taken his elbows off the counter.

'Unfortunately,' I begin to say to the two men in suits, 'we cannot serve pork tonight in this hotel or else – '

'Girl.' The second dark suit is shaking his head and has raised his voice. 'Do you think I am an idiot?'

'No sir, of course I do not.'

'Do you think I do not know that if Mr Dolgov and the owner of this hotel wish to serve pork, there will be pork?'

I nod, distracted by a commotion at the front door. A gang of security gorillas with ear-wires and square coats has spilled in from the street and is attempting to spread out into the lobby. This means that Prime Minister Kaya is about to arrive, with his delegation of forty negotiators, note-takers and baggage-carriers.

The gorillas seem to be looking for trouble and have found it. They are trying to push out of the way a line of journalists and TV cameras whose position Ms N agreed about one hour ago. The journalists, who include a prize-winning TV investigative hot-shot who has been making an expose of the life of our morally irreproachable Prime Minister, do not like being pushed.

'Yes, Mr Burke, how may I help you?' I hear Ms N say.

'I am a Platinum Megastar member of this hotel,' Mr Burke replies, 'and I am not prepared to be treated like this.'

'Pork is a must-have,' the second dark suit says to me.

'We have permission to stand here,' the prize-winning journalist is shouting as a security man pushes him.

I see that a short, swarthy man wearing a black polo-neck under a formal suit has slipped between the security gorillas and is scurrying towards the counter.

A couple of bell-boys have appeared pushing two trolleys loaded with matching Louis Vuitton luggage. The owners of the luggage, a flamboyant Swiss gay couple who have been staying at the hotel for a month, have materialised at the counter ready to check out. They are chatting happily and seem oblivious to their surroundings.

Things are looking busy, I think.

Ms N is looking Mr Burke in the eye and nodding calmly. But I know for a fact that she is logging everything which is happening in the lobby because her left eyebrow is slightly raised. I see her say a few words to Mr Burke, take a deep breath and smile. Then Mr Burke is turning around and sloping off towards the lobby lounge, wiggling his fine buns in his tight chinos as if he owns the place.

Ms N turns to me.

'Thank you, Tatiana,' she says. 'Please can you check out Ms Feuchtwangler and Ms Cladders?' She smiles at the gay couple, who beam back. Then she turns to the two dark suits. 'Let me make you an appointment with the Food and Beverages Director,' she says. Without waiting for a response, she whips out her telephone and talks for a moment, then she pockets the phone and nods at them in a way which signals *all sorted*. 'There,' she says. 'He will see you for a private meeting in the Platinum Megastar Lounge at six o'clock precisely.'

She hands each of them one of the shiny metallic vouchers which grant access to the Platinum Megastar Lounge on the 20th floor.

'A private meeting?' The first dark suit leers at her slyly, as if she has proposed something indecent.

'The Platinum Megastar Lounge?' The second dark suit is actually standing up taller at the thought of gaining access to a venue of such fabled exclusivity.

'But you guarantee there will be pork?' the first dark suit says.

'The Food and Beverages Director will arrange everything to your satisfaction,' Ms N says. She turns crisply away towards the swarthy man in the black polo-neck.

'Theo, darling, lovely to see you, how is the Prime Minister?' she says, and hugs him to her for a second as she brushes her cheek against his. I notice that Theo places one hairy hand on her right buttock as she does so but she seems not to notice and steps back, smiling her fascinated smile. 'I know exactly what you need and all arrangements are made,' she says. 'But I think we need to discuss this in my office, no? Perhaps I could offer you a glass of wine there, in ten minutes. As soon as I have sorted out these troublesome journalists.'

Theo grins with such immense self-satisfaction that pure smugness seems to come welling out of the top of his black polo-neck. 'Your office,' he smiles. 'A glass of wine. I will be there.'

I am busy adding up the astonishing list of extras on the bill of Ms Feuchtwangler and Ms Cladders, but I can see in the lobby that one of the bell-boys has summoned Nigel, the Duty Security Manager, who has arrived with two assistants to try and calm the situation between the journalists and the gorillas who are accompanying the Prime Minister. Next to me, one of the other receptionists is trying to secure my attention to deal with a call from the Canadian Embassy about a cancelled booking for the Sapphire Ballroom this evening; I tell her to say that we will call back in a few minutes.

The fact that our morally irreproachable Prime Minister himself is going to appear any moment makes sorting out the fracas a matter of urgency. In fact, I cannot see how Ms N can restore order in time. Nigel has legs like tree-trunks and a neck to match and his men have physically separated the journalists and the gorillas. But Nigel is not a diplomat, and it looks as if a fist-fight may break out at any moment. I smile to myself and wonder if Nigel has considered calling on Kyoko, our Japanese Executive Chef, who has a terrifying selection of ultra-sharp Chroma kitchen blades and a filthy temper. But clearly Nigel so far rates the potential unpredictability of engaging Kyoko as far riskier than any danger the gorillas may represent and I can see no sign of her.

While I am wondering what Ms N can possibly do, I am surprised to see her ignore all of them and walk across the lobby towards the main entrance. She stops right inside the front door, stands up straight but tiny on her high heels, and straightens her exquisitely-pressed skirt to indicate that she is ready to meet a VVIP, or a Distinguished Visitor as we are learning to call them.

Ms N's authority and calm radiate across the hotel lobby like the shock-waves of some powerful weapon. For an instant the journalists and security gorillas forget about each other and turn, like her, to face the entrance. In that same instant, the bell-boys haul open the door and Prime Minister Kaya enters. Ms N takes a step forward and holds out her hand to greet him. From where I am standing with my hands on the computer keyboard behind the reception desk, I cannot see her face. But I know that she is looking at him inquisitively, with a hint of a smile.

I wish I could be like Ms N.

16.05

I AM SHOWING a customer on a map the way to the entertainment district of the city when I see Ms N approaching the counter. She talks to the other receptionists until I have finished my explanations and then invites me into the back office for a quiet word.

'Yes, Ms N,' I say. 'How may I help you?'

'Tatiana. As you are in charge of reception this evening, I wish you to be aware of several things. The first is that the gentleman from the Prime Minister's entourage, Theo, wished to discuss with me an issue of the utmost sensitivity.'

'Yes, Ms N,' I say.

'Strictly for your own information, the issue is that Prime Minister Kaya has a predilection for a certain type of service which this hotel does not provide.' Ms N looks at me steadily, her face set.

'I understand, Ms N.'

'At 19.00 a woman called Ms Gentle will arrive to check into Suite 1618. This room is of course in a different part of the hotel from the Prime Minister and his delegation. The room has been reserved, and paid for, by Theo. It is for the use of Ms Gentle. I have a copy of her ID here.' Ms N slides across the counter a photocopied page from a passport. It shows an attractive blonde woman with strong features and glasses, like a company executive. 'At 20.00 the Prime Minister will visit Suite 1618 for a period of between five minutes and one hour.' Ms N frowns. 'Probably closer to five minutes. It is vital for the Prime Minister to avoid any kind of publicity for this, uh, transaction. Theo tells me that a number of attempts have been made to expose the Prime Minister's private life, including through the use of false identities. Please make sure, therefore, that the IDs match when you give Ms Gentle the room key. Everything clear?'

'Everything clear, Ms N.'

'Second thing. Mr Burke, the gentleman who has refused to move out of his room, is still in this hotel. I have offered to find him a room in an alternative hotel, but he has declined this. Unfortunately, he has followed up my initial goodwill gesture of a complimentary drink with several more drinks. He is now so inebriated that he is annoying the other guests.'

'This is unfortunate,' I say, 'because we are already one room overbooked. If Mr Burke is refusing to move out, we are two rooms short. Our morally irreproachable Prime Minister and his party have block-booked forty rooms – '

'Forty-one, including their additional guest.' Ms N's face is impassive.

'So we have nil flexibility. I have also received a request this afternoon from four of the TV crews who are covering the Prime Minister's press conference at 18.00 about why he supports harsher penalties for prostitution. The TV crews want a room in which to store equipment and file their stories. Also – ' I wonder whether I should tell her this ' – the Canadian Embassy has phoned to say that, with regret, they must cancel the event in the Sapphire Ballroom because the guest of honour has a bereavement. They have offered to pay, but because they are good customers I have waived the cancellation fee. Unfortunately, this will hit our revenues.'

'Yes. I know we are two rooms short.' Ms N is wearing her inquisitive look. 'And you made the right decision with the Canadians, although this will cost us money. But our main problem is that Mr Burke, our friend in the denim jacket, has insulted our Executive Chef, Kyoko.'

'*He insulted Kyoko?*'

'Yes. He ordered sushi from the lobby bar. This is of course Kyoko's genius, for which we have received the Michelin star. Mr Burke placed a big, complicated order including many speciality dishes. Kyoko, who was engaged personally in the preparation of the food, brought the order to him herself, set out the dishes, and began to explain the individual items. Unfortunately, Mr Burke told her to fuck off.'

I look at Ms N. I know my mouth is hanging open because I cannot imagine anyone telling Kyoko any unpleasant thing and surviving for more than five seconds.

'But this is only the beginning,' Ms N says. 'Kyoko was not pleased by this. But she thought perhaps she had not understood him because her English is not too good. So she continued to explain her art: the fresh ingredients we fly in from Japan, the special way she is steaming the rice, and so forth.'

Ms N falls silent.

'Then what?' I ask.

'Then the customer takes one *Norimaki*, bites into it, and tells Kyoko that her food tastes like shit. He spits out the *Norimaki* on the carpet, then turns over the tray, together with the *Nigiri, Temaki* and *Oshizushi*, and tells her he refuses to pay.'

'Is he still alive?' I try to smile, but actually I am worried.

'Yes. He is still in the lobby lounge, and he is still drinking. Kyoko of course has told me she is unhappy and would like to send in Nigel to throw him out. But I have told her he is a Platinum Megastar member and our options are limited. Also, I have instructed her not to kill him in the lobby lounge as this will be bad for the image of the hotel. Kyoko has told me she understands this and has reserved the Lotus Massage Room in the 10th Floor Spa to undertake some anger management meditation. I think this is a better outcome than the alternative.' Ms N smiles. 'But if you see her approaching the lobby lounge, please call me at once. Especially if she is carrying one of her Chroma knives.'

'And what about Mr Burke?' I say. 'We still need his room.'

'Yes,' Ms N says. 'But some of today's guests are not due to check in until 10 p.m. Perhaps we will have a cancellation by then.'

'Yes, Ms N.' I look at her again and admire her calm and her problem-solving abilities. But she is not finished yet.

'Unfortunately, the Dolgov banquet is still unresolved,' she says. 'Of course, my reference to the Food and Beverages Director was a delaying tactic. The Food and Beverages Director offered our friends in the dark suits a mouth-watering selection of non-pork delicacies. But, as I feared, they are not satisfied. Now Mr Dolgov himself has spoken to the hotel owner, our own Ms Sofia, who is indeed his personal friend. Ms Sofia has spoken to the General Manager, who as you know is on holiday in Bali. The GM has spoken to me. If we do not serve pork at the banquet, the owner will ask our HQ in Atlanta for a new GM and management team.'

'I know a place where we can buy pork in this city,' I say.

'Thank you, Tatiana. But this is a question of ethics. This hotel chain does not break the law. If we break it so we can serve pork, what will we do next week? Also, and perhaps more important, I cannot allow myself to be threatened in this way. This, too, is a matter of principle. I have agreed with the GM that we shall stand firm, and the GM has explained this to Ms Sofia. Unfortunately, Mr Dolgov is not happy.'

'What will you do?' I ask.

'We will have to serve them the best meal we can,' Ms N says, 'and hope that they are satisfied.'

'And what about the camera crews?'

'Please ask them to use the Cigar Bar,' she says.

'That is very crowded,' I say. 'We have a group of Russian businessmen who are watching the ice-hockey championship on cable TV. There is no spare room at all.'

Ms N looks me in the eye. 'Tell them to use the Cigar Bar,' she says. 'If there is any problem they should come and speak to me.'

'Would you like me to speak to Kyoko?' I say. 'Perhaps I can try to calm her down.'

Ms N smiles. 'Tatiana, darling, you are wonderful. You have attention to detail. You have the personal touch. You have a grasp of strategy. Keep it up and you will have a great future in our hotel chain. But think carefully. Do you think it would be safe for you to go and see Kyoko when she has been told by a customer that her *Norimaki* taste like shit?'

I think about this for a moment. Then I slowly shake my head. 'One day, Ms N, I would like to be like you.'

'One day, Tatiana, you will be much, much better.'

Then she turns and goes click, click, click across the lobby, her high heels sending a message of power right through the hotel.

19.00

Ms Gentle arrives exactly on time. My first impression is that she is quite an ordinary-looking woman compared with the ladies who are sometimes seen in the lobbies of five-star hotels. But when she comes closer I see that I am wrong. Her face is finely structured and behind the spectacles her eyes are sparkling. When she hands over her ID she looks at me in the eye as if I matter.

I am so impressed by the interpersonal skills of Ms Gentle that I want to ask her if she enjoys what she does for a living, but of course that would be unprofessional and inappropriate. Instead I check the ID carefully against the photocopy I have been given and study Ms Gentle herself. There is no doubt that she is the woman I am expecting. I hand back the ID and the card-key to Suite 1618.

'Thank you, Ms Gentle,' I say. Then, by accident, I add, 'good luck.' At once I feel awful because this, too, is unprofessional and inappropriate.

But Ms Gentle does not seem to mind. For a moment a beautiful smile appears on her face and she puts one finely-manicured hand on the counter. 'Why, thank you Tatiana,' she says. 'I need all the luck I can get.' She puts her head a little to one side and takes off her spectacles for a moment. 'Perhaps today's my lucky day.' Then she puts the glasses back on, the smile disappears and she walks across the lobby towards the lifts.

For fifteen minutes after the arrival of Ms Gentle the lobby is quiet. Guests arrive and check in. I am still fretting that we are two rooms down, because some of our late-arriving guests are repeat customers who I do not want to bounce into other hotels. The Marketing Director comes over to grumble to me about letting the Canadians off too lightly, but I am able to tell him that Ms N has endorsed my decision. Everything seems quiet in the hotel. But I know that beneath the surface there is a lot of pressure waiting to explode.

At 19.15 I see Ms N arrive in the lobby. She is always cruising around looking for problems to sort out, so at first I do not pay her too much attention. But then I see that she has an unusual expression, less inquisitive than usual. More mischievous. She walks across to the reception counter.

'Hello Tatiana, how are you?'

'I am well, thank you Ms N. But we are still two rooms short and the Marketing Director is complaining about losing the business from the Canadians.'

'We shall live with this. No cancellations yet?'

'No cancellations.'

'Well. It is time to start solving some problems. Is Mr Burke still drinking in the lobby lounge?'

'Yes, Ms N. Shall I call Security?'

'No, thank you, Tatiana. Please could you go to him and ask him politely to leave the hotel. If he refuses, I shall speak to him.'

'Yes, Ms N.'

I am thinking of course that if Mr Burke has not left the hotel since 10 a.m. he is hardly likely to leave now, but I am confident in Ms N's judgement, so I follow her instructions.

Mr Burke is sitting in a corner by the window and at first sight he does not look too bad. He has a glass of whisky in front of him and is cradling a tablet computer in his lap. When I get close I see that the tablet computer is showing a pornographic movie. I do not wish to look at the images which the tablet computer is displaying, but I am unable to avoid seeing that the movie shows a man doing something to a woman which she is not enjoying at all.

As I approach Mr Burke he looks up.

'You're the first bitch who tried to throw me out,' he says.

'Good evening, Mr Burke,' I say. 'Unfortunately, you must leave the hotel now.'

'Is that so?' He moves the screen of the tablet computer so that the images are facing me. 'Do you know that I am a Platinum Megastar member?'

'Yes, Mr Burke I do know that. But we have nil room

availability. We have booked accommodation for you in another hotel. I have ordered a taxi.'

'Do you know what I'd like to do to you?' Mr Burke lifts up the tablet computer, where something is happening which I do not wish even to describe. 'I'd like to do this, for starters. Then I'll do the same with Ms N. Then perhaps the two of you together.'

I am trying not to look at the images on the computer screen and am feeling sick. I know I should summon Ms N, but I do not wish to expose her to this man. Then I feel a hand on my arm.

'Good evening, Mr Burke.' Ms N's voice is calm and professional. I turn, and see she is wearing her inquisitive face.

'You again,' Mr Burke says. 'Are you going to try and throw me out, now? Take a look at this, baby.' He holds up the tablet computer. 'How would you like to – '

'Mr Burke.' Somehow, Ms N is still calm. 'I am pleased that you enjoy our hotel, although I must tell you that you may not use the lobby lounge wi-fi zone to view images which may be offensive to other customers. It is time for you to leave.'

'I'm not leaving.'

'I am sure that once you have seen what I am offering, you will leave. As you know, we have a number of amenities in this hotel which are reserved for our most valued customers.'

'Like me, you mean.'

'That is correct. Have you ever had a massage here, Mr Burke?'

'With no happy end?' Burke drains the rest of his whisky. 'Are you kidding?'

'We have a new massage therapist who offers a very special service,' Ms N says. 'I have booked you a complimentary treatment. Before you attend, you should go to your suite, take a shower, and change into the complimentary dressing gown, as the massage will be full-body.'

'Shower? Why the hell should I shower?'

'When you enter the room, please remove your dressing gown at once and tell the therapist what treatment you would like. Please be quite explicit as English is not her first language.'

'I'll tell her exactly what I want.' Burke is smiling in a way I do not like.

'She will appreciate this,' Ms N says. 'She is an oriental woman. You will find her in the Lotus Massage Room in the 10th Floor Spa.'

'I like the Orientals.' Burke lurches to his feet and leers at me. 'I'll do you later,' he says. 'I still got lots of juice.'

I say nothing as Mr Burke staggers off towards the lift, then follow Ms N back to reception.

'Is that safe?' I ask when he has gone. 'Kyoko may still be in the Lotus Room.'

'I know that she is there,' Ms N says. 'I just texted her to say that I am sending her a treat.'

'What do you think she will do to him?'

'I think she will have some ideas,' Ms N says.

When we arrive back at reception it is just after 8 o'clock. The award-winning journalist is standing next to a tall, heavily-built man in a shiny suit who stinks of cigar smoke.

'Hello, how may I help?' Ms N says.

'I'm from the …' the award-winning journalist says, naming a world-famous news channel. 'Do you really have nowhere for the news crews to hang out? The Cigar Club is full of these guys – ' he indicates the tall man in the shiny suit ' – having a good time and cheering on the ice-hockey. We need a quiet place to file our stories.'

'Tatiana may be able to help you,' Ms N says. She motions me to go behind the reception desk. 'Suite 1618 has just come free. Could you issue a card-key, please, Tatiana?'

I look at her. Ms N is smiling her mischievous smile. I nod, and issue another copy of the card-key which I have already given to Ms Gentle. 'Here it is,' I say.

'Could you give us a couple of spares?' the award-winning journalist says. 'There are eight of us altogether.'

'I am afraid there has been some misuse of duplicate keys,' Ms N says. 'I suggest you make sure that all eight of you arrive and enter the room together. Then co-ordinate your movements after that.'

'OK. I guess I should be grateful,' the award-winning journalist says.

'Yes,' Ms N says. 'I guess you should.'

The award-winning journalist takes the card-key and heads off towards the cigar club to collect his friends and go to Suite 1618. It is ten past eight.

'What would you like me to do now?' I ask Ms N.

'I would like you to wait with me in the lobby,' Ms N says.

For a while, we stand by the reception desk. Nothing much is happening. I want to ask Ms N how we should find our two additional rooms, but I feel confident she has a plan. I am also nervous that the two men in the dark suits will reappear to complain about the pork, but there is no sign of them.

At 20.30 I see the lift doors open and a group of people spill out. I hear raised voices. It is Theo, the man in the black polo-neck, with four journalists. Theo is red in the face. He walks quickly towards the reception desk.

'We would like to hire a conference room,' he says. He looks at Ms N as if he is about to say something, but then he notices that the journalists are watching him. Ms N is wearing her inquisitive look. 'The Prime Minister wishes to hold an additional press conference at nine-thirty. To explain the situation.'

'Certainly, sir,' I say. 'What size room will you need?'

Theo shakes his head and sighs. 'The largest one you have.'

'That would be the Sapphire Ballroom,' I say. 'Unfortunately, there will be a short-notice supplement for us to prepare it by 21.30.'

'Just do it,' Theo says.

Behind Theo I see another lift open. This time it is Ms Gentle. She, too, has four journalists in the lift with her. She looks magnificent: serene, smiling and beautiful. She, too, approaches the reception desk. She ignores Theo.

'I would like to hire a room for a press conference.' She nods at the journalists. 'These gentlemen will pay.'

'Certainly, madam,' I say. 'What size would you like?'

'The biggest you have,' one of the journalists says. He is smiling like a wolf. 'Every journalist in town will be here.'

'Our biggest room is already booked,' I say.

'If it's for the Prime Minister's press conference, we'll take it after him,' the journalist says. All the journalists look at Theo and Ms Gentle. Ms Gentle is looking happy. Theo is not.

'How about an exclusive on the life story?' one of the journalists says to Ms Gentle. 'We'll give you $250,000.'

'I'll go to $300,000,' the second journalist says.

The journalists and Ms Gentle move away from the reception desk, discussing large sums of money. I see the lift doors open again, and my heart sinks. It is the two men in the dark suits. Both of them look angry. Both are walking in a mechanical way, as if their suits are still too tight.

'I wish to speak to the manager about the pork,' the first dark suit says.

I glance at Ms N. She nods imperceptibly.

'The Hotel Manager is here,' I say. 'She will be pleased to assist you.'

'Yes, sir, how may I help?' Ms N says, as if she somehow will be able to magic up some legal pork.

'I have a personal message from Mr Dolgov,' the second suit says. Suddenly, for the first time, he smiles. 'Mr Dolgov wishes me to tell you that he considers the sweet and sour pork prepared by this hotel the best he has ever tasted. He says the flavour is subtle yet tender. He says he will buy the hotel from Ms Sofia. When he does that, he will increase the salary of your chef to twice whatever you are paying him.'

'Thank you,' Ms N says. 'Actually, Mr Dolgov's banquet was prepared by our Executive Chef, Kyoko, who is a lady from Japan. I will pass on Mr Dolgov's appreciation, and his offer. I am sure she will look forward to working with him.'

The second suit looks serious again. 'But Mr Dolgov is not

happy that you are pretending there is no pork available, then you are serving pork. This cause him unnecessary concern.'

'That is because no pork is available,' Ms N says. 'For this hotel to serve pork would be breaking the law.'

The two suits look at each other and frown. Then one of them smiles. Then they are both smiling. They turn to Ms N.

'No pork is available,' says the first suit. 'Of course. Because that would be illegal.'

'So the meat you served to Mr Dolgov was not pork, even though it tasted like pork,' the second suit says.

'That is correct,' Ms N says. 'That meat was not pork.'

'We understand,' the first suit says. 'We will tell Mr Dolgov that you fixed the problem in a very clever way. Perhaps he will recommend a bonus.'

'If there are any bonuses, they should be for Kyoko,' Ms N says. 'She worked very hard to prepare the banquet for Mr Dolgov in good time. Maybe she will wish to buy herself some new Chroma knives.'

The two suits look at Ms N and nod. Then they walk back to the lift.

Ms N turns to me. 'Thank you, Tatiana. Please can you tell Housekeeping to start making up Suite 1618. This room is now free. Also, they can clear out Mr Burke's room. He will not be needing it tonight. This gives us the two rooms we need for our guests arriving later this evening.'

I look at Ms N. She is smiling her mischievous smile. She is good at solving problems. One day, I would like to be like Ms N.

3. THE SWEDISH WOMAN

17.25

'I AM SORRY, sir. But this is a five-star hotel. I cannot arrange services of this kind.'

'Tatiana, my darling. Sweetheart. It is not for me that I am asking. It is for my own dear father. He is eighty-seven years old. He only has six months to live, the poor sweet man. And here he is having come all the way from Ireland to join me and a select group of our friends to celebrate his birthday in style, courtesy of your boss and my good friend the Hotel Manager. Are you sure you cannot be finding someone for him, now?'

Secretly I am impressed to hear that this man and his father are friends of Ms N, the Manager and acting General Manager of this hotel, who is also my boss. But the rules are clear. I have no trouble answering because I know that Ms N would say the same.

'I am sorry, sir. I cannot help you.'

'Tatiana, sweetheart. You may be sorry. But just imagine how my poor, dear father will feel. Here he is, having flown all the way from Ireland for a weekend of fun. And now you tell me: no fun. Please, Tatiana, show mercy!'

The man at the reception is middle-aged and fit, and has green eyes. He wears a tailored grey suit, an open-necked shirt and a cologne which drifts across the counter, reminding me of the fields of herbs which cloak the mountain uplands around my poor village far from the historic capital of our beautiful country. When he talks about his father from Ireland, and when he says *show mercy*, he smiles so kindly that I want to help him.

But of course I cannot.

'Would you like to speak to the Hotel Manager?' I say. 'Perhaps she can help you.'

I am fibbing when I say this. I know that Ms N will not help the man with a kindly smile to obtain the kind of service which he says he wants to obtain as a birthday treat for his elderly father. Ms N is strict about such things. But perhaps Ms N can suggest some other birthday treat.

I am looking over the man's shoulder as I am speaking, because four men and two women are waiting behind him to be served. Three of the men are wearing white *thawb* robes, and *keffiyeh* head-dresses held in place with *agals*. I recognise these items because we receive many Arab visitors and some of them wear traditional dress. I can see no sign of their *janbiya* ceremonial daggers and I am guessing that our security team will have asked them to check these in when they are passing through our full body scanner at the entrance.

The fourth man who is waiting is tall and grey-haired. I recognise him at once as the Regional Director of our hotel chain and Ms N's boss, whose name is Mr Matt Miller. Ms N has told me to treat Mr Matt Miller with care and attention and to call her the minute he appears. Mr Matt Miller is accompanied by a woman who looks as if she might perhaps be of South-East Asian origin and whose booking details, which I have memorised this morning, give her name as Mrs Matt Miller.

The second woman has wild, frizzy hair and no make-up and is wearing a green out-door jacket as if perhaps she has spent the day trekking in the rugged and windswept mountains of our beautiful but not yet economically advanced country.

Actually, the woman in the green out-door jacket is not exactly waiting to be served. She is gazing around our lobby, with its thirty-metre water feature and its sushi bar with a Michelin star, as if perhaps she is not taking such things for granted like most of our guests, but finds them remarkable.

I am pleased that the woman has stopped to look at the lobby because this means that she is no longer my problem, unlike the man with the fragrant cologne and the green eyes and the kindly smile, and the three gentlemen in Arab dress, and Mr and Mrs Matt Miller, all of whom are now at the counter.

'One moment, please,' I say. I pick up the telephone and call Ms N. 'Please come,' I say. Then I terminate the call.

'The Hotel Manager will speak to you in a moment,' I say to the Irish gentleman. 'Please take a seat in the Lobby Bar.'

I turn to the first of the gentlemen in *keffiyehs*. 'Welcome to our hotel, sir. Good choice. Do you have a reservation?'

The man in Arab dress tells me in not bad English that he and his colleagues are here for the World Anti-Corruption Forum, which is opening in the Sapphire Ballroom of our hotel the following morning. I see a note on the computer from Ms N telling me to be helpful to this group of gentlemen, especially if they have special seating needs in the restaurant or Lobby Bar.

I am guessing that these gentlemen must be very rich indeed, and probably also very fussy.

The note from Ms N is unusual, so I look with interest at the first gentleman in Arab clothing, who I now see has dark eyes and cute dimples. He returns the hotel pen to me with a word of thanks when he has finished signing his name, unlike many guests who put the hotel pen in their pocket, or drop it on the floor, or simply leave it lying on the counter so I can put it away.

I like it when customers treat hotel staff as if they are human beings.

While I am admiring the dimples and the manners of the gentleman in Arab clothing, Mr Matt Miller says to me in a loud voice:

'Do you know who I am?'

Of course, when Mr Matt Miller says this I am struggling to stop myself laughing because every hotel worker knows the story about the air stewardess dealing with a self-important customer who asks this same question. In reply, the stewardess turns on her public address system and asks all the other passengers if anyone knows who the self-important customer is, because he seems to have forgotten.

Usually in this story the self-important customer is a man. I do not know why this is.

Luckily, I am a highly trained hospitality industry professional, so I do not laugh but instead turn to the grey-haired customer and his wife and smile my famous thousand-watt smile. 'Mr and Mrs Miller. Welcome to our hotel. Good choice. I will be delighted to deal with you as soon as I have finished with these three gentlemen.'

Mr Matt Miller says nothing but nods his head as if to acknowledge what I have said. His wife, assuming that the woman is his wife and not a woman who bizarrely has exactly the same name as him, also says nothing. In fact, she does not even change her expression, which is one of surprise bordering on shock, or possibly fear, as if she has heard a horrifying piece of news.

I wonder if she is perhaps like one of the rich but sad women we see often in our beautiful but not yet economically advanced country who cannot move her face too much because of plastic surgery. But I cannot imagine that even the worst cosmetic surgeon in the world would leave any customer with a face so shocked, or possibly frightened, as that of Mrs Matt Miller.

As I complete the registration of the three men wearing *thawbs* and *keffiyehs* and *agals* I hear a commotion in the Lobby Bar. I am only now noticing that although the area to which I have sent the man with the green eyes and the kindly smile and the fragrant cologne is packed with people, he has easily found a seat at the centre of the crowd and is talking to two of his neighbours. I turn to look for the source of the noise and realise that half of the people in the Lobby Bar, several of whom seem to have had at least one drink and are mostly dressed in clothes at the "casual" end of the "smart casual" look to which our hotel chain hopes its guests will aspire, must be celebrating the birthday of the eighty-seven-year old Irish gentleman who is the father of the customer with the green eyes and the kindly smile and the fragrant cologne.

All of this group have risen to their feet and are shouting and cheering.

The other half of the customers in the Lobby Bar are not shouting and cheering. These people are mostly heavy-set men wearing dark suits or leather jackets, who include some of the richest businessmen in our beautiful but not yet economically advanced country. One of these gentlemen has recently become Minister of Justice, helped by the fact that our wholly uncensored newspapers and television channels, many of which he owns, have reported definitively that he is 100% untainted by corruption of any kind.

I am guessing that the group of gentlemen in dark suits or leather jackets is also booked into the hotel to attend the Anti-Corruption Forum, since these people, including our untainted-by-corruption-of-any-kind Minister of Justice, are amongst the greatest experts in corruption in the world, let alone in our beautiful but not yet economically advanced country.

The second group look at the first, noisy group like adults watching the antics of badly-behaved but simple children and continue to sip the glasses of Dom Perignon drink which are sitting in ice-buckets between their tables.

Then I see why the people who are celebrating the elderly gentleman's birthday are shouting and cheering. Ms N, the Hotel Manager and my boss, has entered the lobby and is heading our way.

Ms N's high heels click a message of power and control. She is wearing a dark jacket and skirt and a black stretch top and as she passes the Lobby Bar she turns slightly towards the group of less-smart-than-casually dressed people of whom several have had at least one drink. She smiles in greeting before continuing to the reception counter and stretching out her hand to Mr Matt Miller.

'Matthew. Mrs Miller,' she says. 'Welcome to our hotel. I hope we will ensure you have an unforgettable stay.'

'Why, hello there,' Mr Matt Miller replies. 'How wonderful to see you, and how fabulous to see your hotel. I guess the whole chain has a lot to learn from the famous Ms N.'

Mr Matt Miller of course has used Ms N's full name, but I have removed it here because Ms N is a modest person who does not like me to highlight her fabulous qualities.

Mr Matt Miller's voice is so warm that I am surprised to see that he has not shaken the hand Ms N is holding out towards him. In fact, he has not moved at all. He is much taller than Ms N, who even in her high heels is what we call in the hotel industry petite, and while he is speaking he strains to stand up as straight as he can, in order to look down on Ms N from the greatest possible height.

'Yes, we do have a lot to learn from the famous Ms N,' Mr Matt Miller continues. 'For example, I am grateful to you for breaking off whatever important task you were doing in order to come and meet me. I noticed you had laid a trap with Tatiana here, although frankly I should have thought it would have been a courtesy to greet me at the door. In fact, I should have thought it would be strongly in your interests to do so, since as your Regional Director my decisions, and my evaluations of your performance, may powerfully influence your future career.'

Mr Matt Miller's voice is not so warm now. 'Speaking of evaluations,' he says, 'I note that your reception is understaffed; and that the only girl on duty, young Tatiana, can barely speak English and seems to think the main part of her job is to cream her panties while she flirts with the male guests she is checking in while ignoring those waiting to be served. I notice also that you have packed the hotel with a group of your friends who are no doubt enjoying our *chums'n'cousins* staff discounts, lowering the tone of the lobby, depressing profits and eroding the experience of the full-rate customers who have taken the trouble to dress in proper business attire. With the World Anti-Corruption Forum starting tomorrow, you and every other hotel in this armpit of a capital city will have full occupancy. So your *chums'n'cousins* are enjoying their discounts at the cost of higher-rate bona fide customers who would boost your hotel's prestige and bottom line.

'Finally,' Mr Matt Miller concludes, 'I could not help hearing Tatiana being approached by a guest to help him organise a prostitute. Although she declined to help, I noted that she asked him to discuss the matter further with you as if, perhaps, you might be able to resolve the issue.' He glances briefly at his wife, whose facial expression is still one of surprise bordering on shock. 'I have no idea if Mrs Miller is going to enjoy her stay in your hotel and I do not much care. But I can tell you that you have made a bad start with me.'

Mr Matt Miller looks down at Ms N and raises his eyebrows, as if to say *what do you say to that,* or perhaps *eat that, bitch.*

Ms N looks back at Mr Matt Miller. She does not seem upset at his comments, but has an inquisitive expression on her face, as if she is figuring out how to solve some problem. Perhaps Mr Miller is the problem.

'Thank you, Matthew, for your perceptive insights,' she says. 'I know of course that it is for me to learn at the feet of the master. And I am delighted to meet your wife.'

Ms N stretches out her hand towards Mrs Matt Miller. Unlike her husband, Mrs Matt Miller shakes Ms N's hand. When she looks at Ms N's inquisitive expression, Mrs Matt Miller's mouth twists for a moment away from its expression of shock and, perhaps, fear, and a small smile of joy transforms her face. I am thinking that perhaps no-one has smiled at Mrs Matt Miller, or even acknowledged her existence, for many years. When she smiles she is looking maybe twenty years younger than with her shocked or frightened face, which I now realise is caused not by bad plastic surgery but by her husband, Mr Matt Miller.

'Tatiana,' Ms N says, 'please could you check in the lady in the green Barbour, who I think you will find has a Swedish passport and will be staying in one of our deluxe sixteenth-floor Platinum Megastar Suites with lounge access. I will introduce Mr and Mrs Matt Miller to some of our honoured guests in the Lobby Bar. I may also give him a short tour of our back of house, as he is a senior colleague from HQ who has a keen interest in how we run our hotel.'

Ms N leads Mr and Mrs Matt Miller towards the Lobby Bar. I see that she is introducing Mr Matt Miller to several of the heavy-set men wearing dark suits or leather jackets, including our untainted-by-corruption-of-any-kind Minister of Justice. Perhaps she is trying to show Mr Matt Miller the type of senior and well-connected guests who are staying in our hotel.

If I am honest, I am a little surprised that Ms N is introducing Mr Matt Miller to the gentlemen in the dark suits or leather jackets because neither they nor our untainted-by-corruption-of-any-kind Minister of Justice seem very pleased to meet him. Indeed, they are looking as if they would like him to drop down dead at the first opportunity, although of course he does not do this.

Then I see that Ms N is introducing Mr Matt Miller to some of her *chums'n'cousins*, some of whom have had at least one drink.

This also is surprising to me, because I have already heard Mr Matt Miller criticising the presence of Ms N's personal friends in the hotel, as well as the special services requested by the gentleman with the fragrant cologne and the green eyes and the kindly smile.

But I do not have much time to analyse the interaction of Mr Matt Miller with the guests in the Lobby Bar because the wild-haired woman in the green out-door jacket has finally made it to the reception counter and is holding out her ID.

It is, as Ms N has forecast, a Swedish passport.

This is unusual because in our beautiful but not yet economically advanced country we do not receive many tourists, or indeed visitors of any kind, from Sweden. The fact that Ms

N could identify the nationality of the wild-haired woman in the green out-door jacket therefore makes me think that our guest must either be someone well-known to Ms N, or famous, or both. But I do not recognise her.

I look her in the eye and smile my famous thousand-kilowatt smile and take her passport and say *Welcome to our hotel* and *good choice* but her only response is to reach into an inside pocket of her green out-door jacket, which I now see carries the label of the British brand which Ms N has mentioned, and pull out a rabbit.

'Could you ask the chef to prepare this for me?' she says.

They are the first words she has spoken.

I peer at the rabbit and at the woman. The rabbit is dead and is looking at me with glassy, disapproving eyes. The woman is looking at me too, in a distracted and slightly absent way, as if she does not think she needs to say anything more to me and is perhaps waiting for me to deal with the rabbit. I wonder if I have perhaps misheard her amidst all the noise in the lobby but when I consider this, I realise that all the noise in the lobby has ceased and it is now as quiet as a church.

The lobby is so quiet that I wonder for a moment if perhaps the two groups of guests in the Lobby Bar have somehow silently left the building. But when I glance in that direction I see that the group of heavy-set men in dark suits or leather jackets and the formerly cheerful group of Ms N's *chums'n'cousins* have not moved. In fact, they are standing around Mr Matt Miller, staring at him with what I can recognise even at this distance as undiluted rage.

Even the gentleman with the fragrant cologne and the green eyes and the kindly smile, who up to now I have thought of as a sophisticated and gentle person, is looking at Mr Matt Miller as if he would like personally to wring his neck.

Mrs Matt Miller is once again looking shocked, or maybe frightened, and twenty years older than when she was talking to Ms N.

I conclude from this that Mr Matt Miller has been saying

some things which have not made him popular with the people in the Lobby Bar.

Indeed, since Mr Matt Miller seems to take pleasure in saying things which upset people, I am more puzzled than ever that Ms N has been introducing him to her friends and other guests.

But I am even more surprised when I see what Ms N is doing next. She is leaving the Lobby Bar and is heading with Mr and Mrs Matt Miller towards the back of house area.

In fact, Ms N is taking them towards the kitchen.

When I see this, I feel worried on behalf of Mr Matt Miller because I fear that in the kitchen he may meet Kyoko, our Japanese sushi chef, who has a collection of ultra-sharp Chroma knives and is famous for her violent temper. Kyoko has reacted strongly on occasions in the past when someone has said to her something she perceives as being less than 100% polite. The likelihood of a conflict between Kyoko and Mr Matt Miller seems high.

The thought of Kyoko and her knives reminds me of the rabbit, which is still looking at me with its glassy, disapproving eyes, and of the woman in the green out-door jacket, who fortunately does not seem to be in any more of a hurry than the rabbit.

I take the rabbit in one hand and the passport in the other in order to process the check-in, although if I am honest I do not need the rabbit for this.

While I am checking the Swedish woman in I ask her if she would like the rabbit prepared in any particular way. She says 'however you like, my darling,' with a faint smile which, although perhaps lacking the intensity of my own thousand-watt version, has an old-world charm which makes me want to help her. When I take a photocopy of her passport I scan the details for any clue about who she might be; but the name means nothing to me and I can detect no hint of her occupation, or why she might be in our hotel. The only clue is that the passport itself is old and battered, as if the Swedish woman has perhaps travelled a great deal.

I summon a bell-boy and tell him to escort her to the Platinum Megastar Suite on the 16th floor.

When the bell-boy leads the way to the elevators, I notice that the Swedish woman does not follow. Instead, she takes a meandering route. She examines the art on the wall; the thirty-metre water feature; and the menu of our one-star Michelin restaurant. The result is that she arrives at the elevator fully two minutes after the bell-boy.

For reasons I do not fully understand, this behaviour makes me happy.

It is as if the Swedish woman knows how to enjoy things other people take for granted.

By the time the Swedish woman is reaching the elevator, I notice that the noise in the lobby is picking up again. The increase in noise reminds me that Ms N has taken Mr and Mrs Matt Miller to the kitchen to meet Kyoko, with her ultra-sharp Chroma knives; and for a moment I am concerned.

But as soon as I have this thought I put it from my mind. Mr and Mrs Matt Miller are with Ms N. Ms N must know what she is doing; in fact, she must have a plan.

Ms N is good at solving problems. One day, I would like to be like her.

19.30

IN OUR BEAUTIFUL but not yet economically advanced country, we do not have very many old people. In fact, our average life expectancy is only sixty-eight years. So I am excited to meet the elderly Irish gentleman, who the customer with the fragrant cologne and the green eyes and the kindly smile has told me is his father, and who is already nineteen years older than our average life expectancy.

Clearly, although he walks with a stick, many parts of his body are still in good working condition.

I find the father and son in the Lobby Bar having a drink before dinner. Both of them are drinking our hotel's signature Platinum Megastar Sucker Punch cocktail.

The father of the customer with the fragrant cologne and the green eyes and the kindly smile is shorter than his son and is wearing crisply pressed slacks, a polo shirt and a jacket with a red *foulard* which strikes me as being at the smart end of the smart casual range. His face is so deeply wrinkled that it reminds me of the spectacular gorges which cut through the uplands around my poor village far from the historic capital of our beautiful but not yet economically advanced country. But he has the same kindly smile as his son and also a sparkle in his eye.

'Is this her?' he says.

'No, daddy,' his son says. 'This is Tatiana, the guest services manager of the hotel. Please be polite to her.'

'Tatiana?' The elderly Irish gentleman looks me up and down. 'Well, you sure are smashing, darling.' He waves his walking stick towards a group of guests who are sitting in a nearby group of white leather armchairs, and smiles again. 'Isn't she smashing?'

The people in the armchairs raise their drinks, which I see are mostly Platinum Megastar Sucker Punch cocktails, and agree that I am smashing, whatever this means. Even a few of the heavy-set men in dark suits or leather jackets who are visiting our hotel for the World Anti-Corruption Forum smile and raise their glasses of Dom Perignon drink, which makes me think that perhaps they do not mind the behaviour of Ms N's *chums'n'cousins* too much.

I am also thinking that if all of Ms N's *chums'n'cousins* are drinking industrial quantities of Platinum Megastar Sucker Punch cocktails, perhaps the impact of their stay on the hotel's bottom line will not be so bad as Mr Matt Miller has suggested.

Then I notice that one of the heavy-set men in leather jackets is still looking at me, not as if to agree that I am smashing, but in a way I do not like. He has a flat, squashed nose; thick gold rings on three of the fingers of his right hand; and a gold chain around his neck. He is sitting next to our untainted-by-corruption-of-any-kind Minister of Justice, who is also looking at me in a way I do not like. Neither of them is smiling in my direction; but as they whisper together, they are smiling at each other. It is as if they are making plans for me to do something to me which they will enjoy; but which they are not expecting I will enjoy at all.

I look away from the gentleman with the rings and our Minister of Justice and see that the three gentlemen in *thawbs* and *keffiyehs* are sitting nearby. They do not look as if they are planning to do anything to me, but raise their glasses of soda water and nod as if, perhaps, they too are thinking I am smashing. I am looking for the gentleman with the dark eyes and cute dimples, but if I am honest, with the *keffiyehs* and the *agals,* I am finding it difficult to tell which of the three gentlemen is which.

I can see now that the gentlemen in *thawbs* and *keffiyehs* are almost certainly businessmen and are in the bar area to discuss business. I deduce this because one of them has placed a briefcase on the table and is taking some documents out of it, perhaps about fighting corruption, which he is handing to the other two gentlemen. Two of them are also using laptop computers, although these are not on their laps but on the table in the Lobby Bar. Then they are all sitting down and examining their papers and their computer screens and leaving the briefcase on the table.

I remember Ms N saying that these gentlemen were particular about tables and seating arrangements and I am happy to see that their table has a "Reserved" sign on it, showing that they must specifically have asked to sit there.

'Tatiana, sweetheart, hello there. Did you meet your man Mr Matt Miller? The boss?' The man with the fragrant cologne and the green eyes and the kindly smile is not smiling now. 'What a wanker, if you'll pardon my French. He told the lot of us – our whole party – that we had no business being in the hotel at a discounted rate during this so-called Anti-Corruption shindig when top law enforcement officials could be staying here. Ms

N asked him what he thought about corruption. Mr Matt Miller said he thought corruption, and I quote, was a cancer that should be eradicated. I could swear he was looking at us like a few discounted rooms are a crime. Then he turned to my Dad – '

'He turned to me,' the elderly gentleman says, 'and said to my face: *As for you, grand-dad, there'll be no hanky-panky for you in this hotel – even if you can get it up, which I doubt.*' The elderly Irish gentleman shakes his head. 'I mean, the fellow's never even met me, let alone slept with me. How would he know whether I can get it up or not?'

I blink at both of them, horrified and baffled that any hotel guests – however deep their discounts – could be treated in this way by a member of our senior management. But I am distracted from this abomination by the arrival in the Lobby Bar of a tall woman with swept-back blonde hair wearing a beautiful white silk dress and the kind of make-up which makes a woman who is perhaps not completely young look beautiful rather than tragic. The elderly Irish gentleman and his son see her, too, and fall silent. At first I do not recognise her; but when before sitting down she meanders between several possible seats and then begins to examine a print on the wall I have never noticed before, I realise that she is our Swedish guest.

She sees me looking at her and comes across. 'Hello, my darling,' she says. 'Has your chef found a suitably tasty rabbit recipe?'

'Yes. He is making *lapin a la cocotte*.' I am proud of my pronunciation, which I have practised with our French chef in the restaurant, although even at the end he was saying he was disappointed in me.

'A rabbit stew! How rustic! It sounds so much better in French!' The Swedish woman turns to the Irish gentleman and his father and, although I am certain that she has never seen them before in her life, addresses them like old friends. 'Good evening,' she says. 'What brings you to this oasis of civilisation? And what are those cocktails you are drinking?'

The elderly gentleman and his son look as if they have won the lottery. The younger man with the fragrant cologne and the green eyes and the kindly smile almost runs to the bar to buy more drinks. The older man leans his stick against the sofa next to which they are standing. Then, with a huge smile on his wrinkled face, he urges the Swedish woman to sit down, guiding her with one hand on her bare arm in a way which I do not feel is appropriate but which she does not seem to mind. As he does this, he tells her that it is his birthday. The Swedish woman smiles her faint, distracted smile and asks him how old he is.

I do not hear the rest of the conversation because I am distracted by an exchange between one of the heavy-set men in leather jackets and our untainted-by-corruption-of-any-kind Minister of Justice. The heavy-set man is the one with the gold rings and squashed nose who has been looking at me earlier in a way I do not like. The two men are talking in Russian, which is still widely spoken in our beautiful but not yet economically advanced country, and which I learned in school in my poor village far from our historic capital. I hear the words *FBI* and *bastards*.

Of course, these words make me want to listen more carefully. But the heavy-set gentleman and the Minister are speaking in a way which makes it difficult to overhear. All I can understand is that the gentleman with the gold rings and squashed nose is not attending the World Anti-Corruption Forum because he is keen to stamp out corruption, which I understand is the aim of the meeting. On the contrary, he is attending in order to assess for himself the progress which the world's law-enforcement agencies are making in fighting corruption, and to make sure that any such progress does not affect his own operations.

When I listen further, I hear the gentleman with the gold rings say to our untainted-by-corruption-of-any-kind Minister of Justice that he believes one or more agents of the dreaded FBI may be in the hotel in order to identify and maybe take action against any criminal or corrupt elements to whom the bright idea of attending the Forum may have occurred. The idea that FBI agents may be in the hotel is prompting in these gentlemen a range of emotions and colourful words so shocking that I am thinking I should maybe move out of ear-shot.

But as I am thinking this, the gentleman with the gold rings and squashed nose addresses me.

'Hey, *devotchka*,' he says. *Devotchka* is of course the Russian word for a young girl, but when he uses this term he is not meaning it as a compliment. The men of my beautiful but not yet economically advanced country are not skilled in small-talk.

'Yes, sir,' I say. 'How may I help you?'

'Are you eavesdropping our conversation?' he says. 'Are you FBI?'

'No, sir,' I say. 'I am working in the hotel.'

'That is good because FBI – ' he makes a throat-cutting gesture. 'But you, me – we can do other things. You are very beautiful.'

'Thank you,' I say. 'Can I help you?'

'I own three Bentleys, a Rolls Royce and a villa in the south of France.' The gentleman with the gold rings and the squashed nose is resting his hand on his groin and looking at me and smiling.

When I am seeing this behaviour from the heavy-set man with the leather jacket and the squashed nose and gold rings and gold chain I am beginning to sweat and am finding it hard to breathe. This is because the heavy-set man is reminding me of Mr Minas, the former owner of this hotel, who used to impale the junior staff and cause many other problems until Ms N solved those problems using a giant cake and a man wearing glasses who I believe was the President of China.

Before Ms N took action, Mr Minas was a dangerous man.

The heavy-set man in the leather jacket who is attending the World Anti-Corruption Forum and who is touching his groin with his hand is also looking dangerous. In fact, I am wishing he is not a customer who is staying in the hotel tonight and who I and the other staff must treat with as much respect as we treat all our valued and five-star customers.

I nod and smile as if I am not seeing what he is doing with his hand and look around for something else which perhaps may need my attention. I find it at once. Across the lobby, Ms N has appeared in the doorway of the kitchen. She is talking to Kyoko, our tiny but emotional Japanese sushi chef. Kyoko is waving her hands, in one of which she is holding one of her ultra-sharp Chroma knives.

The first time I ever met Kyoko was in her kitchen. I saw then what one of her ultra-sharp Chroma knives could do to an innocent haggis. So I am alarmed when I see Kyoko brandishing one of these knives close to my Hotel Manager. But Ms N seems calm. In fact, I see her put her hand on Kyoko's shoulder, despite the risks of the whirling knife-blade, and pat her gently.

This gesture does not seem to calm Kyoko. On the contrary, the colour rises to her face and she lifts her knife to shoulder-height as if she is about to stab Ms N in the heart.

Then I see that Kyoko is not looking at Ms N. She is gazing across the lobby, past the 30-metre water feature and the Lobby Bar, to the lifts, where Mr and Mrs Matt Miller have appeared.

I have rarely seen Ms N move more quickly. She raises her hand to Kyoko's wrist, removes the knife, and hides it in a single movement in an inside pocket of her jacket. Then she gently but firmly propels Kyoko back through the doorway into the kitchen.

Mr Matt Miller has changed into a dark blue Brooks Brothers suit with a striped shirt and a purple tie. Mrs Matt Miller has also changed. She is wearing a matching pink skirt and jacket, which look also as if they might be from Brooks Brothers. I wonder whether perhaps Mr Matt Miller has taken Mrs Matt Miller to Brooks Brothers to buy their clothes together. She is wearing flat pink shoes, which look comfortable but which make her appear small standing next to Mr Matt Miller.

They are an odd couple. I am thinking that Mr Matt Miller looks dynamic and purposeful in his business attire. But Mrs Matt Miller still looks shocked, or even frightened, as if she knows that something awful is about to happen.

I am afraid that perhaps she knows Mr Matt Miller better than the rest of us do.

Mr Matt Miller begins to walk towards us. I feel a sense of dread: for Mrs Matt Miller; for Ms N's *chums'n'cousins*; for the elderly gentleman and the Swedish lady, who are still talking on the sofa; and even for the heavy-set gentlemen in the dark suits or leather jackets, who although they are bothering me, also seem not to enjoy the company of Mr Matt Miller.

I am also thinking that the three gentlemen in Arab dress, who so far seem to have had no contact with Mr Matt Miller at all, are unlikely to enjoy any contact which may be about to take place.

I take a step towards Mr Matt Miller; but before I can intercept him, I sense an aroma which reminds me of the fields of herbs which cloak the mountain uplands around my poor village, far from the historical capital of our beautiful but not yet economically-advanced country.

The Irish gentleman with the fragrant cologne and the green eyes and the kindly smile is blocking my way. His smile has grown larger.

'Tatiana. Sweetheart, mine. Where, but where, did you find her?' he says.

I stare at him, thinking about Mr Matt Miller. 'Who, sir?'

'The girl. The woman. She is simply too bloody perfect for my dear old Dad. And him with only six months left to live.'

Seeing me frown, the Irish gentleman with the fragrant cologne gestures to his elderly father, who is engaged in conversation with the Swedish woman. The elderly gentleman is leaning so far towards the Swedish woman that his head is almost touching her breasts, and I am beginning to wonder if it is true that he has only six months left to live. The Swedish woman does not seem to notice how far he is leaning forward, but is talking slowly while staring at the top of the elderly gentleman's head and smiling her faint smile.

Suddenly I realise what the two Irish gentlemen are thinking.

'No,' I say. 'You have misunderstood. I have not arranged anything. She is not – '

'Of course she is, as you say, not.' The younger gentleman smiles even more warmly than before. 'And I fully understand that you have not arranged anything inappropriate for my poor, dying father. This is a five-star hotel, after all.' He taps his nose and winks. 'Say no more. But that is what I call service.'

I stare in horror at the Swedish woman. Does she realise what the elderly Irish gentleman and his son are thinking about her? What if the elderly Irish gentleman does something more inappropriate than touching her arm? What if, for example, he asks her to go to his room? I wonder again what it is that she does for a living. Perhaps it is something to do with rabbits.

'No need to look so worried, sweetheart,' the younger Irish gentleman says. 'My father is fully experienced in these situations.'

'On the contrary. I think young Tatiana, and her boss Ms N, should be very worried indeed.'

The voice rings out. The person who has spoken is Mr Matt Miller.

I turn to face him.

'I guess you didn't see me coming,' he says, and fingers the big knot in his purple tie. 'But hey! It looks like I'm here. It's Miller Time!' He looks around the circle of Ms N's *chums'n'cousins* which is surrounding him, and laughs loudly. 'In fact, every day is Miller Time when I'm around. Better get used to it.'

Around us, everyone has fallen silent. I am thinking that this is often the effect of Mr Matt Miller; and that perhaps one of the terrible events which cause Mrs Matt Miller to look so shocked, or even frightened, may be about to take place. Ms N's *chums'n'cousins* group, including the Irish gentleman and his father and the Swedish woman, are quiet. The heavy-set gentlemen in dark suits or leather jackets are watching Mr Matt Miller with dark faces. Even the gentlemen in Arab dress are looking up from their papers and computer screens.

But Mr Matt Miller has not finished.

'I told you I was shocked when I heard this low-life pal of your Hotel Manager approach you in the reception to arrange a *prostitute* for his father. I said earlier that I assumed you had declined to help. I now discover that, far from refusing his indecent request, you have *corruptly and illegally* arranged for a *sexual encounter* for an eighty-seven year old guest, right here in the hotel in which you are working.' Mr Matt Miller draws himself up to his full height. 'You will leave the employment of this hotel group immediately.'

When Mr Matt Miller mentions the words *prostitute, corruptly, illegally* and *sexual encounter* he is almost shouting, as if these are words that deserve special attention.

I am watching the reactions of the men and women in the Lobby Bar as Mr Matt Miller is saying these words. Unfortunately, when Mr Matt Miller says the words *prostitute* and *sexual encounter*, the younger Irish gentleman with the fragrant cologne and the green eyes and the kindly smile grins and shrugs in a "what can you do?" kind of way. But when Mr Matt Miller says the words *corruptly* and *illegally* I see that every one of the men in dark suits or leather jackets, including our untainted-by-corruption-of-any-kind Minister of Justice, makes a sour face, as if they are considering painful tortures which they could inflict on Mr Matt Miller if they were to catch him in a quiet place. I see the gentleman with the rings and the squashed nose with the three Bentleys and the Rolls Royce and the villa in the south of France lean over to the Minister and I think I hear the Russian words for "Federal Bureau of Investigation", although I am not quite sure.

Of course, some of these gentlemen are not speaking English too well, and seeing Mr Matt Miller in his blue Brooks Brothers suit and purple tie and hearing him raise his voice when he says the words *corruptly* and *illegally* I am imagining they might be thinking he is some kind of law enforcement official.

But my main worry is that Mr Matt Miller has told me I am

fired for arranging a prostitute for a guest. This is not fair, as I have done no such thing; and also I am depending on my job to send home money to my family, who are still living in our poor village far from the historic capital of our beautiful country. I turn to him.

'Sir. Mr Miller. You are making a mistake. That lady is a guest – '

'Mr Matt Miller does not make mistakes,' Mr Matt Miller says. 'I have witnessed the whole sordid transaction from start to finish.'

'Excuse me, Matthew. Let me try to clarify things.' Ms N has appeared, miraculously silent on her high heels of power, and is standing next to Mr Matt Miller. She tosses her jacket onto a chair and takes a deep breath. She is wearing her inquisitive expression, perhaps with a hint of a smile. She looks around the Lobby Bar. 'But perhaps someone else is best placed to explain?'

Ms N is looking past Mr Matt Miller. I see that she is looking at the blonde Swedish woman on the couch, who has been talking to the elderly Irish gentleman.

The elderly Irish gentleman has been grinning right across his face since Mr Matt Miller has said the words *sexual encounter*, perhaps because he is hoping that this is what will be happening to him next.

The blonde woman, who Mr Matt Miller has accused of being a prostitute, is smiling her faint, distracted smile.

When I see the Swedish woman's distracted smile I am thinking that she perhaps does not understand English too well and has not quite realised what Mr Matt Miller is saying about her. But when Ms N looks at her she nods slightly and rises to her feet.

Once again, I am struck by the beauty of the Swedish woman, now that she has tidied her hair and put on her white silk dress. When she rises from the couch she stands up straight and seems to grow until she dominates not only the Lobby Bar but actually the entire lobby. Although she is not tall, I have the sense that she is looking down on all of us, and on Mr Matt Miller in particular.

'Thank you, Ms N,' she says, in what I am thinking is sounding like an English accent. She of course uses Ms N's real name but I will not write it here, for the reasons you know. 'I am so sorry to have put you in this position and to have caused such embarrassment for all concerned.'

The Swedish woman looks around the room and frowns as if she is truly very sorry, although if I am honest I cannot see what she has to be sorry about. 'It is not often,' she continues, 'that I have been accused of being a prostitute when I have engaged a gentleman in conversation. But there is a first time for everything, I suppose.'

'Don't give me that baloney.' Mr Matt Miller's voice is loud in the lobby. 'I've heard fairy tales from hookers a thousand times. I know a whore when I see one. Scram! Get out of the hotel and don't come back.'

Still the Swedish woman is smiling. 'I understand that you are confused,' she says. 'Although the strength of your conviction seems to rest on prejudice and preconceptions rather than any actual evidence. Perhaps that is symptomatic of the way in which opinions are formed in this Internet age.' She sighs. 'Unfortunately, prejudice and preconceptions have been my bread and butter throughout my life, because I had the privilege and responsibility to be born into a noble household. There is no particular reason why you should recognise me. But I am the Queen of Sweden.'

The Lobby Lounge is silent. Ms N's *chums'n'cousins* are staring at the Swedish woman with open mouths. The elderly Irish gentleman, still sitting on the couch, is scratching his head. Ms N is smiling her inquisitive smile and I am realising that she is knowing that the woman is the Queen of Sweden all the time.

Mr Matt Miller has turned white. 'But…' He swallows and takes a step backwards. 'What are you doing in the hotel?'

'Tonight, I am hoping to enjoy a peaceful drink before dinner, when I look forward to tucking into my *lapin a la cocotte*,' the

Queen of Sweden says. 'Tomorrow, I shall make the opening speech at the World Anti-Corruption Forum, of which I am the global patron.' She smiles at Mr Matt Miller. 'I hope you will not mind if I finish my conversation.' She turns and sits back down next to the elderly Irish gentleman, who is beaming.

I watch the elderly Irish gentleman with interest, because I am wondering whether he may be disappointed to discover that he is having a drink with the Queen of Sweden, instead of a prostitute as he has expected. I am assuming he must know his chances of enjoying a *sexual encounter* this evening are less than he has been imagining.

But the elderly Irish gentleman looks even happier than he looked when he was thinking the Swedish woman was a prostitute. In fact, when I see how his eyes are gleaming, I feel certain that his son has been lying when he has told me earlier that I should help his poor, sweet father find a female companion because he was having only six more months to live.

Maybe I am optimistic, but I am hoping that maybe his life expectancy is no less than is normal for an eighty-seven year old Irishman; and that he will enjoy chatting to the Queen of Sweden more than any possible *sexual encounter* with a prostitute or anyone else.

Or is the elderly Irish gentleman even more optimistic than I am? Can he be hoping that he might get lucky with the Queen of Sweden? I do not even want to think about this possibility.

Another person I am expecting to look more cheerful after the Queen of Sweden has revealed her identity is Mrs Matt Miller. She has been standing at the edge of the group in her matching pink skirt and jacket and shoes. I am thinking that the terrible event she has been expecting perhaps has not turned out so badly and that she could now lighten up a bit.

But when I turn to Mrs Matt Miller I see that if anything she looks even more shocked, or frightened, than she did earlier.

This is troubling because I am thinking that Mrs Matt Miller is probably knowing Mr Matt Miller well; and that the terrible event which she has been expecting has perhaps not yet happened.

I am also worried that the heavy-set gentleman with the gold rings and the squashed nose and the three Bentleys and the Rolls Royce and the villa in the south of France, and also our untainted-by-corruption-of-any-kind Minister of Justice, are continuing to watch me in a way I do not like; and I am wondering how I, or perhaps Ms N, may be able to stop this.

But the next moment I forget about the gentleman with the gold rings and our untainted-by-corruption-of-any-kind Minister of Justice, because Mr Matt Miller has turned away from the Queen of Sweden and the elderly Irish gentleman and is standing face-to-face with Ms N in the middle of the Lobby Bar.

'So,' he says. 'Congratulations. This is quite an operation you have going here. The Queen of Sweden. *Her Majesty.*' Mr Matt Miller is saying this last phrase loudly enough for everyone in the Lobby Bar and maybe even the street outside to hear. But the Queen of Sweden does not seem to notice him.

'Since I took over as Director of your region six months ago,' Mr Matt Miller says, 'I have heard great things about the famous Ms N.' Again, he gives her full name, although I have not written it here. '*She is great at solving problems,* they say. *Her hotels are the most profitable in the world. Her staff survey ratings show her teams respect and admire her.* Etcetera, etcetera. So I thought I'd come and see for myself what all the fuss was about, and draw my own conclusions.'

Suddenly Mr Matt Miller holds out his hand to Ms N. For a second, her inquisitive smile disappears and she purses her lips; but then she smiles again, holds out her own, smaller, hand and shakes his firmly. 'I have to say,' Mr Matt Miller continues, 'that I have, in the light of what I have witnessed in your hotel, decided to put your name forward for a special award as Platinum Megastar Manager of the Year. What do you say to that?'

I stare at Ms N. I am feeling full of joy that she has won over such a critical gentleman who is also her boss. The fact that Mr Matt Miller is now beaming at Ms N a smile which I am thinking is perhaps almost as brilliant as my own famous thousand-watt smile seems to me to show that he has at last recognised her qualities.

But Ms N is not smiling. Nor, I see, is Mrs Matt Miller, who is continuing to look shocked, or even frightened.

'I know,' Ms N says slowly and clearly, 'that you are focused on stamping out everything which is corrupt and illegal. Your job is to root out criminals and scams. You are very successful at it.' She lowers her voice. 'I am honoured if you believe that my efforts to run this hotel deserve a Platinum Megastar award. But of course, if any prize is due it is my staff, not I, who deserve it.'

In the corner of my eye, I see the heavy-set man with the leather jacket and the gold rings nod slowly when he hears the words *corrupt* and *illegal* and lean over to whisper in the ear of our untainted-by-corruption-of-any-kind Minister of Justice.

'Do you really think you don't deserve the award?' Mr Matt Miller is standing straight again, perhaps in an effort to look down on Ms N from the greatest height possible. He pauses, as if he is thinking about the question carefully. Then he speaks to her in a voice so quiet that I am straining to hear it. 'You know – maybe you're right. On reflection, I think this hotel has to be the shoddiest, shabbiest, sleaziest apology for a hotel I have ever experienced in our chain. Prostitution. A bottomless pit of *chums'n'cousins*. Even your paying guests look more like gangsters and shagged-out sheikhs than genuine business people.' He shakes his head. 'This is your last job in our hotel chain, as Hotel Manager, stand-in General Manager, or anything else. I've already fired young Tatiana. You're fired too. And now –' his voice rises as if he is enjoying himself – 'It's Miller Time! I'm off to the Platinum Megastar Lounge for an ice-cold beer. At least your riff-raff chums won't have access there. Nor will you, for much longer.' He turns and marches towards the elevators, shouting to his wife over his shoulder as he goes: 'Come on, you.'

Seeing Mrs Matt Miller trailing behind her husband towards the elevators, still wearing her shocked or even frightened expression, reminds me of the ultra-sharp Chroma knife which Ms N took from Kyoko at the door to the kitchen and which she placed in the jacket which she threw down in the Lobby Bar.

Where is that ultra-sharp knife now?

Could it have fallen out, and be lying around on the floor where it could injure someone?

Could Mrs Matt Miller have picked it up, and be about to sink it into the unprotected back of her awful husband?

When I think this, I find that I am smiling; but I know that such an act can never happen. It is impossible to imagine Mrs Matt Miller wielding an ultra-sharp Chroma knife in the Lobby. But it gives me pleasure to picture her doing this, perhaps while wearing her shocked or even frightened expression.

It is impossible because I am certain that Mrs Matt Miller is a highly intelligent woman. If she were to wield a weapon against her husband I am certain she would do it in a private place where no-one would observe her, and she would be laughing cheerfully rather than looking shocked or even frightened.

Again, I find myself smiling.

As the elevator doors are closing behind Mr and Mrs Matt Miller, I am surprised to hear Ms N is speaking. She is talking slowly and clearly, and I am thinking that perhaps she is making sure that the thick-set gentlemen in the dark suits or leather jackets, and perhaps also the gentlemen in Arab dress, are understanding her fully.

'I wish to apologise for the actions of Mr Matt Miller,' she says. 'Because the World Anti-Corruption Forum is beginning in the hotel tomorrow, he is wanting to take firm action against any activity in these premises which could be considered in any way corrupt or illegal. And he wishes to ensure that the law enforcement agencies have all the support they need.' For a moment, Ms N seems to address our untainted-by-corruption-of-any-kind Minister of Justice. 'That includes any covert law enforcement agents who may be operating in this hotel.' She winks. 'You never know who could be an FBI agent.'

For a moment there is silence. Then everyone starts talking at once. Ms N sits down with her group of *chums'n'cousins* and I am pleased to see that the fact Mr Matt Miller has just fired her does not stop one of her friends ordering a bottle of Champagne to drink her health. When it arrives, the entire group of *chums'n'cousins*, including the two Irish gentlemen and even the Queen of Sweden, burst into applause.

Again, I am thinking that these *chums'n'cousins* are not harming the profitability of the hotel at all, and that Ms N is quite aware of this.

The heavy-set men in dark suits and leather jackets, by contrast, are quiet. They and our untainted-by-corruption-of-any-kind Minister of Justice put their heads together and talk quietly. Unfortunately, this means that I cannot hear a word that they are saying.

Only the three gentlemen in *thawbs* and *keffiyehs* do not seem to pay any attention to the actions of Mr Matt Miller. They continue to read their papers and look at their laptop computers and drink their soda water and talk softly to one another. From time to time one of them will replace some papers in the briefcase on the table, or take out some new papers to examine and discuss.

In fact, the three gentlemen in *thawbs* and *keffiyehs* do not interact with anyone else in the Lobby Bar at all. This seems to me a pity, since one of them has dark eyes and cute dimples. But as soon as I think about the dark eyes and dimples I forget them again, since this is not a professional thought to have about a guest.

I look across the Lobby Bar. If I am honest, I am astonished by the way in which Ms N has settled the atmosphere and cheered up our guests, even though she is no longer the Hotel Manager, or acting General Manager, of this or any other hotel. A few seconds ago, we had silence, bad tempers and loud voices. Now the gentlemen in Arab dress are enjoying their work; the gentlemen in dark suits or leather jackets are discussing their business; and the group of *chums'n'cousins*, including the 87-year-old birthday boy, are in the best of spirits and running up a large and profitable bar bill for the hotel.

In fact, it is almost a miracle.

Ms N is good at solving problems. One day, I would like to be like her.

22.00

FOR A LONG time after Ms N has restored the atmosphere in the Lobby Bar, everything is quiet. People come and go. Some of the gentlemen in the dark suits or leather jackets wander off to visit our sushi restaurant with the Michelin star, to enjoy Kyoko's specialities. The gentlemen in Arab dress do not go anywhere but order bar snacks and continue to enjoy their soda water and soft drinks. Ms N and her party of *chums'n'cousins*, including the two Irish gentlemen, go downstairs to the Dionysus Bar, our basement luxury venue, to enjoy a specially catered buffet dinner, before drifting back into the Lobby.

It seems that Ms N's *chums'n'cousins* are enjoying the Lobby Bar very much and that many of them are quite thirsty.

Most of the gentlemen in dark suits or leather jackets, including our untainted-by-corruption-of-any-kind Minister of Justice, also return to the Lobby Bar after enjoying Kyoko's sushi. But instead of drinking more of the Dom Perignon drink they are now drinking the hotel's exclusive triple-distilled *horilka* from Ukraine, which is perhaps the greatest vodka in the world.

It seems that the gentlemen in the dark suits or leather jackets also are thirsty, because they are enjoying the *horilka* very much. I am pleased to see this because in my experience, after a man has consumed a large enough quantity of *horilka,* he is less likely to be aggressive or troublesome towards women than before he is drinking it.

Indeed, the mood of the gentlemen in the dark suits or leather jackets seems better than it was earlier, when Mr and Mrs Matt Miller were present. Even the Queen of Sweden has returned to the Lobby Bar, although I notice that she chooses to sit at a table by herself, and is drinking a cappuccino.

During this time, I see no sign of Mr and Mrs Matt Miller. This is good, because I am not thinking that Mr Matt Miller is necessarily contributing in a positive way to the atmosphere in the Lobby Bar. I am also thinking that the longer Mr Matt Miller is not present, the more time we have before he can put into action his decision to fire myself and Ms N.

In fact, I am even beginning to think that this hotel would be better off in every way if Mr Matt Miller were never to reappear.

So I have mixed feelings when the doors of one of the elevators in the lobby are opening and Mrs Matt Miller appears. She is still wearing her matching pink jacket and skirt but she has changed her pink flat shoes to a darker colour and is carrying something in her hand.

When she comes closer, I see that her expression has changed to one I have not seen before.

She continues to look shocked. But she no longer looks frightened. In fact, underneath the shock on her face I almost think that I can see small traces of happiness, although the contrast between the shock and happiness, if I am honest, makes her face hard to read. She comes to the reception.

'My name is Daphne,' she says. 'I am afraid that the elevator needs cleaning. My shoes are dirty.'

These are the first words I have heard Mrs Matt Miller, or as I should now call her, Daphne, speak since she is arriving in the hotel. I am interested to learn that she has an American accent and a soft voice which is much easier to listen to than the voice of her husband.

I look over the reception counter and see that I am wrong to think that Daphne has changed her pink flat shoes. She is still wearing them, but they have been stained a dark brown, or possibly red, colour. When I look back towards the elevator I see that there is a chain of dark brown, or possibly red, footsteps leading across the polished white marble floor of the lobby towards the reception counter.

I look at Daphne. 'Is there anything else in the elevator, madam?' I ask.

'Yes,' she says. 'There is the body of a man. His name was Mr Matt Miller. I also found this.' She places on the reception counter an ultra-sharp Chroma knife, covered, like her hands, in what I am now sure is dark red blood.

All trace of shock, or possibly fear, has vanished from Daphne's face. Now, she is smiling. This smile is once again making her look twenty years younger, and perhaps the happiest person in the whole of the hotel.

I look at Daphne. I look at the knife. Then I look at Ms N, who has left her party of *chums'n'cousins* in the Lobby Bar and is standing next to Daphne at the reception counter.

I am expecting that Ms N will herself be looking shocked, since it is not good for a hotel when a guest has killed another guest in the elevator. Actually, it is not good for a hotel when anyone has killed anyone in the elevator. But if the murderer or the victim is a guest, this is worse. And if both the murderer and the victim are guests, this is the worst possible combination.

But what if the murderer is not only a guest but also the wife of a top regional manager in our hotel chain; and the victim is not only a guest but also a top regional manager in that chain and the husband of the murderer? This seems to me worse than the worst possible combination, and definitely a suboptimal outcome.

But when I am looking at Ms N, I am thinking that perhaps I do not understand too much about murders in hotels, of which today's example is, if I am honest, the first I have ever witnessed. Ms N is smiling her inquisitive smile; and does not look even surprised, let alone shocked.

'Tatiana,' she says, 'kindly call Nigel. Tell him he should quickly review the hotel's CCTV systems to search for evidence as to who carried out this act. Tell him also to send four of his staff to ensure no-one leaves the lobby.'

'Yes, Ms N,' I say. I am astonished to hear Ms N say that Nigel should search for evidence, because it seems obvious to me that Daphne is the murderer. Who else could have done it? At first, I am also surprised to hear that Ms N is expecting Nigel, our Head of Security, with his legs like tree-trunks and his head perhaps made of similar material, to solve this crime; but then I realise that Ms N has not asked him to solve anything, but only to look at some CCTV recordings.

'Second, please call Housekeeping to tell them not to clean the elevator, or these footprints, which could be evidence. STOP!' Ms N has whirled round towards a Housekeeping team, which is approaching the bloody footsteps with a cleaning trolley.

I am thinking that in other circumstances, this would be an excellent performance by the Housekeeping team, since the bloody footsteps have been soiling the polished marble floor of the lobby for only a few seconds. But when the team hear Ms N shout, they take their trolley and leave the scene so quickly that I am almost tempted to wonder whether it is they, rather than Daphne, who have committed the murder.

'Third,' Ms N says to me, 'tell Engineering to lock the elevators, as they may contain evidence. Fourth, can you please ask Kyoko to step preparing her *futomaki* and *chumaki* and *chirashizushi* and join us in the lobby bar. Fifth, and finally, call the police and tell them to come. Tell them there is no danger, but that we are concerned that a murder may have been committed and we need to clear it up urgently.'

Ms N looks at me, and smiles as if this is a day like any other day. 'When you have taken this action, please come and join us in the Lobby Bar. I shall want to have a hotel employee as a witness for what is about to happen. But we should start by taking care of our guest. What is your family name, Daphne?'

'You may call me Dr Daphne Miller,' Dr Daphne Miller says.

'I should be most grateful if you would agree to come with me to the Lobby Bar, Dr Miller,' Ms N says, 'and sit down. We have business to do.'

I watch Ms N as she accompanies Dr Daphne Miller to the Lobby Bar and sits her down and orders her a cup of tea before returning to the reception. I am wondering what this business is which is about to happen; and why she might need me as a witness. I am also wondering why calling the police is only fifth on Ms N's list of priorities.

I am also remembering Ms N's earlier references to FBI agents being present in the hotel in preparation for the World Anti-Corruption Forum; and I am wondering whether Ms N should perhaps think about calling them also. I can see no sign of her doing this. I know, however, that I should not worry, because Ms N always has a plan. So I begin to carry out her instructions while she makes an emergency announcement on our public address system asking our guests and staff to stay where they are and to avoid using the lobby until further notice.

Within a few minutes Nigel's security team, with their legs and heads like tree-trunks, have stationed themselves at the exits and entrances to the lobby. I head to the Lobby Bar, as Ms N has asked.

The atmosphere in the Lobby Bar is, if I am honest, more like a party than the scene of a crime. Everyone is talking to everyone else.

Well, nearly everyone.

The gentlemen in the dark suits or leather jackets are talking to each other in Russian, in an animated way. Several of them, including our untainted-by-corruption-of-any-kind Minister of Justice, are talking on their mobile phones. Ms N's *chums'n'cousins* are also talking with each other, but at much greater volume. The Queen of Sweden, who earlier has been sitting by herself and drinking her cappuccino, has begun a softly-spoken conversation with Dr Daphne Miller.

In fact, only two groups of people are silent.

One of the groups of silent people is very small. It is our chef Kyoko, who is standing by herself looking angry and wearing an inappropriate red, white and black cooking apron with the slogan *Forget Sex, Let's Have Dinner*, which I am guessing she has not removed in order to show that she is upset with being asked to leave the kitchen.

The second group of silent people is consisting of the three gentlemen in *keffiyehs* and *thawbs*. They are still looking at their papers and laptops as if nothing has happened. In fact, I am wondering if perhaps their English is less good than I had thought.

Ms N's heels are again clicking out their message of power as she approaches the Lobby Bar. I am excited to see how she will solve what is surely one of the greatest problems any Hotel Manager, or indeed any acting General Manager, has ever faced. But I am also worried that solving this problem may be beyond the powers even of Ms N. I am relieved, as we reach the Lobby Bar, to see that Nigel, our Head of Security, is hurrying towards us.

Nigel's arrival is good because Ms N has asked him to review the CCTV footage. Most public areas of hotels are monitored by more CCTV cameras than you can imagine. Indeed, I cannot see how anyone could commit even the tiniest crime in a hotel without being found out, let alone a murderer who has left an elevator filled with blood. So I am confident that Nigel will bring us valuable evidence to help Ms N, including establishing once and for all whether the murderer is Dr Daphne Miller.

Nigel walks up to Ms N and stops dead. I know he is making a big effort not to click his heels. This is difficult for Nigel, because he was formerly working in the British army and he is clicking his heels even in his sleep. He leans forward and begins to whisper something to Ms N.

'Speak louder, Nigel,' Ms N says. 'I wish Tatiana and everyone else to hear what you have to say.'

'Yes, Ma'am.' Nigel stands up straight, as if he is perhaps on a parade ground, and barks out the words. 'The CCTV system is not working, Ma'am. We have no CCTV pictures for the last four hours. I cannot understand how this can have happened, because it is designed to be tamper-proof and – '

'Thank you, Nigel. Please stay here.'

I am staring at Nigel in horror, because it seems to me that the task of identifying the murderer has become one thousand times more difficult. But Ms N is calm. She turns to the assembled guests.

'The absence of CCTV pictures is a problem, but not a crisis,' she says. 'I think we can solve this murder. I also think we must do this before the police arrive, for three reasons. First, the police in this country are unfortunately not always fantastically efficient. Second, despite the powerful efforts of the government – ' she turns to our untainted-by-corruption-of-any-kind Minister of Justice and smiles her inquisitive smile ' – there is a risk that the police may sometimes operate on the basis of factors other than an objective scrutiny of the best available evidence. And third, I do not wish the hotel to be a crime scene for longer than necessary. Is everyone happy with that?'

There is a murmur of assent, although if I am honest I do not think anyone is taking too seriously Ms N's proposal to solve the crime before the police arrive, unless Dr Daphne Miller is about to own up to being the murderer. But then I am looking at Nigel standing close to Ms N with his legs like tree-trunks and suddenly I realise that *Ms N believes the murderer is one of the other people in the lounge.*

Not for the first time, I am pleased that our full body scanner at the entrance to the hotel, which we have had installed for many years to prevent customers from accidentally bringing *janbiyas,* assault rifles or rocket-propelled grenades into the hotel, means that in theory none of the people in the lobby is likely to be armed.

Unless it is with one of Kyoko's ultra-sharp Chroma knives.

Ms N looks around the people gathered in the Lobby Bar and takes a deep breath. I realise that although she seems as calm as ever, she knows she is facing one of the biggest problems of her career; and that solving it may not be easy.

I step up behind her and take a deep breath too, to let her know that I am here and am ready to support her in whatever she plans to do. I see her smile as she hears me. Then, at last, she speaks.

'First, the weapon,' Ms N says. 'It seems to me that the Chroma knife used in the attack is the same one I took from Kyoko earlier this evening and stored safely in the pocket of my jacket. I then placed the jacket on a chair in the Lobby Bar. When I put the jacket back on, the knife had disappeared. I assumed it had fallen on the floor; but with hindsight I realise that, perhaps, the murderer may have taken it. Perhaps we can start by addressing this question. Did anyone here take the knife from my jacket?'

Kyoko; the gentlemen in the dark suits or leather jackets; the Queen of Sweden; Dr Daphne Miller; Ms N's *chums'n'cousins;* and the gentlemen in Arab dress all look at Ms N. No-one admits to having taken the knife, or says anything at all.

'That is as I expected,' Ms N says. 'So let us, secondly, look for a motive. I see several possibilities. First, Dr Daphne Miller had a strained relationship with her former husband, who I suspect was not at all times and in all situations the most agreeable life partner for whom a woman could wish.'

I see that Dr Daphne Miller is watching Ms N closely. Dr Daphne Miller is still looking twenty years younger than before, and is no longer looking shocked or frightened. But I am thinking she is wondering what Ms N is going to say next.

'Whether,' Ms N says, 'that strained relationship would justify her killing him, and why she should do so this evening, in the difficult security environment of a hotel, is less clear. Did you kill your husband, Doctor Miller?'

Dr Daphne Miller rises slowly from her chair. Her shoes are still caked with blood and I am wondering whether she might wish to take them off, but she does not seem to mind. Perhaps in fact she likes being reminded that Mr Matt Miller is dead and that she is treading in his blood with every step she takes.

'I did not kill him,' she says. 'Although maybe I wish I had. He left the Platinum Megastar Lounge ahead of me to come down to dinner. After a few minutes I followed. When I stepped into the elevator he was lying there. The knife was on the floor.'

'Thank you,' Ms N says. 'A second motive is that Mr Matt Miller was rude to my friends, who are staying here on a *chums'n'cousins* rate. One of them could have stolen the knife and carried out the murder. This seems to me unlikely, since gratuitous rudeness is not usually a matter for a revenge killing; but perhaps some people might feel it is.' She turns to her friends, who have fallen uncharacteristically silent. 'Did any of you commit the murder?'

Ms N's friends, including the two Irish gentlemen, all say 'no' so quickly that I am again thinking this is quite suspicious; but Ms N pays them no further attention.

'Now we come to your royal highness,' Ms N says to the Queen of Sweden. 'You, too, have been subject to some bizarre and hurtful insults from Mr Matt Miller. Leaving aside issues of *lèse-majesté*, I again hardly see that this is a sufficient motive for a murder. But as a head of state you might have greater resources than other people; and in the interests of equality, diversity and the rule of law, I feel I should ask you, also, whether you committed the murder.'

The Queen of Sweden rises to her feet. Her white silk dress brushes the ground like a milky waterfall; and I am again thinking that she is a beautiful woman.

'Thank you for including me in your suspects,' she says. 'I agree that this shows an admirable absence of preconceptions or prejudice. But for the record, I can confirm that I did not kill Mr Matt Miller, much as I would have enjoyed seeing him die. Nor did I instruct or encourage anyone else to do so.'

'Thank you,' Ms N says. 'Kyoko. Mr Matt Miller entered your kitchen earlier. What did he say to you?'

'He say...' Kyoko hesitates. 'He say no reason why Japanese

sushi chef needed to prepare *sushi* and *sashimi*. Local cook same, only cheaper, he say. Only need to chop up fish. Also, use cheaper ingredients. Better for bottom line.'

'I understand,' Ms N says. 'How did his comments make you feel?'

'I want to *kill* him.' Kyoko makes a frenzied stabbing motion with her hand, which is fortunately empty. Anyone who is seeing our Japanese chef at this moment is thinking that she is almost certainly killing Mr Matt Miller, or any other person who insults her cooking.

'And did you kill him, Kyoko?'

'No.' Kyoko shrugs, instantly calm. 'If I kill him, no body in lift. No blood. No nothing. No clue for anyone. Also, like you say, that knife is one you took from me when I say I want to kill him earlier. How can I kill him with that knife if I do not have it?'

'Thank you, Kyoko,' Ms N says. 'I have good reason to believe that what you say is true.'

Ms N pauses for a moment and I know she is thinking about our customer Mr Burke, who refused to leave the hotel and behaved badly when we were two rooms overbooked. On that occasion, after Mr Burke insulted Kyoko's cooking, we never had any problem with him again.

'Now, I do not intend to question our guests in the *keffiyehs* and *thawbs* for two reasons,' Ms N continues. 'One of these reasons is that they had their dinner in the lobby and have not been out of sight all evening. I will come to the other reason in a moment.' She smiles at the gentlemen in Arab dress, who nod politely. One of them stands and puts some papers in the briefcase. Another peers at the screen of a lap-top computer.

'This brings us to our final motive, which applies to our remaining guests.' Ms N turns to the gentlemen in dark suits or leather jackets. Most of them smile and nod like the gentlemen in the Arab dress; but the man with the gold rings and the squashed nose with the three Bentleys and the Rolls Royce and the villa in the south of France turns to our untainted-by-corruption-of-any-kind Minister of Justice and whispers something in his ear. Our untainted-by-corruption-of-any-kind Minister of Justice nods and makes another phone call, covering his mouth with his hand.

'This motive,' says Ms N, 'is two-fold. First, Mr Matt Miller did not treat our respected business guests, or even the Minister, with one hundred percent respect when I brought him to the Lobby Bar earlier. Could I have foreseen this? Perhaps I could. It may be argued that any normal person coming into contact with Mr Matt Miller for more than a few minutes would want to kill him. But most people would not actually do so.'

When Ms N is saying *perhaps I could* I am thinking that her eyes are twinkling. But I do not have time to think about this as she continues almost at once.

'The situation might be different,' Ms N continues, 'if the people upset and insulted were a group of hardened criminals, perhaps of the sort who are well enough connected to spend time with government ministers in five-star hotels and even to attend an Anti-Corruption Forum opened by a distinguished visitor of the highest calibre. A group, perhaps, who were accustomed to killing and who even had the means to sabotage a hotel's sophisticated CCTV system in order to conceal their actions. One can imagine that such a group, if it existed, might perhaps commit such a killing after being insulted by Mr Matt Miller.'

When Ms N is talking about these hypothetical hardened criminals I am looking at the man with the gold rings and the squashed nose; and when she mentions the government ministers I am looking at our untainted-by-corruption-of-any-kind Minister of Justice. But neither of them seems to be looking too worried, or even to be paying any attention to what Ms N is saying.

It seems to me that these people either did not commit the murder, or else, if they did, that they are confident that no evidence can possibly be produced to link them to the crime.

But Ms N has not finished. 'What if the motive were

stronger?' she says. 'What if the hardened criminals believed that the FBI were closing in on them; and that one or more under-cover FBI agents might be operating in this hotel? Might they, believing that they had identified one of the agents, seek to remove that agent as a threat, perhaps as a diversion using a weapon they had acquired in the hotel? That, it seems to me, might well be a sufficient motive for the crime we have witnessed.'

No-one speaks. I see that two police cars have arrived outside the front doors of our hotel and that the portly Chief of Police of our historic capital is climbing out of one of them. This takes time, because the Chief of Police is not a slim or a fit man.

I am thinking that it is mostly good that the police are here, because they are armed and should be able to prevent any violence, should anyone in the Lobby Bar be tempted to be violent, for example against Ms N.

On the other hand, the portly Chief of Police is well known to be closely connected to our untainted-by-corruption-of-any-kind Minister of Justice, and may not be too enthusiastic about trying to take action against either him or his friends in the dark suits or leather jackets if it is turning out that they are involved in a crime. Indeed, I am also thinking that it is odd that the Chief of Police personally should attend a crime scene, and am wondering whether this may be the result of the phone calls I have been seeing our untainted-by-corruption-of-any-kind Minister of Justice making earlier.

Then I see the mouth of the man with the gold rings and the squashed nose stretch into a smile as he sees the portly Chief of Police entering the front door of the hotel; and I am certain that the Chief of Police is not here by accident.

Perhaps the arrival of the Chief of Police is even making the man with the gold rings more confident, because suddenly he speaks.

'It is a pity,' he says, 'that you have so many bright ideas, *devotchka*.' Again, when he is addressing Ms N in this way, the man with the gold rings is not meaning it as a compliment.

'And yet, you have no evidence with which to back these ideas up. Did I understand your thick-necked friend correctly when he said that your CCTV system is unfortunately not working?'

'My Head of Security did say that, yes.' Nigel's face has turned red. I see Ms N lay her hand on his shoulder as if to calm him down.

'And did I understand you correctly when you said that someone had identified an under-cover FBI agent, and murdered him with a knife they found in the Lobby Bar? That is a tragedy. Especially when there is no evidence.'

'I am sorry if my English is not always perfect,' Ms N says. I see that she is standing up even straighter than usual on her high heels; and that she is smiling her inquisitive smile. 'I did not say that anyone had murdered an under-cover FBI agent. Nor did I say there was no evidence.' She turns to the portly Chief of Police, who has entered the Lobby Bar with two uniformed officers from our country's recently re-branded, retrained and 100% corruption-free but perhaps not yet entirely world-class police force. 'Can I offer you a cup of coffee, sir?'

'Thank you, yes. And a glass of malt whisky,' the portly Chief of Police says. Then he turns not to Ms N but to our untainted-by-corruption-of-any-kind Minister of Justice and asks in Russian if, perhaps, there is any kind of problem with which he can assist.

Fortunately, Ms N is speaking excellent Russian. Before our untainted-by-corruption-of-any-kind Minister of Justice can reply, she takes another deep breath and speaks.

'I fear that the gang of hardened criminals you see before you may mistakenly have murdered a man who, while obnoxious beyond any measure, was not the under-cover FBI agent they believed him to be. Furthermore, I have reason to believe that the true under-cover FBI agents may be able to provide us with all the evidence we need.' She turns to the gentlemen in Arab dress. 'Gentlemen. Is that a highly sophisticated parabolic microphone and video camera that you keep fiddling with in your briefcase on the table, or do you have to keep putting your papers back in your bag to keep them warm?'

One of the gentlemen in Arab clothing rises to his feet. I am pleased to see that it is the man whose dark eyes and cute dimples made an impression on me when I checked him in earlier in the day, and to whom a note on the computer from Ms N told me I should be particularly helpful should he or his colleagues ask to sit in any particular spot in the Lobby Bar. I am also noticing for the first time that the table they have chosen is right next to the table at which the gentlemen in the dark suits or leather jackets, and our untainted-by-corruption-of-any-kind Minister of Justice, are sitting; and that their briefcase is sitting on the table right next to the Minister.

'I am sorry for any confusion,' the gentleman in Arab clothing with the dark eyes and the cute dimples says in English, which I am now realising is not only not bad but is actually perfect. 'You are correct that we are from the Federal Bureau of Investigation. We have of course declared our presence to the hotel's senior management, and also to our friends in the local security agencies at working level.' He smiles at the portly Chief of Police. 'Although I have no way of knowing whether this information has been passed on to the political level.' He nods at our untainted-by-corruption-of-any-kind Minister of Justice.

Now it is not Nigel, but the portly Chief of Police who is turning a deep red. Our untainted-by-corruption-of-any-kind Minister of Justice is looking at the portly Chief of Police without any expression, but I have a sense that he is transmitting a clear message.

'You are correct that you have declared your presence,' the portly Chief of Police says to the three FBI agents in Arab dress. 'But this does not, of course, give you any power of arrest in our beautiful but not yet economically advanced country.'

'Absolutely not,' the FBI man with the dark eyes and cute dimples says. 'Arresting people is your job. But I know you are always searching hungrily for evidence that a crime has been committed. I have that evidence.'

He reaches across the table and takes from the hands of one of his colleagues the laptop computer we have seen earlier; and turns it around so that the screen is facing towards the portly Chief of Police, and Ms N. On the screen we see a frozen close-up of the man with the gold rings and the squashed nose leaning towards our untainted-by-corruption-of-any-kind Minister of Justice.

'Listen up,' the FBI man says. 'Sound quality is terrific.'

The atmosphere in the Lobby Bar is tense and silent. Everyone is looking at the screen.

The FBI man taps a key. On the screen the man with the gold rings leans further towards our untainted-by-corruption-of-any-kind Minister of Justice. His words are clear, even though he is whispering.

'The blue suit is FBI,' he says in Russian. *'Want me to kill him?'*

'Kill him,' our untainted-by-corruption-of-any-kind Minister of Justice says.

I was thinking that the Lobby Bar was quiet before. Now, it is even quieter.

Again, I see that our untainted-by-corruption-of-any-kind Minister of Justice is looking at the portly Chief of Police.

The portly Chief of Police licks his lips. He looks around the Lobby Bar at the crowd of people who have seen the video. If I am honest, I am thinking that his face is showing a kind of panic. He clears his throat.

'I cannot comment on the value of that evidence,' he says. I see that he is looking at the bag and perhaps is thinking that everything which is happening, and everything he is saying, is still being recorded. 'But the problem with all evidence, especially in a country such as this which is beautiful but not yet economically advanced, is that in some cases – even important ones – evidence can be lost. Or even destroyed. We have to proceed with caution.'

I see our untainted-by-corruption-of-any-kind Minister of Justice nod slightly when the portly Chief of Police says the word 'lost' and nod again when he says the word 'destroyed'.

'You are absolutely correct,' the FBI agent with the cute dimples says. 'Which is why we have been transmitting authenticated copies of this recording to your excellent Ministry of Justice; to Europol; and to the FBI itself in the United States in real time. We're still live on air. No need to worry; this evidence is one hundred per-cent secure.' He glances at our untainted-by-corruption-of-any-kind Minister of Justice. 'It cannot be lost or destroyed.'

Now the face of our untainted-by-corruption-of-any-kind Minister of Justice is not smiling. Again, he is looking at the portly Chief of Police. But the face of the portly Chief of Police has taken on a strange expression. If earlier he was embarrassed, and then panicking, now he is looking determined.

If I am honest, I think he knows he has no choice. He may even be thinking that, given this lack of choice, putting behind bars in a high-profile international case two criminals charged with murder, one of whom is our untainted-by-corruption-of-any-kind Minister of Justice, may even give his career a boost. He may also be thinking that if he does the right thing, the position of Minister of Justice, and all the financial opportunities it brings, may be coming vacant very soon.

The portly Chief of Police looks at the FBI agent. He looks at the bag on the table. Then he looks at our untainted-by-corruption-of-any-kind Minister of Justice and swallows.

'You have the right to remain silent and to refuse to answer questions…' he begins. He beckons to the two officers from our country's re-branded and retrained but perhaps not yet entirely world-class police force, who also are looking at him with a kind of panic in their eyes. But when the portly Chief of Police glances at the still-live FBI briefcase with the sophisticated parabolic microphone and video camera, the two of them take out their handcuffs and advance slowly on our untainted-by-corruption-of-any-kind Minister of Justice and the man in the leather jacket with the gold rings and the squashed nose.

Our untainted-by-corruption-of-any-kind Minister of Justice

looks dazed, and does not put up any resistance. But the man with the gold rings raises his fist at Ms N and shouts.

'You said he was FBI!'

Ms N shakes her head. 'I do not know what you are talking about,' she says. 'I am sorry if you somehow inferred that Mr Matt Miller, the Regional Director of our hotel group, was a law enforcement official. Perhaps it was his references to cleaning up corruption and illegality. Perhaps it was his Brooks Brothers suit. But I think you will find, if you examine the evidence, that I at no stage said anything about Mr Matt Miller working for the FBI.'

23.30

A LITTLE LATER, Ms N calls me across to sit with her in the Lobby Bar. The hotel is returning to normal. The police have taken witness statements, and examined the lift, and taken away the body of Mr Matt Miller. Ms N has allowed Housekeeping to clean up the lobby and the elevator. Many of the guests who have been confined to their rooms have come down to the Lobby Bar to enjoy the free drinks Ms N is offering to them as compensation for their inconvenience.

If I am honest, I am thinking that most of the guests are finding the experience has been an exciting one; and they are all keen to talk about it. It is almost sounding as if a party is happening in the Lobby Bar. Perhaps after their free drinks many of the guests will decide to have one or two more drinks at their own expense, which will help boost the profits of the hotel.

Maybe Ms N has thought about all of this before she is offering the free drinks. Or perhaps she is feeling we all have something to celebrate.

Next to the table at which Ms N is sitting is a bottle of Champagne in an ice-bucket. Ms N invites me to join her. The Champagne is cold and delicious.

'So,' she says. 'How was your day?'

'I am glad it is nearly over,' I say. 'I was worried that you or I might be fired by Mr Matt Miller. Do you think we are safe now?'

'I do not know what you mean,' Ms N says. 'I do not remember Mr Matt Miller saying he would fire either you or me, nor any reason why he should have wished to do so. Do you?'

I think for a moment. 'No,' I say. 'I do not.'

'If you have had a difficult day, Tatiana, I should perhaps remind you that you have an admirer amongst the guests.'

I look at Ms N. At first I am thinking that she may mean the elderly Irish gentleman, or perhaps the younger Irish gentleman with the green eyes, the fragrant cologne and the kindly smile. Both of these are fine gentlemen, although perhaps not entirely to my taste. But when I look around the crowds in the Lobby Bar I see that the elderly Irish gentleman and his son are both talking to Dr Daphne Miller, who is still looking maybe twenty years younger now she has lost her shocked or frightened face, and who I see is also drinking a glass of Champagne.

'Other side,' Ms N says. 'On his own.'

The FBI agent with the cute dimples is sitting at a table looking at his laptop computer. I have not spotted him earlier because he is no longer wearing a *keffiyeh* and a *thawb* but is dressed in jeans with a white shirt and a black leather jacket.

The dimples, however, are still the same.

'Perhaps you should offer him a complimentary glass of Champagne,' Ms N says. 'He has helped you and me a great deal.'

'Thank you, Ms N,' I say. 'But what will you do on your own?'

'I thought I might plan my future,' Ms N says. 'I have found it a privilege to work as Hotel Manager in this beautiful country; and an honour occasionally to serve, as now, as Acting General Manager. But since Mr Matt Miller is no longer our Regional Director, I think my chances of securing a substantive position as General Manager of a hotel of my own have improved.'

Ms N looks at me with her inquisitive smile. I cannot help smiling back.

'I have applied for a job as GM,' Ms N says, 'in a country called C—. Conditions in C— are even more difficult than here; and the hotel there has a great number of problems. But I think that perhaps I could help to sort it out. Especially if you were prepared to come and help me. Have a think about it.'

'I will do that – ' I begin to say. But at this moment we are joined by a woman with wild, frizzy hair and no make-up, who is wearing a green out-door jacket. Although I have seen the jacket before, it takes me a moment to recognise that it is the Queen of Sweden because she is looking so different from earlier in the evening, when she was wearing her beautiful white silk dress. Ms N and I rise to our feet.

'Congratulations,' the Queen of Sweden says. She shakes the hand of Ms N and then, to my delight, shakes my hand also.

'I wanted to say to you,' she continues in her English-sounding accent, 'that this is the best hotel in which I have ever stayed; and that you are the best General Manager I have ever encountered. What you have achieved this evening is extraordinary. When I open the World Anti-Corruption Forum tomorrow I shall mention the arrest of the Minister of Justice by the re-branded, retrained and 100% corruption-free police force of this beautiful but not yet economically advanced country as an example of exactly the kind of progress in the rule of law which other countries in this region should emulate.'

'I am pleased you like the hotel,' says Ms N. 'Although I should say that I am only an acting General Manager. And it is staff like Tatiana who make everything possible.'

'Yes,' the Queen of Sweden says. 'Although I do feel that your comments about Mr Matt Miller and your conversations with him in the Lobby Bar could accidentally have led a hypothetical group of hardened criminals, perhaps for whom English was not their first language and who were paranoid about undercover FBI agents, to believe that Mr Matt Miller was perhaps such an agent. It is also most unfortunate that the ultra-sharp Chroma knife which you wisely confiscated from your violence-prone sushi chef should have ended up literally an arm's length from such a group of hardened criminals, who were thus provided both with a motive and a murder weapon. Of course, I am not habitually sympathetic to murderous hardened criminals, particularly those who harass women. But the series of coincidences which has solved the problems both of Mr Matt Miller and of the gentlemen who were hassling your staff strikes me as remarkable.'

'The death of Mr Matt Miller is of course a tragedy.' Ms N glances at Dr Daphne Miller, who is still looking like perhaps the happiest person in the hotel. 'And who can predict the actions of hardened criminals, or the workings of the wheels of justice?' She smiles her inquisitive smile. 'May I help you with anything? A taxi, perhaps?'

'Thank you, no.' The Queen of Sweden gestures towards the lobby with her distracted expression. 'I am going for a walk to clear my head after all the excitement. If you ever come to Sweden, perhaps as the General Manager of your own hotel, please let me know.'

We watch as the Queen of Sweden wanders towards the door – stopping once to look at another artwork I have never noticed, and again to have a word with one of the bell-boys. Then she vanishes into the night.

'Now. Tatiana,' Ms N says. 'Please can you go and look after the FBI gentleman over there. I am worried that he is thirsty.'

I nod; and smile; and pour two fresh glasses of ice-cold Champagne.

For a moment, I look around the Lobby Bar. It is hard to believe that only a few hours ago, the hotel seemed to be full of problems. Now, everyone is happy; and I can see no problems that need solving at all, except perhaps for a thirsty man with dark eyes and cute dimples.

Ms N is good at solving problems. One day I want to be like her.

4. THE WHITE BLOUSE

If I am honest, I do not like border crossings.

It is a lonely place in the passport queue, waiting to enter the country of C—. But what to do?

In addition, I know I should not complain because I am here by choice. It was my decision, to apply for a job in this country. When I was successful I was so pleased that I went out shopping and bought myself a new white blouse, which is folded up in the big black suitcase at my side. But now, waiting in a room which I do not think has been painted or even cleaned for many years, I am wondering if I have made the right decision either applying for this job or accepting it.

The country of C— is remote. There are not even direct flights to C— from most countries. Instead, I must fly to a neighbouring country, R—. R— has a capital city whose airport is a hub for the region. From there I must take a taxi fifty kilometres to the border of C—. Once I am through passport control I will hire a taxi on the other side of the border and continue to my destination.

I have already been waiting thirty minutes.

But now I am at the front of the queue.

The passport officer is a tall man with a black moustache and a khaki-coloured shirt which is stretched out tight by a large belly. He looks down at me in a way I do not like.

'So,' he says in English. 'You are coming to work in our country?'

'Yes,' I reply. My work permit is with my passport on the counter in front of him so I cannot think what else to say.

'You want to work in a hotel. As a head receptionist.' He says this as if it is something dirty. 'Your customers will like that. You are a very attractive woman.'

He smiles at me, but not in a good way.

'Is that a problem?' I say.

'I think we must do a customs search.' He looks at my black suitcase, then he looks for a longer time at me, and licks his lips. 'Come.' He points to a door behind the counter.

I do not like the appearance of this door, which looks as if it has not been painted or cleaned for even longer than the rest of the room. But the passport official is beckoning to me with my passport, which he holds in his big hand like a prize.

I hesitate.

'Actually, there is a problem.'

A woman is walking towards the passport officer on his side of the counter. She has an accent which is hard to understand. Perhaps she is from the Middle East, or from Iran, or from Afghanistan. Although she is on his side of the counter, she is not wearing a uniform. In fact, she is wearing a low-cut top, showing off her breasts, which are seeming to have trouble staying inside the bright yellow material which is stretched across them. She has a mane of black hair which is bouncing around as she walks towards the passport officer, and seems to be smiling at him.

I wonder why I did not see the woman before but then I notice she is tiny – smaller, even, than me.

'Wait, please, one moment,' the woman says. Then she turns to me and smiles in such a way that I realise that she has not been smiling at the passport officer at all. She has been showing him her teeth.

'Tatiana,' she says. 'Welcome.'

I am so surprised, I almost want to cry, because these are the first kind words I have heard for many hours.

The woman in the yellow top turns back towards the official.

'Please treat this case as a priority,' she says. 'We need her at the hotel as soon as possible.'

Her voice carries so much authority that I feel an urge to obey her, even though she is not speaking to me.

The passport official takes a step backwards. He glances at me and his mouth twitches.

'She did not say she was working at your hotel,' he says. 'I was preparing a customs search.'

'A *what?*' The short woman seems to swell in every direction. The bright yellow material is even more stretched than it was earlier. 'If you do not allow her to pass immediately I shall ensure Mr Kagit hears of this and you will remain a passport official for ever.'

When the short woman says "passport" in her hard-to-understand accent it sounds like "piss-poor". The man turns pale.

'No,' he says. 'Of course.' He blinks and moves towards the counter. There is a click and a thump, and he is holding my passport out to me, open at a page showing a red stamp, glistening wet.

He turns back to the short woman, but she is ignoring him.

'Come with me, Tatiana,' she says. 'The Mercedes is waiting.'

'But...' I have to run to keep up with her. 'Who are you?'

'My name is Susan. I am Engineering Manager at the hotel. Ms N sent me.'

'Ms N?' I cannot keep the pleasure out of my voice. 'I thought she was starting next month?'

'She has arrived early.' Susan waits a moment for me to catch up. 'I think we are going to see some changes.'

'I know Ms N from my last hotel,' I say. 'I applied for this job because I heard she will be the new General Manager here. One day, I want to be like her.'

'We all want to be like Ms N.' Susan smiles at the driver of the black Mercedes which is waiting for us. 'But my guess is that not everyone will like her style.'

My arrival at the new hotel is a disappointment.

The first problem is that my job has been taken by someone else. Her name is Maria and she is a tall woman with straight blonde hair and a pretty face who wears high heels which make her look even taller. Her height and her good looks mean that she catches the eye of any customer entering the lobby of the hotel through the main entrance, whose manually-operated swing doors do not seem to have been painted or cleaned much more recently than the waiting room at the border post. Most of the customers are men, so perhaps it is better that they are looking at Maria than looking at the swing doors. Unfortunately, Maria has never worked in a hotel before she started here two days ago, so I cannot understand why she has been appointed as head receptionist.

Susan takes me to the rooftop terrace bar of the hotel. 'The reason is Mr Kagit,' she says in her hard-to-understand accent. 'Mr Kagit is a big man in C—.' When she says "big" it sounds so much like "bitch" that I think she is making a joke. But Susan is not smiling. 'Mr Kagit works in the President's office and his brother is the Minister of Planning. Luckily for us, his favourite place in the country is this hotel. Sometimes this can help us, as you saw at the border. Mostly, it is a problem. Maria is his niece. This is why she has your job. So Ms N has put you in charge of the Platinum Megastar lounge of the hotel.'

When Susan says "Megastar" it sounds like "Monster". Again I wonder if she is making a joke, but she is not smiling. This is good, because the Platinum Megastar lounge is reserved for the most honoured customers of our hotel chain and it would be inappropriate to make jokes about it.

The second reason I am disappointed when I arrive is that compared with the previous hotel at which I worked with Ms N, this one is what we call in the industry a "shitbox". I am sorry to use this vocabulary, but this is the correct professional term. My previous hotel had a twenty-storey atrium and a one-star Michelin restaurant with a genuine Japanese sushi chef. The new hotel has a long, low lobby in which not all of the plants are even alive; and the restaurant has no stars at all.

Susan tells me not to worry. 'Sure the place is a shitbox,' she says. 'But Ms N is working on it. First of all it needs investment. That's why we plan a new conference centre next door, on the site of the old secret police HQ.'

Susan leans towards me. 'Unfortunately, construction cannot begin without the agreement of Mr Kagit, for which he wants thirty thousand bucks. Of course our hotel chain cannot pay a bribe of $1, much less a bribe of $30,000. But Ms N has a plan.'

Actually the third reason I am disappointed when I arrive at the hotel is that Ms N, who is the only reason I have moved to this awful place to start what turns out to be a non-existent job in a shitbox of a hotel, is not here to greet me. I find this surprising because Ms N is usually someone who pays close attention to details such as the arrival of a new member of staff – especially one who has travelled half-way around the world to work with her.

'Don't cry,' Susan says. 'Ms N has a big meeting tonight. She arrived only two days ago. Cleaning up this shitbox is a big job. Usually we call a hotel a shitbox because it's shitty – it's made of shit. But this hotel is worse. Not only is it made of shit, but it's full of shit. Welcome to a truly shit shitbox. Cheers.'

Susan raises her glass and I raise mine, although what she has said does not seem very encouraging.

'Which reminds me,' Susan says. 'When you start work in the Platinum Megastar lounge tomorrow morning the first person you'll see will be our most important guest. Make sure you treat him appropriately.'

'Who is it?' I ask.

'Our most important guest,' Susan says, 'is Mr Kagit.'

When she says his name in her hard-to-understand accent it

sounds like "Mr Ka-shit". But Susan is not smiling.

My first morning in the Platinum Megastar lounge is a challenge. In our hotel chain we are taught to say that a big challenge is a big opportunity, and I am wearing my new white blouse which I have ironed specially this morning to make sure I look my best. But in this case I do not see the opportunity, to be frank.

My first impression is that the lounge is not maintained to the standard which visitors to our five-star hotel chain expect. In fact, the colour and texture of the brown curtains are reminding me of how Susan was describing the hotel the night before. When I pull back these curtains to let in more light and to hide them a little from sight, I find I am choking on a cloud of dust and debris which must have been building up in these curtains for years.

At this moment a guest walks in and starts to help himself at the breakfast bar without even looking in my direction. Perhaps he cannot see me because of the dust cloud. I smile my famous thousand-watt smile, but he is at the buffet with his back to me.

I follow the guest to where he is standing. He is heavily-built and dressed in a well-cut grey suit which I am guessing cost several thousand dollars. I explain that because I have only arrived in C— the previous night, I am not yet familiar with all the Platinum Megastar members who are staying at the hotel. I would therefore be grateful if he could show me his Platinum Megastar pass so that I can remember him in future.

The man slowly puts down the plate of food he is holding and turns towards me. He is good-looking, with well-cut grey hair and a smile which is warm and respectful. He looks at me in a friendly way, and I feel pleased that I am wearing my new white blouse. 'I am delighted to meet you,' he says. 'What is your name?'

'My name is Tatiana.' I try out my thousand-watt smile again.

'My name is Mr Kagit.' He licks his lips and I see that his tongue also is grey, like a lizard. 'Welcome to the hotel.'

I smile. 'Actually, I think that is my job, to welcome you – '

'Tatiana.' When he places his finger on my lips I smell soap and cologne. 'Your job is to keep your guests happy. You are doing a great job so far. Now if you do not mind I would like to eat my breakfast.'

Of course in the hotel we do not encourage the guests to touch the staff; but since Susan has briefed me that Mr Kagit is our most important guest, and since for me all guests of our hotel are important, I do not mention him touching my mouth but smile and return to the entrance of the lounge.

The rest of the morning presents other challenges or, possibly, opportunities. The next guests to arrive at the Platinum Megastar lounge are two women. One of them has short, straight grey hair. She shows me the shiny metal token which gives access to the lounge as if possession of such a privilege is somehow a burden to her. The second woman is younger and darker-skinned and her eyes sparkle as she shows me her token. I notice this because it reminds me that although Mr Kagit was smiling, his eyes did not sparkle at all.

I am interested to see that the grey-haired woman picks a table in the lounge as far from Mr Kagit as it is possible to be. When I bring their coffee, the grey-haired woman places her hand on my arm.

'That man,' she says. She does not need to be specific because there is only one man in the lounge. 'Do you know who he is?'

I smile and say nothing, since of course it would not be appropriate for me to reveal the name of one guest to another and I am not too happy about her touching my arm.

'*Be careful around him,*' the grey-haired woman says.

I smile again. I see the younger woman is also smiling, but the grey-haired woman has screwed up her mouth like a prune.

'We are from a group which is trying to prevent the abuse of women,' the grey-haired woman says. 'I am afraid that in this part of the world this is a big problem.'

'It is a big problem in many places,' I say.

'Margarita is leading a series of workshops on empowering women.' The younger woman gestures at her companion. 'Unfortunately, we are not making as much progress as we would like.'

'We leave tomorrow.' Margarita frowns. 'My colleague Inez is understating the problem.' She says "my colleague" in a way which seems to imply that Inez is a person of limited mental capacity. 'Attendance at our seminars has been appalling.'

'What are you doing to help women?' I say. 'Apart from the seminars?'

'Maybe we should have gone more into the city – ' Inez begins to say, but Margarita interrupts her.

'Our seminars are designed to help women to help themselves.' Margarita is showing her prune mouth again. 'If they do not want to hear our advice, there is little we can do.'

The final guest to arrive before the breakfast buffet is cleared is a small, wiry man with a moustache who does not show me an access token but who tells me he is the Materials Manager at the hotel. I know that as a senior member of the hotel executive team he is entitled to eat in the Platinum Megastar lounge. But I am surprised to see him because in my last hotel, Ms N made a point of eating breakfast in the canteen with the junior staff. I had expected she would encourage the same thing here, even though she has now been promoted to General Manager.

The Materials Manager leans close to me and speaks in a low voice. 'I am Eli,' he says. He has a mouthful of gold teeth. 'You can call me Mr Fixit. You need it? I can fix it. Remember.' He walks into the lounge. Then he surprises me a little bit more by sitting down at the table of Mr Kagit.

Mr Kagit does not seem surprised to find Eli joining him. They begin a conversation which I notice they interrupt when I bring Eli a cappuccino a few minutes later.

The rest of the morning is quiet. This is not good, because

three guests for breakfast, plus Eli, is not sufficient for the hotel to achieve the kind of service, and also the kind of profits, which I know Ms N will wish to deliver in her new role as General Manager.

So I am pleased when at lunchtime a new person enters the lounge; and I am even more pleased when I see that it is Ms N herself. She shakes my hand firmly and looks me in the eye and says 'Tatiana, how are you?' and suddenly I notice that the sun is shining in the window where I pulled back the curtains.

'I see you are looking as smart as ever.' Ms N takes a step back and looks at me. 'Is that a new blouse? Of course it is. Thank you for making the effort.'

I take a deep breath and stand up a little bit straighter. I am wishing now that I had bought two new blouses, since Ms N is noticing these details.

'You are probably thinking that we need to change these curtains,' Ms N says. 'There are many things about this hotel we need to change. Some of them are small things. Some of them are big things. We will start with the big ones.'

When she is saying this she seems to be looking in the direction of Mr Kagit, who is now the only guest in the lounge. I see that she is displaying her professional face, which is a slightly inquisitive expression with the hint of a smile.

Mr Kagit has a computer and some papers spread on the table. He seems to be using the Platinum Megastar lounge as his office. Although he must have noticed that the General Manager of the hotel has entered, he does not acknowledge her.

Mr Kagit is our most important guest. So I am expecting Ms N to go and greet him. But to my surprise she does not move.

A terrible thought crosses my mind. Can it be that Ms N is afraid of Mr Kagit?

But as soon as I have this thought I put it to one side. I know that Ms N is afraid of nothing. If I had doubted this I would not have come to C— in the first place.

'I am glad I am working with you again, Ms N.' I speak

quietly, because I do not wish to disturb Mr Kagit or for him to hear our conversation.

But Ms N replies in a loud voice. 'Thank you, Tatiana,' she says. 'I am pleased you are with us. Together, we will make this a hotel we can be proud of.'

AT MID-DAY I go off-duty. Before my second shift starts in the evening I change out of my work clothes and go for a walk to look at the old secret police site which Susan has mentioned is next door to the hotel.

The site of the new conference centre is not hard to find. It is a hole in the ground like a super-sized swimming pool, the vertical sides maybe four metres deep. The bottom is flat, except for a thicket of metal rods which extends from one side to the other. Right in the centre I see a dark, round hole. If I am honest, I am not much liking the look of this hole, which has the feeling of something one might accidentally fall into, if one were for any reason wandering around the basement of the old secret police HQ in the first place.

'Magnificent, isn't it?'

Susan is standing next to me. I am surprised that she has approached so silently because she is wearing scuffed, steel-capped boots which look as if they are not well-suited to moving without noise. She is also wearing bright yellow one-piece work overalls and a hard hat. The top of the overalls is undone, displaying her remarkable bosom to full effect.

'How long before we start building?' I ask.

'No time, in theory.' Susan plants her feet wide apart in the mud which surrounds the pit and points to the far side. 'We'll use the original foundations and pilings. All we need is to stabilise the construction box.'

Susan's accent is perfectly clear when she is talking about engineering.

'What is a construction box?' I ask.

'See the steel reinforcing bars?' Susan points to the metal pieces I have already noticed covering the floor of the pit. 'One more ingredient and we'll have the best foundations money can buy.'

'What ingredient is that?'

'We'll use the hatch, too.' Susan is looking at the dark hole in the centre of the pit. 'That's the entrance to the old bunker from the secret police HQ. It's a good-sized void surrounded by a solid cube of steel. I've checked it out with Ms N. For me as an engineer it's a challenge. But Ms N sees it as an opportunity.'

'Ms N sees everything as an opportunity,' I say. 'How did you get into the hole?'

'We use the crane.' Susan points across the pit. 'There's a steel basket we can lower in. It's a tight fit. But you'd be surprised how often people want to go in the hatch. Even some guests.'

When Susan says the word "guests" her accent becomes hard to understand again, and it sounds like "gits".

I look at the crane and basket and do not like what I see. The crane looks as if it has been standing by the pit for years and is covered with rust. The basket is a small platform surrounded by steel bars with a hook on the top attached to a cable which trails across the muddy ground to the crane. The thought of riding anywhere in this device makes me feel dizzy with fear; but I smile at Susan.

'I would like to try that,' I say.

Susan smiles back. 'Sure. Unless Mr Kagit gives his approval for the new conference centre, we won't be building anything.'

'Perhaps Ms N can persuade Mr Kagit,' I say.

'Yes,' Susan says. 'Perhaps she can.'

Soon after this it is time for me to start my shift, so I return to the hotel. In C— the night falls quickly, and I am pleased to enter the brightly-lit lobby despite the low ceiling and the dead plants. Maria, the niece of Mr Kagit, is standing at the reception desk like a lighthouse displaying a huge mouthful of teeth framed with red lipstick. Actually I am pleased to see her because she looks glamorous and more full of life than the rest of the lobby.

I am less pleased to see Eli, the Materials Manager. Eli is sitting on one of the not-very-clean sofas which are scattered around the lobby as if someone has been looking for something underneath each one of them and has forgotten to put them straight afterwards. To my astonishment, I see he is with Ms N. Ms N is leaning forward, so close that her face is almost touching his. For a moment I am alarmed, because it seems as if Ms N is planning to kiss Eli. This would be inappropriate. Nor do I like the way they are sitting alone, as though they are plotting something.

But my alarm is over before it has begun.

It is Ms N who is sitting there with Eli.

Ms N must have a reason to be doing this thing.

By the time of my evening shift in the Platinum Megastar Lounge I am starting to believe that perhaps the new hotel is not as bad as Susan has been telling me. This is partly because I am beginning to see that Ms N is active in the hotel, talking to customers and staff. In fact, she is so active that I am beginning to wonder why I did not see her in my first few hours the day before.

Although Ms N is so active I am still worried that she is not quite the same person I knew in my previous hotel. If I am honest, I am surprised that Ms N has been working in the hotel for whole two days but has not yet had the dead plants in the lobby removed or replaced. Nor has she arranged for the dark brown curtains in the Platinum Megastar Lounge to be changed, or even cleaned. Nor can I understand why she is not more concerned that the hotel has a huge muddy building site right next door in which no building seems to have taken place for years. Instead she is talking all the time to guests and staff from the top to the bottom of the hotel.

The night shift in the Platinum Megastar Lounge is different from the breakfast shift. The lights are dim. There is music playing which seems to me sleazy and inappropriate and another thing which Ms N will want to fix. But as usual she is talking to guests. This time it is Margarita and Inez. I am wishing I could hear what they are saying, because Ms N is sitting forward on her chair in a way which suggests she is feeling strongly about something. Margarita is exhibiting her prune mouth. But the young woman, Inez, is smiling and nodding.

The other guests in the Lounge are mostly men. Several of them have with them at their tables the professional women who often can be found in the evening in hotel bars. But this does not trouble me as actually I think it is better for these women to be doing what they do in our hotel rather than in the streets outside.

One man with no woman at his table is Mr Kagit. I am pleased to see this, since despite the bad things Susan and Margarita have said about him he is good-looking, and has treated me correctly. He is wearing a black jacket with matching shirt and trousers which is making him look even more distinguished than before. At one point he smiles at me, and I am pleased that I am again wearing my white blouse, which is still looking clean and smart.

It is around ten o'clock when Eli enters. He is not alone. He is walking arm-in-arm with a woman. I look at this woman and see that she is almost more beautiful than I can imagine. Also, however, she is younger than seems appropriate for a bar at this time in the evening. In fact, I am thinking that it is probably past her bed-time already.

Eli walks to the table of Mr Kagit and says a few words. Then the woman, or perhaps I should say girl, sits down next to Mr Kagit.

Most people in the bar do not react in any way when the girl sits down next to Mr Kagit. But two people do react. Margarita is staring at the young woman and is making her prune-mouth, as if perhaps she is upset that this person has not attended one of her seminars. Inez is looking at Mr Kagit. This is the first time I am seeing Inez when she is not smiling, and if I am honest she is looking more like someone who is wanting to start a fight than someone relaxing in an exclusive hotel bar.

Ms N stands up and from the table where she has been sitting with Margarita and Inez and walks over to me.

'Good evening, Tatiana,' she says. 'Please can you make sure Mr Kagit receives everything he needs this evening.'

'Yes, Ms N,' I say. 'But should I serve the girl? I know that I am new in C—, but in some countries there are laws which prohibit people below a certain age from visiting bars of this kind.'

'Thank you, Tatiana, you are right to ask,' Ms N says. 'But in this case we are seeking to secure Mr Kagit's agreement to begin work on our new conference centre, so it is important that he feels he is receiving the best service he could possibly desire. Although it is true that Mr Kagit has certain tastes of which I personally do not approve, I can assure you that the lady who Eli has organised for him this evening is above the age of consent.' She smiles. 'I have seen her passport.'

Ms N leaves the lounge; and I serve drinks to Mr Kagit and his new friend. If I am honest I am shocked by Ms N's statement that Eli is procuring women for guests, since this is not normally the responsibility of the Materials Manager or any other member of the hotel staff. Nor is it something I would expect Ms N to tolerate. I am noticing also that she has referred to the woman Eli has organised this evening being above the age of consent, as if this perhaps is not always the case.

Again I wonder if Ms N has changed. Perhaps she is afraid of Mr Kagit. Perhaps she is no longer insisting on the highest standards. But when I serve the drinks, I see that the girl is a little older than I have thought at first. I also remember Ms N saying that before she can fix the small things, she has to fix the big things. I wonder what those big things might be.

Margarita and Inez leave the lounge shortly after Ms N. The sleazy music continues to play. Mr Kagit talks to the young-looking woman for several hours in a way which seems to suggest he is respecting her; and I wonder again if he is as bad as others have told me. When they leave the bar together, I see that Mr Kagit has his arm around her waist.

THE NEXT MORNING Mr Kagit is once again the first person to appear for breakfast in the Platinum Megastar Lounge. He is alone. I wonder where the young-looking woman has gone. Then I wonder whether, when I saw him twenty four hours earlier, Mr Kagit had also had a girl in his room the previous night.

I am beginning to understand why people do not like Mr Kagit.

A few minutes later Ms N enters the Platinum Megastar Lounge. She is carrying a red folder. After she has greeted me, she sits down with Mr Kagit. I remember Eli doing the same thing the morning before and I am again surprised, because I am expecting that Ms N will be eating breakfast in the staff canteen.

I am watching to see how Mr Kagit reacts to Ms N joining him. At first I am thinking he is not very pleased to see her. But when Ms N deploys her most inquisitive smile, Mr Kagit smiles also; and when she shows him the contents of the folder, he begins to look very happy indeed.

Shortly after this I go to the table to serve Ms N her coffee. When I arrive I notice that they interrupt their conversation; and that Ms N closes the red file. Again this does not feel right, because I remember Eli interrupting his conversation with Mr Kagit in the same way the day before. Even worse, I see before Ms N closes the file that the thing which she is showing him, and which is making him so happy, is a picture of a girl.

When I see this I am so shocked that my hands begin to shake.

I can hardly pour the coffee, which is splashing on the saucer so much that Ms N places her hand on the pot to steady it. If it has been difficult for me to believe that Ms N is not preventing Eli from procuring women for Mr Kagit, it is impossible for me to believe that Ms N herself, my long-time role model and the General Manager of the hotel, is doing the same thing. And yet this is what I am seeing.

Again I wonder whether I have done the right thing, following Ms N to C—, or whether I have made the biggest mistake in my life. I look at the dark brown, dirty curtains and I look at Ms N showing Mr Kagit whatever is in the red folder, and I think that perhaps I will resign my job – which I am not doing anyway because the niece of Mr Kagit is doing it – and return to the country I have come from.

I am still thinking about this when Inez arrives for breakfast. I am surprised to see her, because I had thought that she and Margarita were leaving today on the 6 a.m. flight from the airport across the border in R—. This required them to check out of our hotel in the middle of last night. But Inez tells me she is staying on to help with an important task which Ms N has asked her to do, but with which the older woman, Margarita, did not wish to be associated. Inez does not tell me what the task is, and when she mentions it her face is looking so grim that I am wondering whether perhaps it is something illegal or unkind.

This does not make me feel any better than I am feeling already, which is not good at all.

Perhaps my face is revealing my thoughts, because when Ms N has finished her breakfast with Mr Kagit she closes the red folder and comes to where I am standing by the entrance.

'Tatiana,' she says, 'I am sorry not to see your thousand-watt smile this morning. But on the other hand, if you were smiling your famous smile when you had seen what is going on in this hotel, I would be worried also.'

I say nothing, because I cannot think of anything to say.

'Tatiana,' Ms N continues, 'will you help me?'

She looks at me with a serious expression which I have not seen before. This is the second shocking thing I have seen in the Platinum Megastar Lounge this morning, and again I find myself unable to speak.

'I know that this must be confusing.' Ms N is holding out a tissue for me to dry my eyes. 'And you may find some of the things I will ask you to do today difficult. But if you can find it in your heart to trust me, Tatiana, by the end of the day we will have solved one of the hotel's most difficult problems.'

When Ms N is saying this she is looking at Mr Kagit. She smiles at him and he smiles back, showing his regular, evenly-spaced teeth.

'So,' Ms N says. 'Can you trust me, Tatiana?'

I look at Ms N. I know that I am not yet recovered from the shocks of this morning because I feel as if I may be sick at any moment. But when I see Ms N's warm brown eyes looking at me I know that there is only one answer I can give.

'I trust you completely,' I say.

'Thank you, Tatiana. Unfortunately, we need to act quickly. So I must ask you to begin helping me at once. Can you do that for me?'

'I will be happy to do that, Ms N.'

'Good.' Ms N hands me two passports. 'The first thing I want you to do is to book two first-class return tickets to New York for the holders of these passports, leaving on tomorrow's 6 a.m. flight.'

I look at the passports and see they belong to Mr Kagit and Eli. 'That flight leaves from the airport of R—,' I say.

'That is correct,' Ms N says. 'The gentlemen will cross the border in their own transport. The second thing I should like you to do is to reserve two suites for three nights at our Fifth Avenue UP hotel, with access to the Platinum Megastar Lounge, for the same two gentlemen.'

I look at Ms N. Our Fifth Avenue hotel is one of our exclusive UP-branded city centre boutique resorts. The UP stands for

Ultra-Platinum, although in our chain we joke that it is standing for Unaffordably-Priced. A suite in our Fifth Avenue hotel is costing more for one night than the average US citizen is earning in one month, and its Platinum Megastar Lounge is legendary even amongst our most elite guests.

'Do not worry,' Ms N says. 'I have authorised the Finance Director to cover all the costs involved.'

'Yes, Ms N,' I say.

'Please bring the passports, together with the flight details and hotel reservations, to the Platinum Megastar Lounge by 10 p.m. this evening.' Ms N smiles. 'I have one more request, Tatiana. This is that you wear your white blouse tonight. The one you had on yesterday.'

'That is not possible,' I say, 'because it is in the wash. Of course I am changing my work clothes every day. I have no other blouse as smart as that one.'

'Perhaps you could ask the laundry to perform their express service.'

I start to smile, because I am thinking that in this hotel, an express laundry service may not be very express. But Ms N is not smiling.

In fact, she is once again wearing her serious expression.

I, too, stop smiling. 'I will wear the white blouse, Ms N.'

IN FACT, THE express laundry service is one part of the hotel which seems to function normally. By the time I start my evening shift in the Platinum Megastar Lounge, I am looking my best. I am not feeling my best, however, because I am troubled that things are happening in this hotel which I do not like, or do not understand, or both.

But I am wearing the white blouse; and I have the passports, tickets and hotel reservations under the counter where I am standing at the entrance.

The shift begins quietly. A few customers come and go. The same sleazy music is playing as the night before. But there is no sign of Ms N, or of Eli, or of Mr Kagit. I serve drinks and I wait.

Mr Kagit arrives at fifteen minutes to ten. He greets me warmly, and when I bring him his first drink he slips a $100 bill into my hand.

'Thank you, Tatiana,' he says. 'I think you and I will be seeing a lot of each other.' He smiles, showing his regular teeth. 'I am grateful that you are looking after me so well.'

I display my thousand-watt smile, which is not so easy after I have seen him with the young-looking girl the night before. Then I return to my place by the door.

The next person to arrive is Ms N. She greets me and tells me to bring the passports, tickets and hotel reservations only once Eli has also arrived. Then she sits at the table with Mr Kagit. In her hand she is carrying the red folder. Once again she opens it and I see she is showing something to Mr Kagit.

Eli arrives at exactly ten o'clock. Again he is walking arm-in-arm with a woman. Again I look at her and see that, while she is at least as beautiful as the girl from the night before, she is looking even younger. In fact, she cannot possibly be more than twelve or thirteen years old, even though she is tall, and wearing make-up and high heels and a short white mini-dress which shows off her long, slender legs. She is looking a little bit scared, so I smile at her; but she does not seem to notice.

When I see Eli and the girl join Mr Kagit and Ms N my hands begin to shake again. I look for a signal from Ms N that to bring a girl of this age into the bar is unacceptable. But she is talking to Eli and Mr Kagit as if nothing unusual is happening.

Eli and Mr Kagit, for their part, seem unable to sit still. They keep looking at each other, and at the girl-child. It is as if they are high on some kind of drug. But so far as I can see, they are not taking any drugs. I think it is the presence of the girl which is exciting them, as though they have somehow been given a chance to do something very bad indeed.

I hope that this cannot be true.

After the four of them have settled down, Ms N gives a sign that I should come to the table. I bring the passports and other documents. I am not comfortable doing this. But Ms N seems relaxed.

'Thank you, Tatiana,' she says. 'Could you bring another chair, please?'

It takes me a moment to realise that she wishes me to sit down with them. Of course it is inappropriate for a member of the waiting staff to join customers. But the situation is already wrong on so many levels that I draw up a chair.

'I wish you to witness a signature,' Ms N says.

She opens the red folder. I do not care to look inside, but when I do I see some kind of official document, with brightly-coloured labels showing where it has to be signed.

'Are you ready?' Ms N says to Mr Kagit.

'I am ready.' Mr Kagit glances at the young girl and smiles. Then he takes from his pocket a heavy, gold-ribbed fountain pen.

'Hold it,' Eli says. 'Where's our stuff for New York?'

'Tatiana has everything,' Ms N says. 'Don't you, Tatiana?'

I hand over the passports and documents. Eli examines them, then sits back. 'It's gonna be one hell of a trip.' He grins at Mr Kagit. 'I know people in New York can find you chicks you wouldn't believe.' He prods the girl with his finger. 'This is nothing. Just you wait. I can fix it.'

When Eli is saying this, he smiles in a way that I do not like at all. Mr Kagit smiles back, and I see his grey tongue lick his lips. 'I look forward to it,' he says.

'So,' Ms N says. 'We have secured the services you requested.' She pauses and looks at the girl with an odd expression as though she is trying to persuade her that whatever she may feel, things are not too bad. 'The special facilities are at your disposal this evening. Immediately afterwards, you will be able to drive across the border to R— and fly to New York. I believe we have met all your conditions.'

'I think you have.' Mr Kagit looks at the girl. 'And when we return, you will make her available again? And others like her?'

'Eli will always be available to you,' Ms N says. 'And we have incorporated the special facilities into the design of the conference centre as you asked.' She opens the red folder at an architectural plan.

'Perfect,' Mr Kagit says. 'I am ready to sign.'

He pulls the top off the gold-ribbed pen.

'Tatiana,' Ms N says, 'could you witness this, please?' When she looks at me her brown eyes are calm.

I hesitate. Close-up, the girl looks even younger than before. She looks as if she is about to cry. From what I can understand, the signature will mean Mr Kagit is granting permission for the hotel to build its new conference centre. In return, Ms N is allowing him to abuse an under-aged girl, tonight and in the future. Ms N is also paying for Mr Kagit and Eli to have a fabulous holiday in New York. Finally, she is providing some "special facilities", for Mr Kagit to use with the girl. What these facilities might be I do not even wish to think.

I remember Susan saying that Mr Kagit wanted a $30,000 bribe to grant permission to build the conference centre. What Ms N seems to have arranged is perhaps cheaper, and can be concealed as a legitimate business expense. Yet it is not only illegal, but sickening and wrong. Should I make it possible by witnessing Mr Kagit's signature?

'Maybe it would be more appropriate if someone more senior was a witness,' I say. 'Susan, perhaps?'

'Susan is busy,' Ms N says. 'Please do it for me, Tatiana.' She looks at me and nods slightly.

I look into Ms N's calm brown eyes and remember her asking if I trusted her.

'I will be happy to act as a witness,' I say.

I watch as Mr Kagit signs with his gold-ribbed pen; then I add my own signature and details below. Ms N waits until the ink has dried. Then she closes the red folder and gives it to me.

'Susan is in the office downstairs,' she says. 'Please ask her to lock this in the safe. Do everything Susan says. Then send Mr Kagit's niece Maria to complete the rest of your shift. I'm giving you the rest of the night off.'

'She has earned it,' Mr Kagit says.

I do not speak, because I cannot trust myself to say anything. I go downstairs to the lobby and send Maria up to take over the Platinum Megastar Lounge.

Susan is waiting in the office. Contrary to what Ms N has said, she does not seem busy at all. Although it is nearly eleven o'clock, she is wearing heavy black overalls and work-boots. The overalls, for once, are zipped up to the neck.

'Thank God you're here,' she says. 'Is that the authorisation?'

I hand it over. The fact that Susan is involved in this shameful series of events as well as Ms N makes me want to cry.

Susan locks the red file in the safe, and then stands in front of me. 'Are you ready? This is going to be scary.'

I remember Ms N telling me to do whatever Susan says, and I nod. 'I am ready.'

Susan opens her arms and squeezes me tight. Unlike the touching from Mr Kagit and from Margarita, the warmth of her body makes me feel strong and protected.

'You won't regret it,' Susan says. 'Let's rock and roll.'

I have no idea what she is talking about, but I follow her into the lobby. To my surprise, she keeps on walking out through the dirty swing doors and into the night.

It is now completely dark and if I am honest I do not much like heading out into the hotel grounds without knowing why I am there. My uncertainty is not made any less when Susan heads towards the huge hole in the ground which is the site of the former secret police HQ and now, it seems, future conference centre.

'Keep moving, sweetheart.' Ahead of me, Susan's voice is muffled. 'We have to reach the cage.'

At once I stop walking. In the darkness, I can feel my feet sinking into the mud around the pit.

'The cage?' My voice is small.

'Quick. They will be here in a couple of minutes.'

'Who will be here?'

'The girl and Ms N. And Eli and Kagit.'

Again, her hard-to-understand accent is making it sound like Ka-shit. In the dark, I cannot see if she is smiling or not.

'They are coming here? Why?'

'Because this is where the special facilities are. Come *on*.' I feel her grab my arm, gentle but firm. 'Tatiana. You can do this.'

'You want me in the cage?'

'Yes. But we have to get there first.'

I stumble forward. My eyes are beginning to adjust to the darkness and I see we are passing the dark pit of the foundations. At the centre floats a disc of blackness: the opening of the old bunker.

The ground is rough. But it becomes easier when we cross a roadway formed of thick wooden planks leading to the edge of the pit.

'What are these?' I say. 'They were not here yesterday.'

'Wait and see,' Susan says.

Next to the wooden roadway is a large yellow machine. Susan leads us around it without a word. I do not remember seeing the machine yesterday, either.

We reach the far side of the pit. The cage is standing upright. It is filthy and frighteningly narrow. Beyond the excavation, the entrance to the hotel glows with light. The ancient crane rises into the night.

Behind us I see that the hill slopes down to a road. A car is there, its engine running. Inez is sitting in the car. When she sees us she walks up to where we are standing.

'Is she coming?' she asks Susan.

'Watch the entrance.' Susan is holding a small yellow box with an antenna sticking out of it.

Then Susan whispers to me what it is that Ms N wishes me to do next.

When Susan finishes speaking my first urge is to run away down the hill and drive away in Inez's car, whose engine I notice is still running. But I do not have time to think much because at that moment I hear Inez in the darkness.

'They are at the entrance.'

Two people are standing outside the hotel. It is Ms N and the girl. Ms N is holding the girl by the arm. The girl is barefoot with her high-heeled shoes in her hand. Without them she looks even more child-like.

'Take your shoes off,' Susan says.

I do not move.

'Where are the men?' I say.

'With luck, Maria is delaying them in the Platinum Megastar Lounge,' Susan says. 'But they'll be down any second.'

Ms N and the girl start to move towards us, more quickly than I would have thought possible. Perhaps this is why the girl has taken off her shoes. Behind them I see Eli and Mr Kagit appear in the door of the hotel. They, too, set off in our direction; but Ms N and the girl are moving faster than the two men, who have had a few drinks and perhaps are having trouble finding their way in the dark. In fact I see Ms N hesitate at a certain point; and when the two men pass the same way, both of them fall to the ground, cursing and laughing. Ms N and the girl are far ahead of them now. I can see the girl's white miniskirt in the darkness.

'Take off your shoes,' Susan says again.

I take them off. Susan puts them into a bag and throws it behind the crane. Under my feet the earth is cold.

The next moment Ms N arrives, almost dragging the girl behind her. In the darkness I see that the girl has been crying. Her make-up has run and she looks frightened.

I take the $100 bill which Mr Kagit has given me and press it into the girl's hand.

Inez steps forward. 'Come,' she says.

Inez and the girl run down the slope, climb into the car, and are gone.

I stare after them.

'Tatiana darling, for this to work you need to be in the cage right now,' Ms N says. 'Did Susan tell you what to do?'

'Yes.' My voice is so tiny I cannot hear it.

'They will be here in sixty seconds. If they find the three of us we are going to be in the deepest shit imaginable,' Ms N says.

'Here's the flashlight.' Susan is pressing a metal cylinder into my hand. 'Don't use it until you're in there.'

I throw my arms around Ms N. Her body is soft and warm and her arms hold me tight. Then I step into the cage.

The cage is so narrow that there is hardly room for one person, let alone two. I see Susan's hands move on the control panel and the cage jerks into the air and swings over the pit. The motion is so sudden that I scream and fall forward, my feet skidding on the steel floor. For a moment I am clutching air, then my arm catches a bar and I haul myself upright. Somewhere I can hear an engine whining as the crane winds in the cable.

Over the centre of the pit, the cage begins to descend. I shield my face with my arm and peer back through the darkness. Ms N, Susan and the two men are watching the cage move toward the hatch. Eli is laughing. Mr Kagit is standing with his hands on his hips, rocking to and fro as if he is watching a sporting event.

The black hole of the hatch is rushing up towards me. It seems impossible that the base of the cage will fit in, but suddenly the motion slows and for the final metre the cage inches its way downwards. For a moment it is as if I am standing on the floor of the excavation amidst the steel rods. Then the cage plunges into the void below.

Inside the bunker, the darkness is intense. The basket stops. I click the flashlight on.

I see a flat concrete surface perhaps half a metre below the basket.

I steady myself against the cage.

I jump onto the floor in my bare feet.

Then I strike the bars of the cage twice with my metal

flashlight, *thump-thump*.

At once the cage rises towards the hatch. It reaches the round hole. Then the movement speeds up and the cage disappears into the night.

I am alone.

I sweep the beam across the ceiling of the chamber. The hatch is in the centre of a sheet of steel. The high walls are concrete – impossible to climb. On the floor behind me lies a metal staircase, the original means of access, which has been cut into small, thick pieces.

I turn the beam towards the other side of the room.

The first thing I see are two chairs and a folding table. On the table are a half-finished bottle of whisky; two glasses; an oil-lamp; and a collection of metal implements and other objects whose purpose I do not recognise.

Set into the far wall I see two steel hooks. From each of them hang chains and something I do not recognise but what I think may be handcuffs. Below the hooks I see what look like black stains on the floor.

I do not want to see these things, but I must, because I am looking for something else. At last I spot it.

Quickly, I take off my white blouse. I walk across to the shop-dummy which is standing near the hooks and handcuffs. It looks clean and innocent in this awful place and I notice it has dark hair painted on. This is the same colour as my hair, and the hair of the young girl.

I pull my white blouse down over the head of the dummy so that it is dressed from the waist up. I drag the dummy to the darkest corner of the room, where it is hidden from sight behind a steel pillar.

Then I turn off the flashlight and crouch down amongst the cut-up pieces of iron staircase on the opposite side of the room.

In the darkness all I can hear is my own breathing. I steady myself on one of the fragments of metal staircase – each piece is so heavy I cannot move it.

The crane engine is whining again. I look up at the hatch and see a dim circle of night sky. Then the sky disappears.

I know this is the base of the cage entering the strong-room but I do not shine my flashlight, even though this means I am in total darkness.

I try to breathe quietly, but to me it sounds as if I am as loud as a hurricane.

I am lucky. The two men in the cage are making plenty of noise.

'Where's the kid?' It is Eli's voice, loudly. 'It's no use hiding, sweetheart.'

'You are a master of procurement,' Mr Kagit says. 'Young, beautiful and all for us. She is perfect.'

From where I am standing, I can see the two of them are standing in the cage, just as I have been doing a couple of minutes before, slightly off the floor of the chamber. They seem to have only one flashlight between them. I am pleased to see that its beam is weak, perhaps because it has been provided for them by Susan. Then, without warning, the basket drops to the ground with a thud.

'Fuck that bull-dyke bitch!' Eli has fallen from the cage and is sprawled on the floor. 'I'll make her life hell for that.'

'If you are talking about the Engineering Manager, I am not sure she is a homosexual,' Mr Kagit says. He steps from the cage and watches Eli climb to his feet. 'But it is true that she is not to my taste.' He turns towards the wall with the hooks and reaches into his pocket. 'Now, where are you, my girl? Is that you hiding in the corner?'

I see he has taken from his pocket another flashlight.

Outside, beyond the hatch, I hear a deep roar of a kind I have not heard before.

The game is over.

The moment that Mr Kagit clicks on his flashlight I run towards the cage and throw myself inside, striking it with my own flashlight as I do so.

Thump.

At once the basket lurches upwards.

'What the hell is that?' Eli says.

'It is a white blouse on a dummy,' Mr Kagit says. 'And the basket is leaving. *Grab it.*'

The cage has risen quickly for the first few seconds, but it slows as it nears the hatch. At that moment I feel the platform sway as both the men jump up and grab the base. With my flashlight I can see their hands: four sets of fingers, white with the strain of holding on.

I wish I was wearing my shoes so I could stamp on those fingers, but my bare feet are soft and I do not want to give one of them the chance to grab me. So I kneel down and try to hammer at the fingers with the base of my metal flashlight.

Either the fingers are tough or the flashlight is not hard, but I cannot seem to loosen them. For an instant I have an image of the two men holding onto the base of the cage all the way back to the rusty crane.

Then, slowly, the top of the cage enters the hatch.

It is a tight fit.

The cage rises.

I hear a bump and a grunt as if someone's head has struck the roof of the chamber. One pair of hands disappears and the cage feels lighter.

The other man is still holding on tight. Perhaps he has swung his body below the cage to avoid his body hitting the ceiling of the strong-room. The fingers are manicured. I think this man is Mr Kagit.

But the cage is a tight fit in the round metal hatch.

As my head emerges into the open, the cage begins to rise more quickly. The base catches hard on the side of the hatch and there is a scream of pain. I look down and see four fingers are still visible on the floor of the cage. But they are not attached to any hand.

The cage is rising faster. I look down at the bunker but can see only a black hole.

In the open, the deep roar I heard from inside the hatch is louder. But I do not understand what it means.

A light comes on where Susan and I passed the wooden walkway. It is the headlights of a truck with a cylinder on its back, slowly turning. It has a pipe running into the yellow machine, which I now see is nearly as big as the truck itself and has a kind of funnel next to it from which a piece of plastic fabric is hanging down, like a long white sock. Next to this machine Susan is standing, her eyes fixed on me as she moves the cage back towards the base of the crane.

A moment later I step out of the cage. Ms N throws me a black T-shirt. I want to hug her but as soon as I step out of the basket she pushes the cage onto its side and detaches the crane cable. Then she looks towards Susan and raises her arm.

I pull on the T-shirt. I hear a whine as the cable disappears up into the dark sky.

Ms N runs forward and embraces me.

'Tatiana. Thank God you are safe.'

'Thank you for rescuing me.'

'You are braver than I can imagine.'

'I think one of the men is hurt.' I look around where the cage is lying and find one severed finger, lying on the ground. 'I think this belongs to Mr Kagit.'

'Perhaps,' Ms N says.

I look at Ms N. Her face has changed. Her expression is one I have seen many times before but never until now in C—. Perhaps she has been too busy trying to solve the big problems of the hotel. This time her smile is not inquisitive. It is mischievous. Ms N shines her flashlight on the finger. Then she picks it up and tosses it into the pit.

'Do you not think Mr Kagit might want that finger later?' I say. 'Perhaps it could be sewn on again.'

'I do not think Mr Kagit will be needing that finger in future,' Ms N says. 'Watch.'

I turn towards the pit. Over by the truck, Susan has attached the hook of the crane to the funnel of the yellow machine. Slowly, the crane lifts the funnel out over the pit, trailing the long plastic sock beneath it. The trucks and the crane are making a lot of noise. At one point there is a lull and I think maybe I can hear a man shouting, but I am not sure. Then an engine roars, and I hear nothing.

The funnel is above the black hole of the hatch. Slowly it descends until the plastic sock enters the circular opening beneath. A long tube connects the yellow machine to the funnel.

There is a pause. Again, I think perhaps I can hear shouting. Then Susan moves closer to the yellow machine and I see a torrent of concrete pour out of the funnel, down to the plastic sock and into the mouth of the hatch. The concrete flows and flows. At last it stops and the machines fall silent.

Now I cannot hear any shouting.

The truck at the rim of the pit backs away and disappears. Another truck arrives. I see Susan connect the new truck to the yellow machine, which I understand now is some kind of pump. A minute later, a fresh flow of concrete begins to pour into the hatch.

Ms N is standing next to me, watching the concrete flowing. She links her arm through mine. 'I think we could go back to the hotel, now,' she says.

'Yes,' I say. 'I think we could.'

To return to the hotel we have to walk past the yellow machine and the wooden road. Walking is easier now that there are lights and construction workers everywhere. I look along the wooden road and see a row of trucks waiting, each with a slowly rotating cylinder of concrete on its back.

'Susan is not wasting any time, now we have the authorisation we need.' Ms N squeezes my arm. 'By tomorrow morning the entire floor of the pit will be covered in a layer of concrete one metre thick.'

'Susan said that she wanted the best foundations money can

buy,' I say.

'These foundations are excellent value,' Ms N says. 'We have not paid any bribes to secure building authorisation. Also, if Mr Kagit and Eli decide not to use their flights to New York we shall benefit from a refund.'

'Perhaps we can cancel the hotel reservations also,' I say.

'Let us wait and see whether Mr Kagit and Eli use their booking.' Ms N is smiling and looking into the pit, where concrete is welling up from the hatch and is flooding out to fill the tangle of steel rods. 'Perhaps they will change their plans.' She scratches her head. 'I promised Mr Kagit that we would incorporate his special facilities into the new conference centre. We have done this, but perhaps not in the way he was expecting.'

'No,' I say. I am remembering also that Ms N told Mr Kagit that Eli would always be available to him. She has kept this promise too, but again not in a way which Mr Kagit might have been expecting.

As we approach the hotel entrance I notice that someone has cleaned the doors to the lobby. The glass is gleaming. Inside, I see that the dead plants have gone. In their place are new plants in brightly-coloured pots, neatly arranged around the edge of the marble floor. In-between, the sofas have been grouped at each end of the lobby, making the space appear larger.

It is as if we have left one hotel, and returned to another one.

'When did you do all this?' I ask Ms N.

'This is the work of Maria, Mr Kagit's niece,' Ms N says. 'I have reassigned her to Susan's team and it turns out she is full of good ideas. I think she will be a better worker, now that her uncle has gone to the United States. If we are lucky perhaps he will stay there.'

'Perhaps he will,' I say.

Ms N turns to me. 'You will start work as head receptionist tomorrow. In the meantime, I think you deserve a good night's sleep.'

She is smiling her mischievous smile. Her suit is immaculate.

If it were not for the mud on her shoes it would be hard to imagine that a few minutes ago I had been embracing her on the edge of the pit which will hold the new conference centre.

'Thank you, Ms N,' I say. 'I think I will enjoy working here.'

As I leave the lobby I turn and see Ms N, standing in by the entrance, running her hand over the chipped paintwork of one of the swing doors. She has started to solve the big problems of the hotel. Now she is planning to solve the small problems.

Ms N is good at solving problems. One day, I would like to be like her.

5. GENTS

THE FIRST PERSON I see enter the lobby is loaded with shopping bags from a major international clothing brand.

I will not name the brand because I do not like to promote this kind of clothes. But it is a brand like a masculine man's name. So I am guessing that the man carrying the bags is hoping that wearing these clothes will make him more of a man than he is perhaps feeling inside.

'Mr Anderson. Welcome to our hotel.' I smile my thousand-watt smile. 'Good choice.'

'Hey. Tatiana. You're using the script.' The man slides his passport across the counter and peers at my name badge. 'Are you Russian?'

I maintain my thousand-watt smile and pick up the telephone, which our brand standards say must be answered within three rings. A Mr Jones in Suite 1295 says he wishes to complain that his shower is not working. I promise that Housekeeping will come shortly. Across the lobby I see a group of men whose uniform of dark trousers and blue smart-but-casual shirts, and the noises they are making, remind me of a party of schoolchildren. They are heading for our signature EcoSystem Lounge Bar.

The man with the shopping bags is right that our hotel chain's core script for reception staff includes the words *Welcome to our hotel* and *Good choice*. But the guidance notes which accompany the script also tell us that *the customer is a human being* and that we should use *originality, humour, respect and the personal touch* in our exchanges. So I add: 'No, sir, I am Ukrainian. You know. We leave the West behind.'

This is actually not the first time I am using this joke.

'Hey Julius. How's it hanging?'

Mr Anderson ignores my attempt at a *personal touch* and turns to greet the three people who have entered the lobby. They are like him: tall, well-built men who were perhaps attractive five or fifteen years ago. Now their skin is mottled from too much sunshine and their bellies are pushing out the fronts of their smart-but-casual shirts.

All of them carry shopping bags from the same exclusive clothing brand.

The four men laugh and make unnecessary physical contact to pretend that they are friends. But all of them are working to keep their places in the queue.

I consider making an original, humorous and personal comment about the fact that they have the same shopping bags and have maybe been on an outing together. But four more men have entered the lobby.

I now have eight customers waiting to check in and two phones ringing.

'What hotel is this?' The eighth man in the queue is grinning as if he is, perhaps, a comedian. 'Don't they have service standards? What happened to the three-minute check-in target?'

'Zero minutes for VIPs. And gents – we're all VIPs!' Man number seven is standing with his legs braced and his shoulders squared. He is wearing a bright orange look-at-me tie and has black swept-back hair, greying at the temples. 'It seems to me that the reception services at this hotel are slightly shit and we should complain to the management!'

I look with surprise at man number seven. Has he not noticed that I am working as quickly as I can to check in Mr Julius Anderson? Man number seven has a shopping bag from the exclusive store like everyone else. His bag is as big as a suitcase.

He has placed it on the ground to block man number eight from approaching the reception desk.

'Actually, I am surprised the hotel General Manager is not here to meet us.' The sixth man is shorter and younger-looking than the others and is perhaps from Asia. 'I understand this is a normal courtesy when another GM is visiting a hotel in this chain.'

'He'd be a busy guy!'

The other seven men did not react much to the Asian-looking gentleman. But when Mr Julius Anderson, at the front of the queue, makes what is really the same joke about the fact that 800 General Managers from our hotel chain are assembling for our annual leadership conference in Florida, everyone makes the kind of roaring, breathless sounds which are meant to show that they are helpless with laughter.

This is because Mr Anderson is Executive Vice President of our chain, and Group President, Europe, Middle East and Africa. This means he decides who will be the General Managers of our two hundred hotels in that region.

GMs in our chain always laugh at Mr Anderson's jokes.

The phones are ringing behind the reception desk. More men in smart-but-casual clothing are descending from taxis outside. At this moment someone who is shorter than everyone in the queue and who is dressed in cream and burgundy and a four-inch wide leather belt enters the lobby.

It is a woman.

It is Ms N, the General Manager of our hotel in C—.

C— is a country which is not yet economically successful and where it is famously difficult even to buy a loaf of bread, much less to run a five-star hotel. But this does not mean that the hotel in C— is no good. In fact, the hotel in C— won the Platinum Megastar award for the best hotel in our chain just one year after Ms N took over as General Manager there. The hotel won the award thanks to outstanding customer satisfaction, and also increased income and higher bookings from its new conference centre.

This makes Ms N something of a celebrity among other GMs.

But for me she is famous for other things, about which only she and I know. These involve, for example, a giant cake; a set of sharp Chroma knives; and many thousand cubic metres of concrete.

These things make me admire Ms N for her problem-solving abilities.

The men at the back of the queue do not know about the cake or the knives or the concrete. But they make way for Ms N as she advances; and gather in behind her once she has passed.

The exception is the man in the orange tie, whose gigantic shopping bag is like a road-block in the lobby. Ms N picks up the bag and rotates it by ninety degrees so that she can proceed.

Perhaps the men allow Ms N to move to the front of the queue because her small mouth is turned up in an inquisitive smile, as if she has discovered something intriguing. Perhaps it is because her eyes are sparkling as if she is excited about a special secret.

Perhaps it is because she is ignoring them. Instead, she is looking at me.

'Tatiana,' she says. 'How are you?' She leans across the counter and kisses me on both cheeks. Her skin is soft, and I smell a delicious perfume. I am impressed by this, because I used to work with Ms N in C— and I know that she has been travelling for twenty-four hours to get here on three separate and perhaps not entirely modern or safe airlines.

'I am well,' I say. 'Congratulations on your award.'

'Thank you, Tatiana.' She leans in close again. 'But I do not care about awards. All I want is to move from our hotel in C— to our luxury new UP-branded hotel in London. A man I care about is living in that city.'

'Good luck, Ms N.'

'I shall need it, because every GM in our chain wants to run our luxury new UP-branded hotel in London.' Ms N looks around and speaks more loudly. 'Why is everyone standing here?'

'They are waiting to check in,' I say.

'Check in?' Ms N addresses the men crowded around her. 'It seems to me some GMs have wrong priorities. Why are you creating congestion here when you could be exchanging best practice in the EcoSystem Lounge Bar?' She rests her hand lightly on the arm of Mr Anderson. 'Julius. Let me buy you a pre-dinner drink.'

Mr Anderson's too-tanned face cracks into a grin. 'I'll get the drinks,' he says.

'He says the drinks are on him.' Ms N sets off across the lobby. 'Let's go.'

The next moment Ms N and Mr Anderson are leading a gang of GMs to the bar and I am facing an empty space dotted with luggage and shopping bags.

The only person left is the man in the orange tie and the improbably large shopping bag.

'Losers.' He gestures at the retreating crowd. 'Lead, follow or get out of the way is my motto. And I'm a fucking leader.' He slaps his passport on the counter. 'See if you can check me in without saying *Welcome to our hotel* or *Good choice*.'

I glance at the passport and smile my thousand-watt smile. 'Sure will, Mr Knox.'

'I need a room on floors four to six,' he says. 'Facing north. Not near elevators, stairs or lounges. If you're on floors one thru three any low-life can climb in your window. Above floor seven if there's a fire, the ladders don't reach. And switch off the fucking fake smile, Tatiana, or I'll switch it off for you.'

I stop smiling. 'The room is booked, sir. Will there be anything else?'

'Not now, honey,' he says. 'But watch that name. Mr Buddy Knox. You'll be hearing a lot about me.'

'Yes, Mr Knox,' I say. 'I am sure I will.'

From my seat at the back of the hall, where I am operating the sound and lighting technology for the conference, the eight hundred General Managers of our hotel chain are like ants in a colony.

Nearly every GM, whether male or, occasionally, female, is dressed in dark colours. All sit at tables, clustered around electronic display-boards in the pit of the room. On the stage above, the gods from our Houston senior leadership sit in armchairs, sometimes rising to address the throng below.

The man doing the addressing right now is Mr Julius Anderson, Executive Vice President and Group President, Europe, Middle East and Africa.

'Gents,' he says. 'It's time for us to take a long, hard look at a paradigm shift in experience optimisation for the female guest. We're talking vanities, hairdryers and nail-files.'

To me, Mr Anderson's words do not seem to mean anything at all. I am not even sure he is addressing me, or Ms N or any of the other female GMs, of whom there are twenty-three in total, as none of us is of course a gentleman. But the response from the GMs in the pit is a rapturous burst of applause.

The rapture is because the ants who crowd the conference room floor are not ordinary arthropods. Instead, they form what I have read can be described as a super-organism. Each General Manager in the room is belonging to a sub-group with a specialised task; and these sub-groups, linked in a hierarchy, are meant to help the whole colony of GMs – our hotel chain – achieve its goals.

The result is that when one of our armchair gods speaks into the microphone, the super-organism pulses with life as GMs make notes, pick up tablet computers, or even take photos of the great men on stage in the distance and use social media to send these to each other.

Each General Manager is seeking attention. As they huddle around display-boards or rise to address the conference, each is hoping to make a mark with the armchair gods.

One of the top attention-seekers is Mr Buddy Knox. He is wearing the same dark suit as everyone else, set off by a crimson tie. His swept-back hair gleams in the spotlights. Each time the conference divides into groups, Mr Knox is eager to lead the discussion. When one of the armchair gods mentions the luxury new UP-branded hotel in the city of London, Mr Buddy Knox explains his concept for making that hotel the most profitable in the history of our chain.

When he says this I think of Ms N, who has told me she wishes to become GM of the new UP-branded hotel in London because a man she cares about is living there; but that other people also wish to take the position.

Clearly, Mr Buddy Knox is one of those people.

Clearly, Mr Buddy Knox is skilled in attracting the attention of the armchair gods who make decisions on where to move the GMs in our hotel chain.

Clearly, Ms N is facing tough competition if she is to achieve happiness.

Ms N is not one of the attention-seekers at the conference. It is true that she is wearing a designer dress from the mountains of C— made of silk and traditional fibres which is not blue or black but is a combination of reds, oranges and greys and comes with a little fitted jacket in matching colours. It is also true that she has applied a little make-up, which with her inquisitive expression makes her look more like a politician or company boss than a hotel manager.

But Ms N has chosen a table in the shadows, far from the stage. She seems more interested in her mobile phone than in the conference. Perhaps she is texting the man she has mentioned she cares about who is living in London.

To see Ms N taking no active part in the conference makes me sad. It seems to me that she risks losing the battle to become GM of our luxury new UP-branded hotel in the city where the man she cares about is living. Unless she fights for her dreams, she will lose her chance for happiness.

At the next break, I see Mr Buddy Knox pushing through other GMs to reach the armchair gods who are mingling with the crowds in the pit. Competition is fierce; but Mr Buddy Knox is telling the truth about leading, following or getting out of the way, and I see him penetrate as far as Mr Julius Anderson, Executive Vice President and Group President, Europe, Middle East and Africa. The two men hold a short conversation and they put their heads together perhaps a little more closely than I would have expected. When Mr Julius Anderson steps back he wears a big smile.

Ms N is sitting at her table in the shadows, playing with her phone. I walk towards her.

'Hello, Tatiana, how are you?' Ms N stands up and kisses my cheeks.

'I am worried, Ms N. I think that Mr Buddy Knox is working with Mr Julius Anderson to become GM of our new UP-branded hotel in London.'

'Yes, Tatiana. You are correct.' Ms N glances at her phone, where a new text message has arrived. She types for a moment, then smiles. 'These so-called gents have a habit of fixing up appointments amongst themselves. It is a kind of male-bonding. Of course, I could not play these games, even if I wished to do so.'

'But what will you do? Your hotel won the Platinum Megastar award last year as best hotel in our chain. You deserve the job in London more than Mr Buddy Knox. And a man you care about is living there.'

'I will do what I can. I will ensure our hotel in C— is run to the best standards possible in that challenging country. I will treat my staff as human beings. I will even socialise with our senior leadership so long as this is fun and does not go beyond certain limits.'

'Yes, Ms N. I know what limits you mean.' I am thinking of thousands of cubic metres of concrete.

'Now, Tatiana, I am afraid I must ask you to excuse me.' Ms N squeezes my arm and picks up her mobile phone. 'I am texting my special friend in London. Some things are more important even than this conference.'

When I go back to my seat amidst the sound and lighting technology I find that I too am smiling. It seems to me that Ms N has a good understanding of what things in life are important, and what things are less important.

THE LAST SESSION of the day is entitled *Wash-up and Special Announcements*. To be honest I think everyone is looking forward to this session because as soon as it is finished we can enjoy the "Active Evening".

The notes which General Managers have received in their conference packs say that the "Active Evening" is *to ensure team-building and active networking at the end of a hard day's excellence-growth*. What this means is that we all will get together with any special friends we have amongst the eight hundred GMs and head out for dinner and maybe a drink in town.

The *Wash-up and Special Announcements* session has been running for fifteen minutes when Mr Julius Anderson, Executive Vice President and Group President, Europe, Middle East and Africa, rises from his armchair and approaches the podium.

A hush falls over the ant-colony.

'Gents,' says Mr Julius Anderson, 'I want to thank you all for an outstanding day.'

In the pit I see Mr Buddy Knox stand up and clap his hands. At once a dozen, then a hundred people around him stand, then everyone is on their feet. Applause echoes round the room.

Ms N remains seated at her table in the shadows, studying her mobile phone.

'Please, gents, please.' Mr Anderson waves for everyone to be seated. 'After such a hard day's work I know you're eager for the evening to begin. We all want to savour the delights our conference city has to offer.' He grins, and a rumbling roar of manly laughter swells and fades. 'But to round off, I want to make a special announcement.'

Silence.

'It is about our luxury new UP-branded hotel in London,' Mr Anderson says. 'We need a General Manager for that project. I know there are eight hundred people in this room who are qualified, ready and eager to do that job.'

Again, Mr Buddy Knox is on his feet applauding. Once more, everyone except Ms N is following his lead, as if Mr Anderson has made a witty and perceptive observation.

Mr Anderson looks around the room. His gaze seems to rest on Mr Buddy Knox. Then he scans the room again, as if he is searching for someone else. He pauses at the table where Ms N is sitting. She is still looking at the mobile phone.

Mr Anderson frowns.

'In our hotel chain we believe in openness and transparency,' he says. 'So I must tell you that we have two lead candidates for the job in London. The first is the General Manager whose hotel last year won the Platinum Megastar award as the best hotel in our chain just one year after this manager took up her appointment there. I am referring of course to our hotel in the incomprehensibly difficult-to-operate country of C—.' He pauses. There is silence as the eight hundred GMs wonder where in the world the country of C—, which is not exactly a household name, might be. 'That General Manager,' Mr Anderson continues, 'is Ms N.'

Mr Julius Anderson of course says Ms N's full surname and given name. But I have removed it here because I know Ms N does not like me or anyone else saying publicly that she is fabulous, although in my opinion such a word as fabulous actually does not do justice to her qualities.

A light dusting of applause echoes around the room as delegates rotate in their seats in search of Ms N and discuss with their neighbours whether the country of C— might, perhaps, be in Asia, or in Africa, or in South America.

'The second candidate on our short-list,' Mr Anderson continues, 'is the manager of our Unter den Linden UP-branded boutique hotel in Berlin. I do not need to remind you that the UP stands for Ultra-Platinum, not, as we sometimes may joke, for Unaffordably-Priced.' He smiles as a roar of hysterical laughter sweeps around the conference. Ms N is again looking at her telephone. I am surprised she is not more excited when she is on a short-list of just two candidates to become GM of the hotel of her dreams. But perhaps she knows something that I do not.

'I would like to invite the two candidates on stage,' Mr Anderson says.

Mr Buddy Knox leaps up from his table at the centre of the room and runs across the pit to the stage in a bounding, loping sprint. It looks as if he is wearing special shoes with springs inside them. He shakes Mr Anderson's hand in a pumping two-handed grip. Over in the shadows, Ms N also rises, shrugs her tiny jacket onto her shoulders, and sets off for the stage. I can see she is wearing heels, because although she is petite and is walking slowly, her gait is authoritative.

To reach Mr Anderson and Mr Buddy Knox, Ms N has to climb a steep, narrow staircase to the stage. I see her hesitate for a moment at the foot of these stairs and I remember that Ms N does not like heights. In fact, heights terrify her. Even to climb to the stage in her high heels will be difficult for her.

But Ms N hesitates only for a moment. Then she carefully climbs the stairs, one step at a time.

By the time Ms N reaches Mr Julius Anderson and Mr Buddy Knox on the stage, the body language of both men is making clear that they wish that she would walk more quickly.

'Gents.' Mr Anderson addresses the audience. 'We have here two of our organisation's finest young talents. It reflects well on our policy of inclusion and diversity that we have a short-list for this key job which is 50% female. That is because our chain prioritises women in leadership, just as it prioritises the needs of the female guest.'

He directs a huge grin towards Ms N. Buddy Knox claps energetically, setting off a wave of applause from the pit. Ms N does not grin or clap but gazes around the room as if she is wondering what she is doing there. Perhaps she is looking for some of the other twenty-two female GMs.

'But enough about us,' Mr Anderson says. 'It's time to announce the new General Manager of our luxury new UP-branded hotel in the city of London.' He takes an envelope from his jacket pocket; opens it; and withdraws a slip of paper. 'The successful candidate who will be appointed to that post is... Mr Buddy Knox!'

This time the applause from the GMs in the pit seems to me less than whole-hearted, but I see Ms N is clapping and so I join in too. It seems that Ms N is not going to be General Manager of the hotel of her dreams.

THE TEXT Ms N has sent me is short. She asks if I would like to spend my "Active Evening" with her and tells me, if so, to meet her in the lobby at eight o'clock. She adds the words *Don't dress up*.

This invitation from Ms N strikes me as friendly. Not only are most of the GMs keen to spend maximum time with other GMs, but many are still trying to get face-time with the armchair gods. So it is good that Ms N wants to spend the "Active Evening" with me, a member of the support staff. It is even better that she tells me not to dress up, since of course I cannot compete with the kind of beautiful clothes which Ms N is tending to wear in her spare time.

I am in the lobby at 7.55. At first I think Ms N is not there, but then I spot her sitting in one of the artfully-clustered leather sofas which our hotel chain places in its lobbies. One reason I do not see her is that she is so small that she almost disappears inside these sofas, which are not perhaps designed for "female guests". But I also understand that I have not seen her because she is wearing jeans and a casual jacket, which make her appear by her standards rather anonymous.

'Hello, Tatiana, darling. Do take a seat.' Ms N gestures to one of the sofas. 'I am glad that you are happy to spend your "Active Evening" with me, because to be honest I can use some company.'

I sit down on the sofa. I can hardly see over the sides.

'Let's have a drink,' Ms N says. She summons a waiter and orders two gin and tonics. I am surprised by this, as the purpose of the "Active Evening" is usually to escape the convention hotel. But I guess that Ms N knows what she is doing.

'Let me say how sorry I am,' I say, 'that you were not chosen as GM of our luxury new UP-branded hotel in London. I know this was important to you for personal reasons. And I think you are a better General Manager than Mr Buddy Knox.'

'Thank you, Tatiana. Mr Buddy Knox has many qualities. I am sure he will do a good job whatever his next assignment may be.'

'You are always generous, Ms N. But what will your next job be, if not London?'

'I will try to be ready for any opportunity which may present itself.' Ms N raises her glass. 'Tatiana. Would you be able to help me with something, tonight? If you are free?'

'For you I am always free, Ms N.' I raise my glass, in turn.

FOR SOME TIME I am not sure what help Ms N wants, because we sit and chat and drink our G&Ts and after half an hour has passed Ms N orders two more. This is of course as good a way to pass the "Active Evening" as any other and I am delighted to be doing so with Ms N. But shortly after the new drinks have arrived, Ms N places her hand on my arm.

'Now. Tatiana. Tell me what you see.'

I kneel up to see over the giant sofa-back.

'I see a group of ten men in the lobby. I think they are General Managers from our chain because they are wearing dark-blue smart-but-casual shirts. They are making a lot of noise.'

'That is because they are excited,' Ms N says. 'Do you see anyone you recognise?'

'I see Mr Buddy Knox. And Mr Julius Anderson.'

'Thank you, Tatiana. Let me know when they leave the hotel.'

Ms N takes another sip of her drink as if nothing unusual is happening. But as soon as I tell her that the men have left, she jumps to her feet.

'Let's have some fun.'

For the first time today, Ms N is smiling her mischievous smile. We walk onto the street and see the men walking in a tightly-bunched group. Their similar clothing making them look like an elderly, overweight sports team.

Ms N squeezes my hand. 'Thank you for coming with me. Tell me if anything happens with which you do not feel comfortable.'

If I am honest I am feeling highly comfortable because being with Ms N for our "Active Evening" feels like an adventure. But I know that sometimes Ms N can do things which are not comfortable at all. So I am not surprised as we follow the men past some turnings and down smaller streets to find that we are entering a part of town which is different from the area around the convention centre.

In fact we are in what is sometimes called the Red Light District.

The absence of many people on the streets makes it hard for Ms N and myself to remain unobserved. Fortunately, night has fallen. Our colleagues do indeed seem excited and are not looking in our direction. We are less than fifty yards away when we see them enter a building via a flight of stairs, which descends steeply from street-level.

The building is in need of restoration. Its bricks seem to have crumbled to pieces over the years. But there are two neon signs on the facade. One is showing a woman moving up and down on a pole as the neon is flashing on and off. The other says GENTS in large white letters, with the words *Gentlemen's Club* underneath.

Ms N takes my hand. 'Let's go in,' she says.

'Why?'

'Tatiana. It is not for you and me to tell other people how they should behave. But we can perhaps encourage them to ask themselves whether what they do is correct and normal. Also, to see inside a Gentlemen's Club will be interesting.'

To be honest, I am not sure I am liking the idea of entering a place which says it is for gentlemen, since I am guessing that most of the customers will be men rather than women. But Ms N seems relaxed, and this helps me to relax also.

When we reach the top of the stairs down to the entrance I see that they are steep. In fact, it is almost like a ladder. In addition, there are two tall, heavily-built men outside the door at the foot of the steps. They do not look friendly, and I am wondering whether they are gentlemen themselves. But Ms N does not hesitate. She holds onto the hand-rail and goes down the stairs one at a time.

To see Ms N overcome her fear of heights to enter the Gentlemen's Club, despite the two large men, makes me proud to be with her.

The bigger of the two men looks down at Ms N and then at me.

'Can I help you ladies?'

Ms N points to a sign by the entrance, which says *Ladies! Entry & First Drink Free!*

'Am I right in thinking women are welcome here?' she says.

'They are.' The man looks at Ms N again and frowns. 'Your first time?'

'Yes,' Ms N says.

'Well, the one rule is, no soliciting,' the man says. 'What you do if a man asks you to do something is up to you. And don't steal tricks off other girls or they'll scratch your eyes out.'

'Thank you for the heads-up,' Ms N says.

To be honest my first impression when we enter the Gentlemen's Club is disappointing. In the movies I have seen, these places are full of women with beautiful bodies dancing on stages with light-shows and music, watched by badly-behaved, rough- but handsome-looking men and waitresses in sexy costumes. In most of these movies something shifty is going on in a room upstairs, with video-cameras, an under-cover detective and a Mr Big wearing a gold belt-buckle.

But Gents is not like this at all.

Four women are sitting at the bar by the entrance. None of them is beautiful or ugly. They are normal-looking women, all wearing short skirts and tight tops and enjoying the free first drink which Gents provide for women guests and looking as if they may be about to die of boredom. I am guessing these women are prostitutes, since I am used to seeing such women in hotels of our chain and, if I am honest, many other hotels, too.

Further into the room is a small stage, surrounded by red benches. On the stage is a naked woman dancing around a shiny metal pole. On the benches sit twelve men – I count them – all staring at the woman on stage as if they have never seen a woman before who is dancing, or not wearing any clothes, or both of these things. Also on the benches are sitting four more women, although these ones do not seem so bored as the ones at the bar. In fact they seem delighted to be sitting next to the men on the benches, most of whom are not paying them too much attention but are staring at the naked woman on the stage.

Actually the naked woman on the stage is not bad-looking and is making a good effort to dance in time with the music as well as to display to the men on the red benches those parts of her body which are not usually visible when women are anything less than fully naked. Why the men are so keen to look at these parts I am not sure but I am guessing that the naked woman knows from experience that this is what they want to see.

'There's our guys,' Ms N says.

Mr Julius Anderson, Mr Buddy Knox and eight other men in dark blue smart-but-casual shirts are sitting on the red benches staring at the naked woman. Mr Julius Anderson has his arm around one of the prostitutes, and I see there are two drinks in front of them. I am wondering whether Mr Julius Anderson will charge these drinks to his expense account. I am also wondering what Ms N is going to do next. But she does nothing except to go to the bar and order us a couple of drinks of our own. We sit down at a table at the back of the room.

Although the Gentlemen's Club is not how I imagined it, I am interested to see what the naked woman will do next and how our colleagues from the hotel chain will interact with the prostitutes, and whether some more people will come in to liven up the atmosphere.

In fact the next thing which happens, is that at the end of the dance, a waitress approaches the two men who have been watching the show who are not from our hotel chain, and asks them to leave or buy another drink.

They leave.

This does not seem to me likely to liven up the atmosphere in the "Gents" Gentlemen's Club.

When the two men stand up to leave, one of the General Managers from our hotel chain turns and notices Ms N and myself at the back of the room. He does not look pleased to see us. He leans across to a colleague, and soon all ten of them are peering in our direction and having a conversation. The music has started again and another woman has come onto the stage, this time wearing some clothes, which I am guessing she plans to take off. I feel sorry for her because her audience is now only ten men, all of whom are more interested in Ms N and myself than they are in her.

While our colleagues talk to each other, the woman on the stage takes off her T-shirt and her spangly hot-pants and begins to wrap herself around the pole. By the time Mr Buddy Knox gets up and comes to talk to us, I am almost relieved, because I do not like to see the girl doing her best to entertain the guests at the Gentlemen's Club while nobody is watching.

Mr Buddy Knox stops opposite Ms N. He does not seem to see me. He does not sit down.

'What the hell are you doing here?' he asks.

'I am having a drink with Tatiana,' Ms N says. 'What are you doing here?'

'You know what I mean, bitch.' Mr Buddy Knox's face is red. 'Did you follow us?'

'I am not sure I need to answer questions addressed to me in that way,' Ms N says. 'What I do in my "Active Evening" is up to me. Same for you.'

'Yeah, right.' Mr Buddy Knox frowns. 'Are you trying to embarrass us? By coming and spying like this?'

'I do not think it is possible for one person to embarrass another person. A person's embarrassment comes from within them, not from outside,' Ms N says.

'Seems to me you're behaving like shit,' Mr Buddy Knox says. 'Is this about London?'

'This is about how we choose to spend our "Active Evening",' Ms N says. 'How is yours, so far?'

'It was going great before you showed up,' Mr Buddy Knox says. 'But I won't give you the pleasure of asking you to leave. In fact, I don't give a flying fuck what you do.'

'Congratulations on London,' Ms N says. 'I'm sure you'll do a great job. And we've finished our drinks, so perhaps if Tatiana doesn't mind we'll be off. What are you doing for the "Active Day" tomorrow, by the way?'

Mr Knox blinks at her. 'I thought I'd try the alligator trip,' he says.

'Me too,' Ms N says.

'I guess you'll fit right in,' Mr Knox says.

THE "ACTIVE DAY" is the second part of our free time during our hotel chain's annual leadership conference. According to the conference notes, the "Active Day" is for *enhanced group dynamics in a stimulus-rich environment ahead of the climactic Conference Gala Dinner.*

Because there are 800 Conference attendees, the "Active Day" is designed around choices to meet all tastes. In addition to the "Alligator Frenzy" outing chosen by Ms N and Mr Buddy Knox, options include a "Studio Tour Adventure"; a "Mall Meltdown"; a "Speed Track Raceday"; a "Theme Park Themed Party"; and a "Brunch munch-a-thon".

Although support staff do not qualify for "Active Day" outings, the conference organisers have allocated some of us to accompany the delegates. I am with the "Alligator Frenzy" General Managers. This suits me because in my country there are no alligators. Also, the excursion includes a trip in something called an airboat. I have seen films of airboats and they look like the most exciting form of transport I can imagine.

If I am honest, the start of the tour is mediocre. Our two buses, carrying seventy-six General Managers, arrive after one hour and thirty minutes at a long low building with a covered auditorium, where a man in a ranger's uniform gives us a talk about different kinds of wild animals.

Most of these animals are not very wild.

The ranger shows us peacocks; parrots; a snake, which we can hold if we want; a kind of monkey with a striped tail; a turtle; and some baby rabbits, which we can also hold. The baby rabbits are cute, but not wild at all. The ranger also shows us a video, which I think we could have watched on-line.

I do not want to hold baby rabbits or watch videos. I want to see the alligator frenzy.

I am watching Ms N and Mr Buddy Knox and I can see that they also are not interested in the bunnies. Mr Buddy Knox is looking more quiet than he has been looking during our leadership conference up to now and I am wondering whether he has had more than one drink in the Gentlemen's Club or perhaps is feeling embarrassed at meeting myself and Ms N there. Or perhaps, like me, he is waiting to see the alligators.

After we leave the auditorium, the ranger takes us outside to an alligator sitting in a pool of water behind a low fence. This alligator is not in a frenzy but looks about as bored as I am feeling. The ranger climbs over the fence and gently opens the alligator's jaws so that he can put his hand inside its mouth. I am hoping the alligator will grab the ranger's arm and perhaps bite it off or exhibit some other more frenzied behaviour but instead the alligator closes its eyes and the ranger withdraws his hand safely.

Ms N comes and stands next to me.

'Tatiana, how are you?' she asks.

'Not too good, Ms N,' I say. 'First, you have not got your job in London. Second, the alligator is drugged.'

'This show sucks,' Ms N says. 'I hope the airboat ride is better.'

'Maybe some alligators will attack the airboat.'

'Maybe they will.'

ACTUALLY, THE AIRBOAT ride also starts badly. In the films I have seen of airboats they skim across the water at high speed carrying one or two passengers looking each other in the eye, while the sun sets and everything is beautiful.

On the "Alligator Frenzy" tour, by contrast, each airboat takes twenty people and looks about as exciting as the coaches we have taken to arrive here. Before we even step onto the airboat the driver, whose name is Tex, gives us a lecture about how it is dangerous to stand up on board and makes each of us sign a piece of paper called a disclaimer. This paper says that we understand that we should not stand up on the airboat and that if we do leave our seats and then have an accident, this is our own responsibility.

Driver Tex briefs us on the safety features of the airboat including the life-vests stored under the pop-up seats; the high sides designed to make it impossible for an alligator even to think of climbing on board; and the flotation tanks which ensure that the airboat cannot sink. Driver Tex tells us he is armed with a hunting rifle which will be used only in extreme circumstances and that if we see him holding it we must all sit down fast.

The disclaimer and safety features seem to take away the fun of going on the airboat ride, since in the films I have seen the passengers are always standing up, sometimes enjoying a European-type cocktail drink in a tall glass with one hand and driving the airboat with the other while they are kissing their boyfriends at the same time.

On the other hand, it would be exciting to see Driver Tex blast an alligator with his hunting rifle.

I notice also that although Driver Tex is saying we must not stand up, he is also saying that if he takes out his hunting rifle we must all sit down. So I am understanding that perhaps it is quite usual to stand for people to stand up on these trips and perhaps the whole experience will not be as boring as I am by now fearing.

But there is no sign of cocktails or any other drinks.

The General Managers board the airboat. At once a complicated dance takes place. This is because everyone wants to be at the front, or on the sides of the airboat, and not on the inside or at the back surrounded by other people.

Ms N is at a disadvantage in this dance because of her fear of heights. Although she is wearing trainers which make her look even smaller than usual, she is cautious about stepping from the dock onto the airboat and she is also slower than some other GMs in manoeuvring around once on board.

But I see also that Ms N has planned her route and has a good sense of timing. So while some other General Managers are discussing which seats on the airboat have the best view, she has made her way direct to a seat at the front left-hand corner. I see her lift up the seat to look at the life-vest and pop-up mechanism, which Driver Tex has mentioned, then sit down.

I am thinking that, although I know for a fact that Ms N is brave, she is making sure that if there is an accident, she will know what she should do.

Mr Buddy Knox, who does not seem to be afraid of heights, is also good at this dance. I see that he takes the seat at the front-right corner of the airboat, rushing to ensure that he sits down at precisely the same moment as Ms N.

In fact, Mr Buddy Knox is in such a hurry that he does not bother to check the life-vest under his seat.

Of course I am in the middle at the back of the airboat with several rows of General Managers in front of me and on both sides, so I will not see any alligators even if twenty of them attack the airboat and are blasted by Driver Tex, but I cannot complain because I am only support staff.

When the airboat sets off I stop being disappointed right away because I am too frightened to remember why I was being disappointed in the first place. The boat has a giant propeller at the back. When Driver Tex, who is sitting up above and behind us like the slave-master on a rowing galley, activates the propeller, the boat shoots forward so fast that the seat slams into my back and I squeak in surprise. At the front of the boat a huge bow wave rises up on each side and I see that Ms N and Mr Buddy Knox both receive a bath of swamp-water.

Ms N, who is wearing a white T-shirt with a red and pink pattern on it, laughs out loud and shakes her hair, spraying some other people around her with spare swamp water. Mr Buddy Knox looks down at his soaking smart-but-casual trousers and shirt and turns as if to tell Driver Tex to take more care. But at that moment the spray of water from Ms N's hair catches him in the face and he turns and sees her laughing.

Actually I am impressed by Mr Buddy Knox, because in the

space of one second his face turns from looking as if he would like to kill everyone on the boat, starting with Driver Tex, to looking as if he has never had so much fun in all his life.

Mr Buddy Knox lifts up his right arm and shouts out 'Whooooooo!' as the airboat shoots forward through the water. He says it with so much enthusiasm that three or four other GMs and Driver Tex also shout out 'Whooooooo!'

Ms N does not say anything but I see that she is smiling as she pushes her wet hair out of her face.

Now I am not frightened any more but I am enjoying the ride.

After ten minutes we are in the middle of the swamp, with thick grass growing up around us on the edges of the open water. The trees under which we began our excursion are miles away on the horizon.

Driver Tex slows the airboat down.

'Guess this is 'gator country,' he says. 'Please stay seated.'

Of course he is telling us to stay seated because as soon as he says there may be alligators nearby, everyone is standing up and peering at the water and the supposedly unsinkable airboat is wobbling in a way which I thought earlier I would find exciting but which I am now finding scary.

Then I realise that I, too, am standing up. Maybe the urge to see alligators is stronger than the urge to stay alive.

I sit down.

But other people are still standing. Mr Buddy Knox is standing right at the front of the airboat, looking down at the water. 'I don't see nothing, gents,' he says.

Ms N is also standing. If anything, it seems she is making a point of standing even closer to the front of the airboat than Mr Buddy Knox. I am surprised by this, because there is nothing to hold onto and I know that with her fear of heights she must be terrified to be standing where she could fall into the water so easily.

Ms N does not say anything, but is peering towards the sides of the creek as if she thinks this will be where the alligators will be lying in the sun, or swimming, or whatever it is that alligators do.

'OK everyone, heads up,' Driver Tex says. 'Looks like we have a group of 'gators in the next creek. Once again, I must ask you to remain seated.'

I realise that the reason Tex is so high above us is so that he can look for alligators over the top of the grass.

The airboat eases into the next creek. I am sitting down. But many people are standing. It seems that some of them are trying to show the other people on the airboat that they have no fear of falling or of alligators and are determined to ignore whatever Tex is saying.

Again to my surprise, Ms N is one of these people. She is standing with her body so far over the water that when the airboat begins to turn I am frightened she will fall.

To her right, Mr Buddy Knox has at first taken a step back when the boat begins to move. But when he see Ms N, he, too, moves forward and adopts a position even more extreme than hers, hooking his foot under his seat so that he can lean out over the water at the front of the airboat.

I am thinking that actually his position is more secure than hers because his foot is safely wedged under the seat, whereas she has no support of any kind. But at this point I stop thinking about Ms N and Mr Buddy Knox because we see the alligators.

To be honest, after the animal show and the sleepy creature we have seen at the display area, I am not expecting too much from the alligators in the swamp. So I am excited to see in the creek maybe thirty alligators, many of them lying in the mud at the edge of the grass and some in the water around the boat. Of course this is not the frenzy we have been promised because the alligators might as well be stuffed for all the signs of life they are exhibiting. But when the wash from our slow-moving airboat hits the alligators I see a few of them open their eyes and look around, as if perhaps they are a little less sleepy than they appear.

Suddenly I do not feel good for Ms N, who is still standing in her trainers on the wet slippery surface at the front of the airboat. But I do not say anything because I do not want to distract her while she may be frightened at the thought of falling into the water.

Instead it is her who speaks.

'Hey, everyone. Check out this bad boy.'

The next moment I am astonished to see Ms N stretch one foot out from the front of the boat, as if she is wanting to step on top of whatever alligator she is describing. Of course I stand up to take a look, and so does everyone else on the airboat.

'Once again,' Driver Tex says, 'I advise all of you to sit down. These are dangerous wild animals.'

Of course no-one is paying any attention and in a moment all twenty of us are on our feet trying to peer over the front of the airboat.

I say trying, because from my lousy position in the middle of the passengers I cannot see much. I especially cannot see much of the big alligator which Ms N is describing. I can see what I think is its huge head, at the front of the airboat on the left side next to where Ms N is holding her outstretched foot, and am guessing that its body extends across the airboat and towards the right. So I look to the right side of the airboat to see if I can spot the tail. While I am doing this I see that one of the other GMs has his hand on the back of the seat in the front right-hand corner of the boat which Mr Buddy Knox is using to balance himself over the water. I see also that Mr Buddy Knox is looking at Ms N's precarious position and frowning. Then he, in turn, stretches out his hand above the giant alligator.

'Better we all sit down, gents,' he says, imitating the voice of Driver Tex. He stretches out his hand just a little further than Ms N's foot and turns to grin at everyone on board. Ms N, as if admitting defeat, steps back so that both her feet are safely on the boat and takes hold of her own chair for added security.

It looks to me as if Ms N is relieved that she is no longer balancing over the water.

Mr Buddy Knox, on the other hand, looks so bold with his

hand held out in front of him over the prow of the airboat that I see Ms N look at him, then look at the seat under which his foot is hooked, then take from her pocket her mobile telephone to shoot a picture.

This seems to give an idea to the GM who is resting his weight on the chair that Mr Buddy Knox is using as a balance, who takes his hand off the chair and reaches into his pocket, perhaps to take out his own phone or camera.

There is a click and the chair pops back, to reveal a life-jacket which is stowed underneath.

In the same moment Mr Buddy Knox says: 'Hey!' and falls off the boat.

I think maybe I have misjudged these alligators when I said that they might as well be stuffed.

Unfortunately, because I am sitting near the back, I cannot see where Mr Buddy Knox falls. It sounds as if he may have landed on an alligator rather than in the water because I do not hear a splash. But I do see what could be the big head of an alligator turning; and what might be jaws opening much wider than the jaws of the alligator we saw in the show on dry land; and what possibly is the swirl of a huge tail in the water on the other side of the airboat.

For a moment I see the hand of Mr Buddy Knox trying to grab the front of the airboat but of course it is too high because it is designed to keep out alligators. At the same time Driver Tex shouts out 'everyone down I may shoot!' and something whacks into the bottom of the airboat which I am guessing is the big alligator as it rolls its body round to pull Mr Buddy Knox under the muddy water in its giant jaws, and we are all thrown backwards with everyone grabbing hold of chairs and each other and Driver Tex shouts 'oh, shit!' and we hear a splash as the hunting rifle he has been trying to aim falls into the water.

'Man in the water!' Driver Tex is yelling into a walkie-talkie even while I am trying to grab hold of something as the airboat rocks and all the alligators that have been lounging on the banks slide smoothly into the water. Next moment, Driver Tex is throwing two life vests into the water, one on each side.

At first I think this is strange because Mr Buddy Knox must be on one side of the airboat or the other. But then I realise Driver Tex cannot see Mr Buddy Knox because Mr Buddy Knox is under the water or under the boat and so Driver Tex is trying to cover every base by throwing life vests anywhere he can.

Other passengers on the boat get the idea pretty quick. I see several other GMs throwing life vests in every direction, in front of the boat, behind the boat and to either side.

But there is no sign of Mr Buddy Knox. On the contrary, what we are now seeing is a genuine alligator frenzy. The water around the airboat is boiling with alligators. In fact, if we had not seen Mr Buddy Knox fall into the water a few moments earlier, we would perhaps have guessed that the alligators were attacking each other.

The tour is proving more exciting than in my wildest dreams.

Most of the passengers, including me, are now huddling in the centre of the airboat trying to keep as far from the sides as possible. But there is no sign that any alligator understands that there are people inside the boat. On the contrary, they are fully occupied with doing whatever they are doing in the water. Driver Tex is still shouting into his walkie-talkie that there is an emergency. So I decide it may be safe to stand up, holding firmly onto the chair in front of me, and try to see what is happening.

For a moment I think I see a pale white hand come to the surface about ten feet away, close to where a good-sized alligator is turning from side to side in the water.

At the same moment there is the splash of a life-vest, precisely on the spot where what may be the hand of Mr Buddy Knox is rising from the water.

I turn and see that while everyone else on the boat is huddling down, Ms N is standing high, precariously, on a chair, scanning the water like myself, and has thrown the life-vest onto the best possible spot to rescue our unfortunate colleague.

But the instant the life-vest lands on the surface of the water, the hand – if that is what it was – is jerked back beneath the surface.

And that is the last we see of Mr Buddy Knox.

IT IS A disadvantage of working in hotels that you are not impressed by second-rate opulence. So when I see the tables set for the climactic Conference Gala Dinner, I am what we call underwhelmed.

The organisers have done their best to lower the lighting and to decorate the tables with flowers and the hotel's best crockery. But to anyone who has attended the leadership conference, it is obvious that these are the same tables around which we were sitting in plenary yesterday.

One other thing which has not changed is the us-and-them layout. Three tables stand on the stage. The rest are in the pit.

Of course they have had to make some changes.

No alcohol will be served during the climactic Conference Gala Dinner. The music is more sombre than would be usual at an event of this type. Impressively, someone has prepared an A6-sized card for each table setting with a black border; a picture of Mr Buddy Knox in a dark suit; a summary of his career in our hotel chain; and selected words of sympathy.

Our Human Resources team has excelled itself.

I think that perhaps it would have been more appropriate to use my picture of Mr Buddy Knox stretching his hand out over the alligator-infested swamp. I know they have this picture, because I have sent it to the special e-mail account set up to collect evidence for the police inquiry.

Of course, by the time the police arrived in their helicopter at the place where Mr Buddy Knox fell into the water, and where we were still watching for any sign that he somehow could have survived the alligator frenzy, all the alligators had disappeared.

So whatever the result of the inquiry, I do not think we will be seeing an alligator in court any time soon.

In fact my photograph and all the other evidence will only make clear what is obvious. This is that Mr Buddy Knox leaned out too far over the front of the boat despite the clear instruction from Driver Tex that we should all sit down. Even the GM who took his hand off the back of the chair under which Mr Buddy Knox had wedged his foot has been persuaded that the accident cannot have been his fault.

The conference room is beginning to fill. I make myself busy with the sound and lighting technology. Even though the mood of the Conference Gala Dinner is not celebratory, the armchair gods will make some announcements. It is important that the General Managers in the pit are able to hear what they say.

One of the exciting things at the Gala Dinner is seeing who sits where. This says a lot about who is going up in our hotel chain and who is not. The biggest question is who will sit at the tables on the stage.

I am hoping that Ms N, as General Manager of the hotel in C— which won last year's Platinum Megastar award, will be on one of the top three tables. The fact that everyone is discussing her heroic attempt to rescue Mr Buddy Knox, when everyone else on the airboat was trying only to save themselves, might also be a reason to put her on the stage.

But I can see no sign of her.

I see Mr Julius Anderson arrive, and check his watch, and look around the room. I see other armchair gods and some young and upwardly-mobile General Managers arrive at the top tables and shake hands in a way which expresses both grieving for the tragedy which has occurred and smugness for the fact that they are alive and, especially, on the top tables.

When the time comes to dim the lights and switch on the podium microphone, there is no sign of Ms N.

But the show must go on.

Mr Julius Anderson steps into a pool of light and a moment

of silence.

'Ladies and gentlemen,' he begins. Again he looks around the room. This makes me wonder if he is looking for Ms N, and whether the new form of address he is using may mean something good for her.

Mr Julius Anderson's voice sinks to a whisper. He introduces the subject of the afternoon's tragic accident and the sense of loss which this has cast over our conference. He mentions the career of Mr Buddy Knox; the honour which he feels in expressing on behalf of our hotel chain condolences to the two grieving ex-wives Mr Buddy Knox has left behind; and the generous compensation provisions we make in cases of this kind.

Personally I am not so sure that the ex-wives of Mr Buddy Knox will be grieving too much.

I wonder how many other people in the room are having the same thought.

'The final question which I have to address is the General Manager position at our luxury new UP-branded hotel in London,' Mr Anderson says. 'This was a project for which we believed Mr Buddy Knox would be the best available candidate. Tragically he is no longer with us.'

At this moment there is a swell of applause in the room.

I am thinking at first that although it may be natural for eight hundred General Managers to welcome the alligator frenzy which has removed Mr Buddy Knox, it is inappropriate for them actually to applaud.

Then I see that the crowd are applauding Ms N, who has wandered onto the stage. She is dressed entirely in black, including a necklace of black pearls; black stockings with a daring seam; shiny high-heeled black shoes; and even black nail polish and lipstick.

Ms N looks like a million dollars in mourning.

Mr Julius Anderson pauses and then begins to clap also.

Ms N does not seem to notice any of this. She is concentrating on her mobile phone, as if perhaps she is sending a text to her special friend in London. Then she looks up and smiles her inquisitive smile, as if perhaps she is wondering why everyone is applauding; and allows Mr Julius Anderson to guide her to the empty seat by his side on the top table.

LATER THAT NIGHT, after the speeches are over, a number of conference delegates gather in the EcoSystem Lounge Bar. It seems that everyone agreed with the decision that the Conference Gala Dinner should be dry in honour of the late Mr Buddy Knox. But no-one feels the need to refrain from alcohol now that the Dinner is over.

Ms N has sent me a text from the stage during the Gala Dinner to invite me to the EcoSystem Lounge Bar for a "post-commemoration celebration".

What this means is a bottle of Champagne.

'When will you start at our luxury new UP-branded hotel in London?' I ask her.

'I do not wish to rush things,' Ms N says. 'Of course I am keen to see my friend who is in London. I also wish to start work as soon as possible on ensuring that our luxury new Ultra-Platinum hotel there is as eye-wateringly luxurious in every department as it should be. But our hotel chain is in mourning for Mr Buddy Knox. It would not be appropriate for me to start work there too early.' She sips her glass of Champagne. 'I fly to London tomorrow morning.'

I smile. 'Did you notice that Mr Julius Anderson changed the way he addressed the Gala Dinner this evening?'

'Yes.' Ms N orders a second bottle of Champagne. 'I think perhaps this conference has helped our senior leadership understand one important thing.'

'Our armchair gods, you mean?'

'Yes.' Ms N smiles and refills our glasses. 'Our armchair gods.'

'What is that thing, Ms N?'

'I think they have learned that not every one of our General Managers is a gentleman.'

I raise my glass and clink it against the glass of Ms N. 'To strong women, Ms N,' I say.

'To strong women. And also to strong men, who are the ones who appreciate strong women,' Ms N says.

For a moment she looks as happy as I have ever seen her.

Ms N is good at solving problems. One day I would like to be like her.

6. ASK FOR SCARLETT

Arrival

I ARRIVE EXHAUSTED. In the shady arbour that is the lobby of the Caravanserai, I slip off my hiking boots, exhale and put my feet up. A breeze caresses my hair. An emerald gecko darts up the wall then stops, a living sculpture on the hand-hewn mountain stone.

For a long moment he stays frozen, as if considering his options. Only his eyes betray his animation.

Could the hotel have arranged a welcome gecko?

At the Caravanserai Ultra Platinum, they tell you everything is possible.

But to me, that gecko looks too cool to be corporate.

'Would madam like to try the complimentary, locally-sourced, hand-woven, virgin-combed, glacier-cured mohair moccasins? We have a choice of natural and hypoallergenic. Or some customers prefer to go barefoot: our carpets have the deepest shag on the market.' The woman kneeling at my feet, who is wearing a name-badge which describes her as Scarlett, guest services manager, allows her gaze briefly to meet mine and moistens her bee-stung lips. 'You can leave your feet *au naturel.*'

I blink. She has veered off-script. I have already marked her as exceptional: attentive, clever and not merely attractive but beautiful. Beautiful, smart women are desirable in the public areas of hotels. The question is how they use those attributes. I cock my head and smile.

'Au naturel? Is that an option?'

'At the Caravanserai UP, everything is an option. You simply have to ask for Scarlett.' She moves her hand to her bosom and tilts her name-badge in such a way as to highlight both her name and the spectacular curve where her breast meets her slender waist under the hotel day uniform – the latter tailored and hand-stitched, I am beginning to suspect, by indigenous craftswomen from sustainable, recyclable, planet-pampering, all-natural fabrics.

Showing off your body is not part of our hotel chain's standards. No matter how spectacular that body may be.

The Caravanserai UP boasts that it is the coolest and most ecological as well as the most luxurious hotel on earth. It is also managed by a dear friend of mine. Yet in one hundred and eighty seconds, to my horror, I have observed two irregularities.

'Scarlett, is it possible for me to wash my feet before I go to my room?'

'Yes, madam. I will be pleased to offer you this service.' Scarlett is back on script. She pours water from a tall pitcher into a heavy enamelled bowl. On the wall, a hand-written message on a chalk-board informs me that the water is neither chilled nor warmed, but precisely room-temperature.

This strikes me as an excellent touch: low-tech; ecological; ironic; and, best of all, dirt-cheap.

Scarlett washes my feet with a touch both gentle and professional. I begin to relax.

Perhaps I have misjudged her.

Then, while her left hand is cradling my right foot, she brings her right hand round to my heel and slides her fingers a few inches up the soft flesh of my calf. In the same instant, she sighs audibly through those moistened, prominent lips and shakes her head as though lost in a moment of pleasure.

No, no and no.

'Thank you, Scarlett.' I jerk my leg away and make to stand, conscious that my feet are still wet.

'Please, madam, remain seated.' She has taken a heavy, unbleached, long-cotton Egyptian towel from the pile and makes to dry me, professional once more.

To confirm my suspicions, I tip her immensely. But her response is from the good hotelier's handbook: a humble shake of the head, as if I have been inexplicably generous. The temptress of a few moments earlier has vanished. In her place I see a humble, hard-working hotel employee.

I am puzzled. In my experience, three strikes mean you are out. Could I be mistaken?

The Caravanserai UP boasts of its bio-sustainability and ethno-chic. I am beginning to feel it may need a little more emphasis on natural selection and survival of the fittest.

'When can I see the General Manager?' I ask.

'In thirty minutes, madam.' Scarlett's gaze is calm.

'Could you show me around the hotel before then?'

'It would be my pleasure.' She places the soiled towel into a rustic hand-woven wickerwork basket and leads me down a tunnel into the mountain.

'There is no air-conditioning in the corridors of the Caravanserai UP hotel,' she says. 'At this altitude, the nights are freezing and the days are hot. But the stone of the mountain dome maintains a constant temperature that happens to be perfect for human beings. As a back-up, guest rooms and common areas are equipped with eco-radiant hydronic climatic amelioration systems. This is the Alexandria Library.'

She steps through an archway into a zone of high-backed leather armchairs, oak shelving and countless books. The seats and bookshelves are bathed in low-wattage lighting so empathetic I have to fight the urge immediately to select a book and settle down to read. The carpet-pile beneath my feet is, as promised, soft, clean and so deep I can barely see my feet. 'How is it – ?' I begin.

Scarlett raises a finger to those lips and beckons me back into the corridor.

'The Library has a strictly enforced code of silence,' she whispers. 'But there is no need to talk. You may use our C-UP app on your own mobile device, or on our complimentary tablets, to order books, drinks, snacks, noise-cancelling headphones or any other service you desire. If you prefer to reduce energy consumption, or are concerned about the carcinogenic impact of electromagnetic radiation, simply insert a written note detailing your wishes into the stone wish-holders at each library-station.'

She hands me a tablet from a stack by the door and nods towards an armchair, where a man with wild grey hair and thick glasses is poring over a fragment of parchment.

'Professor Ahmet is responsible for all library services. He is an expert in the conservation and interpretation of Aramaic scripts; but he is also deaf and dumb, promoting our diversity policy and reducing the risk that any customer could be tempted to speak out loud. You will see we have installed sound meters to alert him to any noise and its provenance. The manuscript cabinets contain a climate-controlled selection of scrolls up to two thousand years old.' Scarlett smiles. 'Our wine cabinets contain a selection of vintages of similar rarity, although our oldest bottle is a mere seven decades in age.'

Scarlett shows me the Ion Restaurant, with its array of locally-sourced specialities; the Chrysalis Wellness Zone, where a display advertises "Zen Secrets of the Billion-year-old Mountain"; the Cavern Eco-Pool, occupying a stalactite-studded void deep within the rock; the *Baykal Banya*, an ultra-hot Russian sauna whose Eagle's Nest frigidarium features an icy plunge-pool on a terrace overlooking a lake hundreds of metres below; the Koh-i-Noor diamond Boutique, which seems out of place and is mercifully shut; and the Moonrise and Sunset bars, each with cinemascope-sized windows and sublime panoramas over the ecologically-pure landscapes and barely-researched archaeological treasures of the countryside below.

No expense has been spared.

Nice.

As a brand-new UP-branded hotel, the Caravanserai does not have a Platinum Megastar lounge of the type our chain usually offers for the exclusive use of elite clients. Rather, the whole hotel is designated Ultra-Platinum, with a pricing structure to match. Scarlett shows me the Creativity Club, a hi-tech play-den of artworks, artists' materials, computer terminals and alcoves.

As a test, I click the C-UP app on my complimentary tablet. It tells me that the Creativity Club is "*designed to bring out the genius in you*" and that "*Here, each evening from 5 to 7 p.m, the Caravanserai's award-winning executive chef Massimo san Giulio sets out a range of complimentary culinary créations based on famous food-based artworks.*"

Tonight, Mr san Giulio has chosen as his artistic reference *Cakes,* by Wayne Thiebaud, which strikes me as hard on those customers who wish to scrounge a cheap meal by dining on the snacks.

Perhaps that is the idea.

As any hotelier can tell you, the relationship between wealth and parsimony is often a direct one.

So it is tonight. Despite the absence of any remotely savoury flavours on the buffet, several of the hotel's well-heeled guests have gathered in the Creativity Club to engage in a serious way with the complimentary cakes. One obese gentleman has in front of him eight or nine slices, each individually presented on what I assume is a colour-co-ordinated range of hand-cast artisan-sourced earthenware dessert plates.

He also has lined up in front of him a row of three gin and tonics, concocted from the London speciality craft gins lined up at the free bar and served in our exclusive Ultra Platinum-branded hand-blown English crystal balloon glasses.

I look at his arrangement of plates, cakes and drinks and am struck by its symmetry and vivid colours. In his way, the obese gentleman has created an artwork of his own – a performance piece, since two of the slices of cake have disappeared while I am watching – which Wayne Thiebaud himself would probably appreciate.

It is good to see the Creativity Club living up to its name.

Next, we visit the Sunset Bar. Given that the Creativity Club is still offering free drinks, I am surprised to find the place full of paying customers. In fact, most of them are women in a lively, boisterous group: made-up, finely dressed and apparently ready to party, even though the sun is not due to set for several hours. Two balding, heavily built men in suits strike a jarring tone. Both have glasses of mineral water and laptop computers and glance at me in an appraising way as I appear in the doorway. The only other customer is a solitary young man dressed in black jeans, sneakers and T-shirt, chatting quietly to two of the party women.

By contrast, the Moonrise bar is empty except for a single group of three customers.

A gentleman with a brushed-back mane of white hair and a handsome, deeply-creased face is sitting between two women. One is a young, full-breasted, clear-skinned girl who I am guessing is from the rural regions of the spectacular but corruption-plagued country in whose mountainous fringes the Caravanserai UP nestles so elegantly. The other, who is wearing a blue Chanel suit, is old enough perhaps to be the man's wife or the young girl's mother.

I do not think that she is either of these things.

The three of them appear to be engrossed in a difficult conversation. It looks as if the old man and the young girl do not have a common language and the older woman is translating.

The man is frowning. For some reason, he strikes me as a distinguished person – a retired diplomat, perhaps.

A transaction is taking place. I have seen such groups before.

We continue our tour. Throughout the hotel, the fittings are costly and tasteful, including a range of retro titanium cocktail shakers and ice scoops, tastefully distressed to match the hotel's ethno-theme. The eco-chic décor barely misses a beat. The idea of a hotel library where a rule of silence is not only in place but enforced gives me a frisson of high-concept delight.

Here and there, in the warren of tunnels connecting the rooms and amenities, waist-height stone columns stand in back-lit alcoves. A sculpture stands on each column.

I stop at a polished metal head, with polished metal hair streaming behind it.

'That is an extraordinary piece,' I say. 'Where is it from?'

'They are all for sale, madam.' Scarlett stops next to me, so close that I can smell her scent. 'They are hand-crafted by a local artist in his charcoal-fired Zoroastrian-style foundry. Each piece is designed to fit into your suitcase for the journey home; or we can ship them if you prefer this. This one is called "ecstasy". It costs ten thousand euro. But I can offer a cash discount of twenty per cent.'

'Twenty per cent? Does the artist mind if you offer a discount?'

Scarlett does not hesitate. 'No. He is always delighted to sell a piece.' Her voice drops a tone. 'The offers at our in-house diamond merchant are even more remarkable.'

Instead of following her cue about the diamonds, I lean in to examine the artwork. 'I would like to purchase a masterpiece like this. But first I would like to discuss a price with the artist.'

'Certainly, madam. We can arrange this.' But Scarlett does not tell me how this might be possible. Instead she walks briskly on, stopping at a crescent-topped, fabric-covered door set in a frame of natural stone. 'I would ask madam please to stand opposite the room number woven in the felt,' Scarlett says. 'The facial recognition software will permit you access.'

I step forward. As I stand facing the door, with its simple combination of form and function, I feel calm wash over me. What a hotel this could be.

With a quiet click, the door opens precisely ninety-five degrees. Scarlett stands to one side, her palm pointing inside. 'This is madam's room,' she says. 'Please enter.'

For a moment, I am concerned she may follow me into the privacy of my suite; but she remains anchored in the corridor.

The reason is obvious.

'Tatiana!' I open my arms and step forward.

'Ms N!'

In a moment, we are embracing; then I step back to admire her.

It is wonderful to see Ms N. Her skin is smooth, her eyes are bright and her mouth is set in a kind of mischievous smile that makes me wonder whether she is already working, here in the Caravanserai UP.

I am not sure if I want her to be working or not.

This is partly because I know she must be tired after sixteen hours of flying on three separate and perhaps not entirely modern or safe airlines to reach this most remote corner of our beautiful but economically still backward country.

But there are other reasons too.

'Welcome to my hotel!' I say.

'Congratulations. You deserve it, darling. You have created a paradise.'

'You are going to tell me that every paradise contains a serpent.'

'No. You are going to tell me.' Ms N turns her head slightly and smiles. 'You already know all the answers, Tatiana. The only reason I have come is to help you to express them.'

'I think, I – '

My voice breaks, and her arms are around me. 'Tatiana,' she says. 'This is your first hotel as General Manager. No-one said it would be easy.'

'But I am doing everything as you taught me. I had hoped it would be perfect. I am sorry that the Caravanserai UP is failing. I am sorry you have had to come.'

'Nothing is perfect, darling. The best any of us can do is to create the illusion of perfection. Like all illusions, once a single customer sees behind the curtain and realises that all is not as it seems, the whole thing may go up in a puff of smoke.'

'I cannot believe my survey results and profitability can be so bad. Look at my hotel! Look at the service! It should be perfect!'

Ms N holds me at arm's length and fishes from her pocket a miraculously fresh white tissue.

'Tatiana. Do not cry.'

Stay

THE TIME ZONE in this country is many hours ahead of my usual workplace. As the sun sets over a range of snow-capped peaks and the shadows of the ancient arches and towers on the plain grow longer and fade to darkness, I change into a not-too-creased all-black outfit and low heels and vow to try and stay awake until midnight.

What are the problems of Tatiana's hotel? Can I really help to solve them? Where to begin?

I glance at the antique thermometer on the balcony outside my panoramic window. Already it is showing two degrees below zero. I note that the scale goes down to minus forty. Yet within the thick stone walls, the temperature is perfect.

All with minimal use of electricity — another reason why the hotel's revenue per available room should be better than it is.

In the Creativity Club a tall, slender guest services operative, possibly of Indian ethnic origin, is clearing the buffet. She is clad in the hotel's evening uniform, which emphasises her gracefulness. The obese man is still sitting at his table with what the unique hand-crafted patterns suggest to be four new plates of cake. Lined up alongside are three more gin and tonics, whose bright beading of moisture shows that they, too, must have been refreshed within the last few minutes.

Despite the plethora of technology with which the Creativity

Club is equipped, the obese man is not reading, writing, drawing, painting, sculpting or even using a computer. He is simply enjoying the refreshments and observing the events taking place around him.

Who is to say that this, too, is not creative?

The man's forehead is beaded also, but with sweat; and his thin hair is plastered back over his head.

All the other guests have left, probably when the Creativity Club was scheduled to stop serving free drinks and food thirty minutes earlier.

The slender guest services operative, who is making more noise than necessary tidying away the glasses and crockery, sees me and smiles.

'Ms N. Welcome to the Caravanserai UP. It is an honour to host such a famous hotelier.'

I glance at her name badge. 'You are kind, Parand. But it is Tatiana who should be famous.'

'She told me a story about a guest you once had who would not leave a hotel,' Parand steps closer and lowers her voice, 'and how you dealt with him. I would like to do the same for this cheaposaurus.' She grinds together the plates she has collected from the buffet and glances at the obese man. 'He has consumed eight gin and tonics this evening and twelve slices of cake. Since he arrived in the hotel he has eaten all his meals in the Creativity Club except for lunch, when the Club is closed. Actually, at lunch-time he seems not to eat at all.'

'Is he bothering the other guests?'

Parand hesitates. 'It is our other guests we are worrying about. We are trying to create the most sophisticated environment in the world and attract the most discerning clientele. How can we do that when this man is defacing our hotel?'

I do not reply. But when I make to move on, the obese man rises slowly to his feet and follows me towards the Reception. The plates and glasses are empty.

At the Reception desk, two customers are complaining. One

is a tall, elegant man. The other is his young, blonde companion.

It is the man who is doing all the talking.

'The sheets are totally stained,' he says. 'Instead of being white they are crimson. Or orange. I have never been so embarrassed in my life.'

'How did this happen?' The guest services manager, who is my friend Scarlett, looks first at the stained-sheet man, then at the stained-sheet woman, who is staring at the floor in what seems to be abject misery. The woman is wearing a miniscule white brushed-cotton top which exposes a great deal of her shoulders, breasts, arms and midriff. All of these magnificent features glow with a remarkable tan.

'You tell me how it happened,' the stained-sheet man addresses Scarlett. 'We need new sheets, for a start.'

Scarlett lowers her manicured eyelashes towards her computer screen, her face hardening. 'Of course, sir.'

While Scarlett is busy with her terminal, a tall man wearing a pin-stripe suit approaches me. He has a severe, business hair-cut, thick lips and a square jaw which reminds me of a Hollywood action hero of rather less than "A"-list stature. In fact, I am thinking more of C- or possibly D-list. On his wrist hangs a colossal timepiece of the type designed primarily to broadcast the wealth of the wearer. Behind him I see the cheaposaurus, standing back from the Reception desk and rocking his considerable weight from foot to foot. His face is pale and I wonder if he is about to be sick.

I also wonder how professionally Scarlett or Parand would respond if this were to happen.

'Are you the General Manager?' the D-lister says.

'No,' I say. 'I am a guest. I expect the ladies at the Reception can help you.'

'I am the General Manager.'

Tatiana is dressed in our hotel chain's unofficial senior management uniform of dark skirt, blouse and jacket. The blonde hair cascading over her shoulders frames her petite features exquisitely. Her dark, practical heels lend her grace and authority. Her eyes are clear and steady.

But being a young hotel General Manager is not always easy.

'You're the GM?' The man in the suit shakes his head. 'Seriously? Did they run out of experienced guys?'

'How may I help you, sir?' She is smiling her famous 1,000-watt smile.

Tatiana's smile is so intoxicating I feel happier immediately.

But the D-lister is strangely immune to her charms.

'I don't like the atmosphere in this hotel,' he says. 'For six hundred bucks a night, I expect something exclusive. Sophisticated. Yet the atmosphere in the Sunset Bar is like a cattle market. The Moonrise Bar would make a cattle market look classy. It is more like slave-trading.'

'That's right.' The cheaposaurus speaks for the first time. He takes a step towards the Reception desk and stands next to the D-lister. 'You need more entertainment in the Moonrise Bar.'

Tatiana looks from the D-lister to the cheaposaurus and back again, no doubt registering that their requests are incompatible. But her smile never flinches. 'Could you explain the problem in more detail, sir?'

'If you can't see the problem, kiddo,' the D-lister says, 'you shouldn't be doing a grown man's job.' He draws himself up to his full height, but before he can speak he is pushed aside by three on-rushing women.

I recognise the women from the group I encountered earlier in the Sunset Bar. All three are wearing well-cut designer clothing, and sufficient heavy and high-quality jewellery to impede the movement of their limbs. Their hair, manicures and pedicures are a testament to the artistry of the beauticians in the Chrysalis Wellness Zone.

The Zen Secrets of the Billion-year-old Mountain clearly include the very latest make-up products, rejuvenation treatments and hair-dyes.

The women form a phalanx at the desk opposite Tatiana. 'I

want to complain about harassment in the Sunset Bar,' says one in an English accent, slamming her hand on the counter. Each of her fingers has a different pattern painted on the nail. 'You got to do something.'

'Too right.' The second woman has a bosom which appears to have been sculpted by at least three plastic surgeons, perhaps working in shifts. 'We come halfway round the world for some peace and quiet, and some randy toy boy starts pestering the girls.'

'And the bleeding diamond shop is closed,' the third woman says. 'I had my eye on one of them colliers for two hundred and fifty thou. Instead we have to put up with this harassment.'

'I am sorry to hear this,' Tatiana begins to say. 'But – '

'I wish to make a complaint.' The woman in the blue Chanel suit from the Moonrise Bar sweeps up to the Reception desk, dragging her beautiful, voluptuous companion. Her accent sounds Russian. The younger woman looks as if she may have been crying. 'I have been approached by an old man in your Moonrise Bar who seems to think he can pay money to have sex with my daughter or even to traffic her back to his own country. What kind of a hotel is this?'

I see that the diplomatic type with the mane of white hair and deeply creased features is standing at the entrance to the tunnel to the Moonrise Bar. He is wearing a suit perhaps not of the latest cut, but which nevertheless shows unmistakeable signs of Savile Row manufacture. He is staring at the woman in the blue Chanel suit. His handsome but desiccated face displays a mixture of dislike and fear.

Perhaps it is his good looks, or his antique suit; but I feel sorry for this man. So when I see the woman in the blue Chanel suit lean across to whisper in the ear of her curvaceous but teary-eyed companion and the young girl replies, I lean forward to eavesdrop the exchange.

Both are, indeed, speaking Russian. Fortunately, this is a language I understand.

What they are saying clarifies a part of what is happening this evening at the Caravanserai UP.

For a moment, it seems as if everyone is speaking at once. Tatiana is holding her hands up, trying to create order. Scarlett and Parand are trying to hold separate conversations with individual guests.

The level of noise is so great that I am worried a fight may break out. This could be a serious incident given, for example, the amount of silicon some of the well-dressed ladies are carrying. But this is not my hotel; and I am keen to do nothing which might undermine the authority of Tatiana.

Suddenly three loud *cracks* ring through the room. The wild-haired Professor Ahmet has appeared at the centre of our group, as if from nowhere. In one hand, he is clutching a wooden gavel which he has brought down hard, three times, on the receptionist's desk.

In his other hand the Professor holds a dark, polished cane like an old-fashioned walking stick. The far end is split to accommodate a sheet of paper. I am guessing this is the tool he uses to collect the orders for drinks, books and other services from the stone wish-holders in the library. Today, however, the crack holds a large piece of yellow paper, folded once, displaying a text written in easily legible letters.

Standing in the centre of the silenced crowd, his face set and his shoulders hunched, Professor Ahmet executes a slow-motion revolution, displaying the text to guests and hotel staff in turn.

I am witnessing an outstanding piece of communication.

'QUIET, PLEASE,' the sign says.

If I am honest, I think this is the worst day of my life so far.

I am including the day when Ms N asked me to wear a white blouse and climb into a steel cage dangling over a construction site, many years ago.

I am including also the time, before I even met Ms N, when

the owner of my hotel stuck his tongue in my ear while I was being forced to stand on a table in a night-club with him and he asked me to do things which I knew were not appropriate and I could feel a part of him, pressing against me, which I did not wish to feel.

This is worse.

Before, I was a junior hotel employee and there were other people to help me solve my problems.

Now, I am the General Manager of the Caravanserai UP and it is my job to solve them.

What is more I have asked Ms N, the best General Manager in the world, to come and help me; and she is watching every move I make.

I have always thought that one day I wanted to be like her.

But now I am thinking that even in a million years I will never be like Ms N. This is because I do not have the faintest idea what I should do to solve the problems of the Caravanserai UP. In fact, I do not even know what those problems might be. This is why I have asked Ms N to visit, flying for sixteen hours on three separate and perhaps not entirely modern or safe airlines.

So far, all she has told me is that I already know all the answers.

She is wrong. I do not know all the answers. In fact, I do not know any of them.

But then I look at Ms N, standing among all the complaining customers at the Reception desk, and I see that her small mouth is turned up in an inquisitive smile, as if she has discovered something intriguing. I see that her eyes are sparkling as if she is excited about a special secret.

To see Ms N looking like this in the middle of the worst day of my life gives me courage and confidence.

I can see she maybe has some ideas about what should happen next. But she is doing nothing because she knows this is my hotel and I have to solve my problems myself.

What would Ms N do now?

I stand up a little bit straighter on my compact but significant heels; I clear my throat; and I speak.

'Thank you, Professor Ahmet,' I say. 'Ladies and gentlemen, I apologise on behalf of the Caravanserai UP for any disturbance or discomfort you may have experienced.' I dial up the 1,000-watt smile and beam around the room. 'To express our heartfelt regret,' I say, 'I would like to offer you each a special compensation package.'

It is at times like this that I am pleased that I have Scarlett and Parand to help me. Nearly all the problems of our hotel are caused by men; and these two young women have a special talent in dealing with our male guests. Sometimes, in fact, I am worried that they are dealing with our male guests a little too much; but I have had no complaints about this and so I am guessing that the men they are dealing with are mostly satisfied.

First of all, I send the customers, including Ms N, to the Moonrise Bar for complimentary cocktails. Then I call Scarlett and Parand to my office.

'I have made a plan,' I say, 'to solve our problems.' I try to smile as if I am in control; and think about Ms N. I am wondering whether Scarlett or Parand ever think that they might one day want to be like me.

'First of all, the cheaposaurus,' I say. 'It is wrong that our fat friend is eating all his meals in the Creativity Club when he could be enjoying our signature four-hundred dollar twelve-ounce massage-pampered mountain-air-cured Wagyu steak in the Ion Restaurant. In fact, he is making a mockery of our Ultra Platinum concept as well as eroding our profitability. As soon as he returns from the Moonlight Bar we shall tell him we have a double-booking and bump him to the other hotel in this town.'

'Terrific.' Parand smiles. 'This is what he deserves. Do you know he had eight complimentary gin and tonics today? Of course, he will not be pleased to be bumped to the Happy Yak. This is not a five-star or even a four-star hotel but has no stars at all.'

'Perhaps that will make him appreciate the service he has

received here,' I say. 'Next, the unfortunate couple with the stained sheets. Presumably he is carrying out some kind of sado-masochistic activity.'

'Yes.' Scarlett licks her lips. 'She was so ashamed she was looking at the floor.'

'I think we need to make an example of him,' I say. 'We will offer him a complimentary massage in the Chrysalis Wellness Zone. But instead of our ultra-slim four-handed Balinese ladies we will deploy Igor, our maximum-muscle ultra-Swedish massage specialist. We will instruct Igor to give our abusive sheet-soiler the bone-crushing dislocation massage designed to enhance the double-jointed qualities of our country's improbably supple oil wrestlers. The sheet-soiler will think twice next time he considers hurting a woman.'

'What about his partner?' Scarlett says.

'Arrange for her a complimentary aromatherapy massage in the adjacent suite,' I say. 'She will enjoy hearing his screams of pain.'

'That leaves the customers from the Sunset and Moonrise Bars,' Parand says.

'I have a plan for them,' I say. 'First of all, I am shocked to hear that the elegant women in the large party are being harassed. This must stop at once.'

'But who is harassing them?' Scarlett says.

'The only possible candidate is the young man in the Sunset Bar,' I say. 'I believe he is the trouble-maker. I suggest we offer him complimentary use of the *Baykal Banya*. But when he exits onto the Eagle's Nest frigidarium he will find that the door has no outer handle; and that he is stuck on a bare rock shelf two hundred metres above the valley floor with only a towel and an ice-filled plunge-pool for company. That will cool his ardour.'

'Perhaps we should ask our diamond-merchant friends to re-open the Koh-i-Noor Boutique until midnight,' Scarlett says. 'The ladies said they wanted diamonds. We should do what they ask.'

I look at Scarlett. She is a talented and capable girl and I am pleased she is coming up with a constructive idea of this kind.

'Yes,' I say. 'Open up the Koh-i-Noor. They can do some good business.'

'The only sensible man in the hotel is the handsome gentleman in the pin-stripe suit,' Scarlett says. 'His complaints about the atmosphere in the Sunset and Moonrise Bars seem right on target. I wonder if he could be a mystery shopper?'

'For someone sent anonymously by our hotel chain to check on our standards, he seemed rather rude,' I say.

'I do not like him.' Parand touches the corner of her mouth with one finger. 'He is creepy.'

'Not every man is a creep,' Scarlett says. 'I think he has been sent by Houston to check up on us. I will give him an upgrade.'

She smiles. Parand does not. I frown but do not intervene. I must trust my staff.

'That leaves the old man with the white hair,' Parand says. 'The mother of the girl said he tried to pay money to buy her daughter as a kind of arranged bride. That kind of behaviour is disgusting. It is inappropriate to our values and our brand.'

'It is,' I say. 'I think a massage with Igor is too good for him. Perhaps we should suggest the Moonlight Serenade.'

Scarlett and Parand look at me. Neither speaks.

'Do you think that I am being too severe?' I say.

'Ms Tatiana.' Parand's face is grave. 'The Moonlight Serenade is recommended only for experienced mountain walkers. The path may be icy. The cliffs at the top of the mountain are more than three hundred metres high. The moon is new – barely a sliver – and the night is dark. Reinhold, our Austrian guide, is away this week. If a visitor were to go without the correct equipment and guidance, he could suffer a fatal accident – even if he were younger than our guest.'

I look from Parand to Scarlett, who gives a little shrug. What would Ms N do? Is our woman-trafficking sex-beast any better than Eli or Mr Kagit, who Ms N put out of harm's way when she was fixing the first hotel in which she herself became a General

Manager, with the help of me and my white blouse? Is he any better than Buddy Knox, her rival for the position of General Manager at the UP-branded boutique hotel in London, who visited a night-club called "Gents" but was not really a gentleman at all? Or what about Mr Burke, who refused to leave our hotel and was so rude to the other guests when we were two rooms short? Ms N made sure he was never rude to anyone again.

Surely a man who is seeking to buy a woman under the roof of the Caravanserai UP deserves a similar fate?

Ms N would not let him go unpunished. Of that I am sure.

'Leave him to me,' I say. 'I will make sure he sees the entire route of the Moonlight Serenade. Even if the new moon is unfortunately not very bright.'

I LOVE TATIANA. For many years, I have watched her develop from an inexperienced waitress, fresh from the steppes of her spectacular but corruption-plagued country, to taking up her first position as a General Manager in our world-class but male-dominated hotel chain.

It gives me pleasure to see her succeed.

I believe she can reach the peak of our profession.

But Tatiana is not perfect. I know from my own experience that even the best hotel General Manager can make a mistake. Sometimes, a small mistake can lead to a larger one. Sometimes, a large mistake can lead to a tragedy.

This is why, when I see Tatiana, Scarlett and Parand leave the office and stride off in different directions, I sense that it would not be wise for me to continue drinking the improbably strong UP-Tail Mai Tai which barkeeper Amanda has mixed for me in the Moonrise Bar, however responsibly sourced and environmentally sustainable the three types of rum it contains may be. Instead, I decide to follow them.

As a hotel General Manager, I am accustomed to walking

silently and to using the service stairs to arrive unobserved at any part of a hotel. But I am alone; and without knowing what Tatiana has planned, it takes me a little while to track the three colleagues down.

First, I follow Scarlett. When I peer around the corner of one of the tunnel corridors I see that she is talking to the D-Lister in the pin-stripe suit and not, so far as I can see, doing anything abnormal. I listen for a moment to what she is saying.

It is not what I have expected.

Quietly, I turn back the way I have come; and see Parand, her back straight and her comportment demure, heading towards the Chrysalis Wellness Zone.

I observe Parand explaining to the Wellness Zone manager the treatments to be given to the stained-sheet man and the stained-sheet woman when they arrive for their complimentary massages.

What I hear makes my joints ache and my toes curl and I feel sorry for the stained-sheet man.

I wait until Parand has left, and then have a word with the Wellness Zone manager. She is surprised at my instructions at first, but when I explain that Tatiana has asked me to help solve the problems of the Caravanserai UP, the manager says she understands what is required and it will be her pleasure to ensure that the stained-sheet man gets the treatment he deserves in the Chrysalis Wellness Zone.

Having heard the treatment planned for the stained-sheet man and what Scarlett was saying to the D-lister, I am beginning to reach conclusions about the problems afflicting the Caravanserai UP.

Perhaps, after all, I can help clean up the ecology of this hotel.

From the Chrysalis Wellness Zone, I therefore run up the stairs to the Reception area. Between the blinds of the office behind the Reception desk I have a good view of Scarlett arriving, accompanied by the square-jawed D-Lister. She takes a magnetic card from a drawer below the computer terminal; swipes it; then enters her four-digit access code on the screen. So far as I can see this card is the only thing in the hotel with no environmental features whatsoever. I see her give a new room-card and a thick brown envelope to the D-Lister, who smiles with his big lips and shakes his oversized watch down on his wrist before heading down the corridor.

I must act quickly.

I am relieved, therefore, when Scarlett, apparently also possessed by a sense of urgency, returns her magnetic card to the drawer, logs off and hurries away.

Like Tatiana, I started my work in hotels at the bottom of the food chain, first cleaning rooms and restocking fridges and later working my way up to front officer manager.

Thus it is that it takes me less than ninety seconds, using Scarlett's card and code, to identify the transactions she has entered on the hotel's property management system; and to enter some instructions of my own. I also make a phone call to one of the guests to pass on some good news.

When I speak to the guest, I suggest there are good reasons why he might want to stay in the Bar and enjoy another complimentary cocktail. In fact, I recommend the pleasantly powerful UP-Tail Mai Tai.

While I have access to the hotel network, I send a couple of e-mails; and check one or two other bookings and reservations.

What I see fills me with foreboding. I may have even less time than I thought. Moreover, I have reached the limits of what I can do at a computer terminal.

I put Scarlett's magnetic card in my pocket; and set off for the *Baykal Banya*.

The staff in the Chrysalis Wellness Centre are pleased to see me again. From the massage suites, I hear the sounds I have been expecting. But I head in a different direction, towards the ladies' changing rooms. Once there, I strip; wrap myself in an unbleached long-cotton Egyptian towel of reassuringly Ultra Platinum size and sumptuousness; and walk into the inferno.

I know well the countries of the Former Soviet Union. I have no fear of the baking temperatures of the Russian version of the sauna. The designers at the Caravanserai UP have done a fine job: the rough stone walls and curved yet tightly-fitting wooden doors create an ambience which blends perfectly the medieval origins of the *Banya* with the Ultra-Platinum sophistication of the world's best hotel chain.

But the *Baykal Banya* is empty. The only sign of life is a towel, as voluminous and soft as my own, discarded on the floor near the door.

I pick the towel up. It is damp, and carries the pleasing scent of a clean man's sweat.

Where is that clean man?

I look around and see a heavy door. It carries an elegant piece of signage depicting a white raptor soaring over a glacier.

The Eagle's Nest frigidarium.

I swing the door open.

The young man I saw earlier wearing black jeans and chatting to the women in the Sunset Bar is huddled naked against the rock wall in the far corner of the terrace, trying to shelter from the wind. I notice for the first time that he is a good-looking boy; and that, despite the cold, his nakedness has much to recommend it. I step onto the terrace to pull him back into the warmth. Instead of rising to greet me, he howls out:

'No!'

I turn to see why he is shouting. The heavy door through which I have stepped has swung shut behind me. There is no handle on the outside.

But I am a hotelier. I do not trust doors, particularly onto freezing outside balconies. I have left the man's discarded towel on the floor to prevent the door from closing behind me.

'Come,' I say. 'Am I right in thinking that you are an artist? And that you have made a good friend tonight?'

The boy looks up at me and nods mutely. When I reach out to help him to his feet, his grip is icy.

Together we re-enter the *Banya*. I shut the door, and hand him his towel. When we have dressed, I borrow a service trolley from one of the maids' rooms; and we take a zig-zag route towards the Koh-i-Noor, which is packed with women examining diamonds. After a short exchange, I leave him there – perhaps the happiest, as well as the luckiest, man alive.

The two balding diamond merchants are not so happy; but they do not stay long.

In fact, I am confident that they will not be visiting the Caravanserai UP again.

I long to stay and watch the young man do his business; but there is no time for this. Instead, I run up what a chalk-board proclaims to be a low-energy, eco-friendly, muscle-toning, fat-burner staircase – in fact, it is simply a staircase – which leads to the Moonlight Serenade.

I have taken the precaution of fetching my black padded jacket and woollen hat before I approach the Moonlight Serenade. But when I open the door, the wind robs me of my breath.

Many high mountains of the world have via ferrata trails. The Hua Shan plank walk of China is legendary. The via ferrata of the Punta Penia in the Italian Dolomites requires crampons and ice-axes. But the Moonlight Serenade of the Caravanserai UP, circling the smooth rock dome atop the mountain that houses the hotel, eclipses all of them.

A single strand of high-tensile steel and a narrow, ice-crusted ledge run like a tonsure around the dome at precisely the point where the rock face steepens to five degrees from the vertical. Poised over the drop to the relic-covered plain beneath and encircled by snow-capped peaks, the adventurous hotel guest may use this miracle of engineering to use his or her complimentary head-cam to take home a stomach-churning day- or night-time vertigo-video.

The Caravanserai UP highlights the ecological soundness of the night excursion by proclaiming it to be "powered only by moonlight".

The first thing I see is the signing-in book, perched in a windproof Perspex box on a steel shelf beneath a light. Our guest, who has given his title as "Ambassador", has signed the standard waiver absolving the hotel of all responsibility in undertaking a potentially dangerous activity. Tatiana has countersigned.

'Tatiana!' My voice is lost in the wind.

'Tatiana! It is not what you think!'

Below me, shallow steps cut into the stone lead to a corrugated steel platform which marks the start of the via ferrata.

The steps are thick with snow and ice.

Did I mention that I do not like heights?

But Tatiana's future is at stake.

Tatiana is my friend.

I shrug on a safety harness and examine it in the moonlight. I study the Y-shaped lanyard, equipped at each end with a D-shaped carabiner. I begin to descend the stairs. As I do so I sense something approaching up the slope and feel a brace of bats hurtle past my face in the moonlight, close enough to touch.

If there is one thing I fear more than heights, it is bats.

'Tatiana!'

Silence.

For a moment, I wonder whether it would be acceptable, or even honourable, for me to return to the warmth of the hotel and enjoy another of Amanda's confusion-inducing UP-Tail Mai Tais in the Moonrise Bar.

Then I snap one of the carabiners onto the cable of the via ferrata.

Tatiana needs my help.

I set off around the smooth, nearly vertical curve of the rock dome, gripping the freezing high-tensile cable with my bare hands.

I try to jam my feet into the narrow, icy ledge, chipped into the rock face in such a way that you can – if you have a good sense of balance – place your weight upon it as you walk.

Below, the rock wall drops into blackness. But I do not

attempt to look anywhere but straight ahead.

I know what Tatiana has planned.

Wherever the cable of the *via ferrata* meets one of the steel bolts which anchors it to the rock-face, the guest must clip the second carabiner onto the cable on the far side of the support. He or she can then safely detach the first carabiner, and proceed.

Easy, if you don't look down.

Easy, if you haven't forgotten your gloves.

Easy, if you aren't afraid of heights.

But it is not only Tatiana's future which is at stake. So, too, is the life of an innocent man.

My fingers are numb. The black trainers I hastily fetched from my hotel room give me a precarious foothold on the ice-free patches of the rock ledge. As I near the halfway point, the moon goes behind a cloud and I am plunged into darkness.

'Tatiana!'

'Ms N – is it you?'

'Do not harm that man!'

'What? I am letting him go now.'

'Do NOT harm that man!'

The rock face has become vertical. Beneath my feet I can feel that in place of the stone ledge, a narrow wooden plank has been set against the cliff to provide a foothold. Blackness surrounds me.

The sliver of moon emerges from behind the cloud.

Below, the great rock dome into which the Caravanserai UP has been burrowed drops away towards the luminescent darkness of the plain. Another bat shoots up the cliff, brushing through my hair.

Tatiana and her guest are ten metres ahead of me.

The diplomat type is slumped against the rock. His arms are splayed, but the stone is as smooth as glass. His eyes are closed. His mouth hangs open.

Tatiana stands close to him. She is gripping the metal D of one of his carabiners in her gloved hand. The lanyard connecting it to his safety harness is all that is preventing him from tumbling into the night. His second carabiner dangles into the void.

She has only to release her grip and he will fall.

Tatiana turns her face towards me. The wind gusts through her blonde hair. 'Do not harm him? Ms N – I never believed I would hear you say these words of a man like this.'

'Tatiana. You are making a mistake. All is not what it seems.'

She shakes her head. I can see her trembling under the man's weight. 'I want to make my hotel better.'

'Tatiana – do you trust me?'

In the darkness, I see her lips move. But I hear no sound. Suddenly, a bat looms out of the night, *heading for my face*. I flinch. A chunk of ice on the wooden plank breaks loose and spins out of sight. My foot slips on the frozen wood. I fall back into the night – and the lanyard catches my weight.

I am breathless.

I am alive, hanging from the cable.

Above, I see the sliver of moon, cold and bright.

Slowly, my frozen fingers stiff against the high-tensile steel, I haul myself back onto the ledge.

'Tatiana!' My voice is faint. 'I said: do you trust me?'

Again, her lips move. This time her words are louder. 'Always, Ms N.'

'Snap him back onto the cable.'

For a moment, she does nothing. Then, in the darkness, her hand moves.

Departure

IF I AM honest, I am ashamed. I am remembering how Ms N had to overcome her fear of heights even to go down a steep flight of steps to enter a so-called gentleman's club, or to climb onto a stage to receive an award.

Now, I have forced her to walk at night around the Moonlight Serenade *via ferrata* in order to save me from myself.

She may also have saved the Caravanserai UP.

'Tell me,' I say, 'where did I go wrong?'

Ms N takes a sip of the Massimo san Giulio signature XO organic Cognac-infused Jersey-cream-drizzle-topped low-carbon Spirit of the Forest Chocolate Libation, which she has selected using the C-UP app on her tablet, and gazes into the darkness beyond the window. The Moonrise Bar is fuller than I have seen it for months; but where we sit, away from the bar, I feel a pool of calm.

'Is there anything else you would like, madam?' Parand has appeared silently at our table. I wave her away with a smile.

Of course, Parand is taking good care of us. I have promoted her to Guest Services Manager.

This was previously Scarlett's position.

'You have done nothing wrong, Tatiana,' Ms N says. 'The hotel is beautiful. Standards are good. But you had a bad member of staff. She has led you in the wrong direction. I have been partly at fault, too.'

'That is impossible, Ms N.'

'The problem began with the Koh-i-Noor. I am guessing that this so-called diamond outlet was suggested by your former employee, Scarlett.'

'She did propose it.' I feel foolish saying this, now. 'She argued that it would help attract the type of elite guests we seek.'

'Of course, the two bald gentlemen were friends of hers and were giving her a cut. The second problem was the statuettes in the corridors. They are beautiful, and fit the concept of the hotel. I expect that they were your idea.'

'They were. But Scarlett offered to set up a sales and incentive system.'

'Naturally she did. Scarlett was making money on commission from the Koh-i-Noor diamonds. She realised could make even more by selling statues. Her salary from the hotel became like pocket-money for her. She began to believe the Caravanserai UP existed to enrich her, rather than the other way around. This can be a problem in any hotel.'

'You are thinking of Mr Eli, the Materials Manager at the shitbox hotel in C——,' I say.

Ms N smiles her mischievous smile. 'Scarlett, too, began to believe she could do as she pleased. She neglected her duties as Guest Services Manager and developed inappropriate relationships with the guests. She devoted her efforts to earning commission. She ripped off the artist. No wonder your revenues declined and guest satisfaction fell, as it were, off a cliff.'

I stare at Ms N. 'But why did it all go wrong tonight?'

'That is my fault,' Ms N says. 'I suspected that Scarlett was a problem when I arrived. *Ask for Scarlett,* she said. I underestimated her. I should have spoken to you at once. But I thought I should stay silent and gather further evidence.

'Scarlett was a dangerous adversary. When I jumped to my feet in the lobby and over-tipped her, she recognised she was in danger of exposure. Her response was brilliant. She devised a plot to destroy you; and, quite possibly, me as well.'

'But how could she control the guests?'

'Her genius was to integrate their behaviour into her plan. First, she brought her lover, the D-Lister, into the hotel to stir up trouble. You will recall it was he who first complained to us about the behaviour of the guests in both the Sunset and the Moonrise Bars. Even though another guest said that in his view, the atmosphere was rather on the quiet side.'

'The fat man?' I look across to where he is sitting next to Professor Ahmed. Neither of them is speaking. Both are watching other people in the bar. Both seem content in one another's company. 'But how could we take seriously anything he said?'

Ms N smiles. 'Because his physiology is irrelevant; and because he is the mystery shopper sent by our headquarters in Houston to test our quality standards. A mystery shopper will always behave in a way that tempts staff to treat him or her badly. Parand fell into the trap.'

'Is she part of this?'

'No. But she was susceptible to Scarlett's narrative that everything going wrong was the fault of the guests. Many hotel staff are inclined to believe this. Parand began to treat the guests less well than she should have done.'

'You gave the fat man an upgrade?'

'Obese, Tatiana, obese. Yes. I had observed Scarlett give her lover, the D-lister, an upgrade. I cancelled the D-lister's reservation – which I saw was complimentary – and called our somewhat overweight colleague to tell him that he, in turn, had been upgraded. I also suggested that he might like to return to the Moonrise Bar to observe the evening's events.' She sweeps her hand around the packed lounge. 'I believe he will leave here persuaded that the hotel is well run.'

'So did the D-lister leave?'

'He had no choice: he no longer had a room at the hotel. When the staff prepared the D-lister's room for our mystery shopper and evicted his luggage, I asked them to look out for an envelope of cash I had seen Scarlett give him. This was her thousands of dollars of illicit takings from the sale of statues. We have returned the money to the artist. I also used my access to the hotel network to cancel Scarlett's access and, via our Houston head office, her employment. I am sorry not to have consulted you but I felt we needed her off the premises immediately.'

'You sent her out into the cold? With her lover? But it is minus 20 degrees.'

'Tatiana. Do not worry. I gave them each fifty dollars in cash and made a reservation at the Happy Yak.'

'If the D-lister was trying to stir things up, what was really happening between the young man and the group of women in the Sunset Bar?'

'I suspected as soon as I saw them that this was a hen party from the United Kingdom. They are wonderful for the hotel's bottom line. They love to eat and drink. They pack out the Wellness Centre and beauty salon. They have fun. Only two things can go wrong.

'First, they can be diverted to spend their money elsewhere. Scarlett hoped to ensure they spent as much as possible in the Koh-i-Noor, earning her commission and cutting the hotel's income. Second, every hen party is an oestrogen-packed time-bomb of lust, desire and the jealousies which can accompany this.

'It was no fault of our young artist friend that he happened to have come to the hotel to talk to you about the missing commission on his statues. Nor was it his fault that he happened to be good-looking and the only young single man amongst the guests; or that he started talking to one of the most attractive women in the hen party. That drove others in the group mad with jealousy, stirring up a complaint.

'Scarlett knew you would tend to blame the man in any dispute. She wanted to get rid of the artist because he had realised she was ripping him off. She set you up to arrange for the poor fellow to be unjustly punished in the Eagle's Nest. He might have frozen to death if I had not reached him in time.'

'And then you closed the Koh-i-Noor.'

'Correct. The young artist and I collected all his sculptures on our way from the *Banya* to the diamond shop. Once I had kicked out the proprietors – Scarlett's friends – and closed the shop, the artist offered to sell the sculptures, in person, to the women in the hen-party. They were delighted to oblige – in fact they competed to out-bid each other in order to catch his eye. It was a win-win: they could interact with the best-looking man in the hotel; he sold his sculptures for high prices without commission; and we end up with more revenue because the women can't buy diamonds. They are all in the bar now.' Ms N points to the other side of the bar, where a dozen women are sitting in a ring around the happy-looking young artist.

By now I am feeling like the sadistic man's blonde girlfriend; ashamed, and wanting to look at the floor. But I have to ask.

'What did you do about the sheet-soiler?'

Ms N smiles. 'The orange-sheet man and woman? That was easy. Didn't you see her shoulders? I could see that she had used too much of an artificial tanning product to try and make herself attractive to her boyfriend. Not that she need have worried; he was crazy about her anyhow. The first time they made love in the hotel bedroom, their sweat and the energy of their exertions caused her fake tan to come off all over the sheets. She didn't want to admit to him what had happened. Result: he came and complained at Reception. No wonder she was staring at the floor.'

'But Igor – '

'I got to our maximum-muscle ultra-Swedish massage specialist before Igor got to him. I allocated the gentleman two Balinese girls instead. Our stained-sheet couple both had the best massage of their lives – I could hear them sighing with pleasure when I went down to the *Banya* later.'

'So that leaves – the ambassador.' My voice cracks again. 'Oh, Ms N, I was going to let him fall!'

'That was understandable, Tatiana.' Ms N is smiling. 'We have all seen these threesomes in our hotel lounges and restaurants. A foreign man; a beautiful young local woman; a fixer, sometimes a man, often a woman, who translates and makes an agreement between them. At first I, too, thought that the diplomatic type was the guilty party.'

'The D-lister – he talked about slave-trading in the Moonrise Bar.'

'Correct. That was part of Scarlett's plan to persuade you that the ambassador had done something awful, so you would seek to harm him. But Tatiana, she was trying to force you to make a mistake. Have you ever heard of a body being found in one of the hotels where I have worked?'

I think of a sweet and sour pork dish. 'No, Ms N.'

'Your chosen method would have left a corpse at the foot of the mountain. At best, the resulting inquiry would have seen you lose your position as General Manager of this hotel. You could even have found yourself with a murder charge, if Scarlett had testified against you. In any case, her position in the hotel would have been strengthened, and she would have been free to continue making money from her diamonds and statuettes.'

'But how did you know the man was innocent?'

'Partly, it was his face. I saw a victim, not a criminal. Second, you should never make assumptions about who has power in these relationships.

'When the woman in the blue Chanel suit came to the Reception, I saw that the younger woman had been crying. The older man looked upset, too. The complaint from the D-lister about a slave market struck me as too convenient. I listened to what the woman in the blue suit had to say in Russian to her young friend. She no doubt thought no-one would hear or understand her in the turmoil of the Reception area.

'She said: *The contact commission he is offering is too little. We can double it.* The young woman replied: *But he is caring; and gentle. I like him.* The older woman replied: *I make the decisions around here.*

'The exploitative person in the trio,' Ms N says, 'was the woman in the Chanel suit. The man might be pathetic, or stupid; but he never planned to harm anyone. The girl was the real victim.'

I look across the bar to where the diplomat and the young woman are enjoying their third cocktail of the night. Both look radiantly happy. Six cocktails between the two of them will have increased the turnover in the Moonrise Bar by nearly two hundred dollars. The woman in the blue suit is nowhere to be seen.

'Tatiana.' Ms N is suddenly serious. 'I am glad I could help. Your hotel is a gem. Would you permit me to stay awhile before I return to head office? Today, I glimpsed a beautiful emerald-green gecko, whose values I admired, considering his options. I should like to escape the corporate world for a day or two, and do the same.'

'Ms N. Please stay as long as you want. And thank you for

solving my problem.'

'It is often difficult to identify a problem you see every day. Fresh eyes can help. Scarlett made it easy for me by making three errors the minute I entered the hotel.'

'The biggest mistake Scarlett made was to underestimate you, Ms N.'

'No, Tatiana. Her biggest mistake was to underestimate you. You had a problem. It is solved.'

'How can I thank you?'

'Well, you could start by booking me into the Chrysalis Wellness Centre. I want to look my best tomorrow evening.' Ms N smiles, takes a sip of her chocolate drink, and looks around the bar. Is it my imagination, or does her gaze rest for a few moments on the handsome young artist she has seen naked at the Eagle's Nest?

Ms N is good at solving problems. One day, I would like to be like her.

AUTHOR'S NOTE: THE Hua Shan plank walk of China and the via ferrata of the Punta Penia really exist. Try Googling them.

7. THE THREE HEADS

'Tatiana, my sugar plum. You are looking beautiful today.'

'Thank you. But – '

'I mean it, buttercup. I never forget how lucky I am to have you.'

'Pablo. I am grateful.' When I gaze into Pablo's warm brown eyes and see his soft lips smiling at me, I find it hard to think straight. 'But we need to talk about your plans to promote the hotel. Our Caravanserai Ultra Platinum is in trouble.'

'Our hotel promotes itself, turtle-dove. It is the coolest, most luxurious and most ecological destination on earth, and the only hotel located entirely within a hollow mountain.' He gestures around the Sunset Bar, with its outrageously exclusive Ron Arad stainless steel sofas and its panoramic views of the sun-drenched, relic-covered plain far below.

'The Caravanserai UP may be cool, luxurious and ecological. But do you see any guests? We are losing a quarter of a million dollars a month.' I tap the rock wall, hand-hewn using local labour and authentic bronze-age-style stonemasons' chisels, as if I am perhaps thinking that the secret to boosting our profitability might lie in some form of redecoration.

Pablo laughs, showing his regular white teeth. He smooths back his crinkly hair and takes a gulp of the bog-water-fed, floor-malted, oak-mashed, peat-kiln powered, quadruple-distilled, treble-oaked, 25-year-old Isle of Staffa "New Moon Harvest" single-malt ultra-Scotch, for which paying guests must cough up one hundred and seventy-five dollars a glass.

'I know, honeybun, I know,' he says. 'Everyone else has to fork out six hundred bucks a night to stay here. You and I pay nothing to sit in the same chairs, with the same view, and market-test the same drink. And you, my angel, are the motor that drives this whole Rolls Royce arrangement. That is one more reason I adore you.'

When I hear Pablo saying such sweet things about me I want to throw myself into his arms and smother him in kisses. But we are both on duty in the hotel and surrounded by staff and, in theory, customers. So I sit up straight, extinguish all traces of my famous 1,000-watt smile and shake my head.

If I am honest, I am trying to model the kind of power pose I have seen my former boss, the legendary hotel manager Ms N, adopt when she is projecting authority.

In secret, I am worried that Ms N could project more authority than I am doing even if she was standing on her head dressed in a clown outfit, but since she is not in the hotel, or even in the country, I do not think anyone will try to compare us.

'This hotel will not be a Rolls Royce machine for long without customers,' I say. 'It will be more like a bicycle with square wheels. And barbed-wire handlebars. And a saddle filled with starving tiger ants. I think this will not be a comfortable kind of transport.'

'No.' Pablo grimaces.

'Since I appointed you Head of Sales and Marketing, we have spent more than thirty thousand dollars on digital promotions. Yet the Caravanserai Ultra Platinum is emptier than it was before.'

'Princess.' Pablo places his hand on my knee and squeezes. I know I should not enjoy this because it means my efforts to project authority have failed. But the touch of his hand is wonderful. 'I told you before – we need to reach critical mass. To do this, I need help. An assistant. With ingenuity and application.'

'I know. You want to recruit the voluptuous Scarlett from our competitor hotel the Happy Yak, who you think has plenty of these attributes, as well as other attributes which I do not wish to discuss.'

'I know she behaved badly last time she worked at this hotel.'

'Behaved badly? She tried to murder two of our guests to get me fired. The Happy Yak may be delighted to give her a job since I threw her out that night. I never will. If you want to kick-start your campaign, you must think of something else.'

Pablo gazes at me mournfully with his brown eyes. 'Do you doubt me, love muffin? If you want me to leave, you have only to say.'

'No!' I cannot stop myself. 'I need you! But I also need profits!'

Pablo turns and gazes out at the plain. When he turns back, his beautiful face wears an expression I have not seen before: quizzical, yet challenging.

'Digital campaigns take time, sweet peach. You must understand this. I have a big idea. A gigantic idea, in fact. But I can only do it if you trust me.'

His words hurt, but I try to keep my voice steady. 'Of course I trust you.'

'It will involve a small investment.'

'I know you have to invest money to make money. What is your idea?'

'I want to bring a celebrity to the hotel. I have made contact with the social media team of DaGurl.'

'DaGurl? The music and fashion and glamour icon? What does she know about hotels?'

'She knows nothing about anything. What matters, honey-bun, is that she is the most famous social media celebrity on earth. She has one hundred million Twitter followers and one hundred million on Instagram. She has more glamour than the Kardashians and higher credibility ratings than The Pope. Hundreds of journalists report every time she farts.'

'I may not know much about social media, but I cannot see how DaGurl farting will help fill beds in my hotel.'

Pablo laughs as if I have made a joke. 'Of course I do not mean they are literally writing about her farting. But when she visits our hotel's Chrysalis Wellness Zone for an unforgettable complimentary massage by our ultra-slim eight-handed Balinese ladies and tweets this out – '

'Complimentary?' I am pleased that Pablo is talking about "our" hotel, but I do not wish to tell him this. 'How much will this cost?'

'My treasure. We will not pay DaGurl one cent to visit our hotel. Usually, she charges one hundred thousand dollars a day for her services. But she is coming for free because I have persuaded her marketing manager that we can offer her an unforgettable experience and a unique opportunity.'

'You are suggesting she should enjoy two nights in our Ultra Platinum Jade Emperor Suite including Via Ferrata access? For free?'

'The point, my cherub – ' Pablo's voice has risen a fraction ' – is not the Jade Emperor Suite. The point is that when she floats in the gold-ionized water of the Cavern Eco-Pool, two hundred million people will share her bliss. When she visits the Alexandria Library and our wild-haired Professor Ahmet shows her our collection of Aramaic parchments, two hundred million people will long to view them too. When the moon is full and DaGurl braves the Moonlight Serenade on our supremely vertiginous Via Ferrata, and when our elegantly-muscled, tastefully tattooed and ultra-reliable Austrian mountain guide Reinhold checks the safety bindings around her famous chest and thighs, the bookings will come flooding in! I have checked, by the way, that the moon will be full and Reinhold is available.'

Pablo orders another whisky. 'In any case, since the Jade Emperor Suite is not occupied, the additional expenditure will be minimal. The only costs will be complimentary food and beverages.' He pauses. 'And the air fares.'

'How much is her air fare?'

'Her PR team were insisting on first class, but I beat them down to business. I think they did not realise that on the three separate and perhaps not entirely modern or safe airlines they will fly to reach this remotest, wildest and ruggedest corner of your beautiful homeland, there is no first class or, in any meaningful sense, business.'

'We are paying her fare. How much?'

'Six thousand dollars.'

'That is not so bad.'

'Six thousand per person. She will be accompanied by her publicist, her manager, her social media technician and her curator.'

'Another thirty thousand dollars. Did you say her curator? I know my English is not too good, but – '

'My pumpkin's English is perfect. The only thing the most beautiful and brilliant hotel manager in the world, who happens to be my beloved, is lacking is maybe very occasionally – trust. Even in those you love.' Pablo bites his lower lip. 'Perhaps you are right. I should cancel this project. But at least let me explain the curator. Because, you see, I have not been fair to you.'

Pablo leans forward, his brown eyes sparkling. 'Do you remember I said I planned to lure DaGurl and her team down here without charging us a fee, by offering them a unique opportunity? I am sorry: I have not explained this properly. Tatiana, will you let me explain? Even though I have let you down?'

If I am honest, Pablo's speech has confused me. Have I let him down by not trusting him? I do not want this, because he is a dear, kind and also handsome man who I love. Or is he saying he has let me down? If so, how?

'Of course I trust you, Pablo. What is this opportunity DaGurl's publicity team are excited about?'

'It is an opportunity to display her heads. She has three.'

'She has three heads? No wonder she has two hundred

million followers.'

'They are the most famous heads in the world. An Austrian artist called Messerschmidt created fifty-six of them in the 1770s. Forty-nine still exist. DaGurl owns three of these heads, which are called The Hanged Man, The Yawner, and The Vexed Man. The Hanged Man is maybe the best known of all the Messerschmidt heads. *And she wants to bring them with her to the Caravanserai UP!*

Pablo is looking so happy, so triumphant, that I want to share his joy. Instead, I am frowning. 'That is wonderful, Pablo. But how will these Messerschmidt heads fill our rooms?'

'It is a full house strategy,' Pablo says. 'DaGurl, and her social media, will attract the young and adventurous. The heads will attract the sophisticated, intellectually bold and, perhaps, less young. The unveiling by DaGurl of the Three Heads in the coolest, the most luxurious and the most ecological hotel on earth will be the social media event of the year. Together, this will fill our hotel to bursting point. Do you not see?' Suddenly Pablo's face crumples. 'My lamb-chop does not see anything, does she? You no longer love me, or trust me. Forget the campaign. I am leaving the hotel. Perhaps they can give me a job at the Happy Yak, with Scarlett.'

'Pablo! No!' Suddenly, although we are sitting in the Sunset Bar and this is inappropriate, I am in his arms. His embrace is strong; his smell is rich and warm. 'I am sorry,' I say. 'Of course I trust you. Please go ahead with the promotion. If even one half of one percent of DaGurl's followers visit the hotel, we will be full for months. We are already losing a quarter of a million dollars a month. Why not invest an extra thirty thousand?'

Pablo's eyes have filled with tears. But when I say I love him, his mouth twitches into an almost-smile. 'My poppet! Are you sure? We go ahead?'

'Yes. I am sure.' I am smiling inside because again he has said "we". When I see him look so happy I want to kiss him, although I decide to wait until later for this.

But when I say I am sure, I am lying. I am not sure that DaGurl and however many heads she has will help the hotel as much as Pablo says. But how can I say this to him, who loves me so much, and who I love so much in return? How can I risk him leaving me?

For a long moment, I lie close, feeling his strong arms around me and smelling his beautiful smell. Whatever else I am unsure of, I know this must be right.

THE PROMOTIONAL WORK of DaGurl begins well. I am thrilled when I see her Facebook post from a white-sand beach in the Maldives that she is planning a break at the famous Caravanserai UP, the coolest, the most luxurious and the most ecological hotel on earth, located in the remotest, wildest and ruggedest corner of our beautiful but still economically backward country – even though this means that she must travel on three separate and perhaps not entirely modern or safe airlines to get here.

In fact, DaGurl makes the journey to our hotel sound like a life-threatening but fun adventure. I am not sure she realises how true this is, except for the "fun" part.

Her post has been re-tweeted twelve thousand times.

When DaGurl posts on Instagram a picture of one of our celebrity chef Massimo san Giulio's culinary creations themed on food-based artworks – in this case a lobster painting by Willem Kalf – and when Pablo points out that this picture has twenty-six thousand "likes", I find myself trembling with excitement.

I am even happier when DaGurl tweets to her followers that our Alexandria Library, with its code of silence, high-backed leather armchairs, oak shelving, Aramaic scriptures, stone wish-holders and deaf and mute wild-haired librarian, Professor Ahmet, is maybe the best location to chillax on the entire planet.

Pablo shows me that our Caravanserai UP Facebook page has doubled its "fans" from two thousand to four thousand since

DaGurl has started her work. I am so happy that I throw my arms around his neck and kiss him.

'Pablo! Thank you!'

'Thank you for trusting me, snuggle-bun. It is working. We will have two thousand more fans tomorrow. And DaGurl is not even here yet.'

'I am even looking forward now to seeing her Three Heads.'

'Everybody in the world wants to see DaGurl's Three Heads. We will live-stream their unveiling in the Creativity Club, and her social media technician will send pictures to her sixty million Instagram followers.'

'This is wonderful. But I thought she had one hundred million Instagram followers? And one hundred million more on Twitter?'

'Sixty million, one hundred million, it is all the same, my little pussycat.' Pablo taps the screen of his iPad. 'Everyone knows editorial content is worth four times more than paid advertising. The Caravanserai UP is making marketing history.'

I am so pleased about our marketing success that I decide to discuss progress with our Director of Finance, Parand. She has been telling me for months that we need more guests, so I am looking forward to showing her our new Facebook fans.

On my way to see Parand I run up our high-tech, low-energy, fat-burning staircase to the rock dome which marks the summit of the mountain inside which our hotel has been carved, to see if the Via Ferrata is busy.

I am thinking that the type of young person who is following DaGurl on Twitter or Instagram or Facebook and is admiring her travelling to this remotest, wildest and ruggedest corner of our beautiful but still economically backward country on three separate and perhaps not entirely modern or safe airlines will be exactly the kind of customer who want to clip herself or himself to the stainless steel safety rail under the guidance of our elegantly-muscled, tastefully tattooed and ultra-reliable Austrian mountain guide Reinhold. Such young, tech-savvy and well-heeled guests will be thrilled to feel their hearts rise into their mouths and their stomachs perform a double somersault as they teeter in the cool air on the narrow ledge which circles the mountain three hundred metres above the sun-drenched, relic-covered plain below. In fact, the Caravanserai UP Via Ferrata makes the legendary Hua Shan plank walk of China feel like a walk in the park.

Maybe the most adventurous of these new guests will even be tempted to attempt the Via Ferrata after dark, in our legendary Moonlight Serenade.

I burst through the doors at the top of the fat-burning staircase and see Reinhold suspended from the safety rail at the lip of the mountain. He has removed his shirt in the bright spring sunshine and I am thinking that if DaGurl could tweet out a picture of his elegantly-muscled, tastefully tattooed and I suspect ultra-reliable upper body poised over the sun-drenched, relic-covered plain below, every woman and perhaps every gay man on earth would be flocking to book rooms at the Caravanserai UP double-quick.

But Reinhold is alone. In fact, his eyes are closed, as if perhaps he is enjoying a quick combined snoozing and tanning session in his perilous position. I can see no sign of any guests, young or old, accompanying him on the Via Ferrata. Nor is a single guest enjoying our Pop-Up Apres-Scare bar which I have set up to maximise revenue from the Via Ferrata in the summer months.

It seems that until DaGurl gets here, the only guests who are likely to be lured into trying our Via Ferrata by the sight of Reinhold's elegantly-muscled, tastefully tattooed and ultra-reliable upper body are those who may happen to see him after climbing the fat-burning staircase to get a bit of exercise.

That will not save my hotel.

I leave Reinhold to his relaxation, descend the staircase – contributing to the environment as I do so – and head for the Alexandria Library.

I see the shock of wild grey hair poking up from behind a high-backed leather armchair before I see the rest of Professor Ahmet. He is leaning forward over a fragment of parchment preserved in a flexible silicone skin on a hypoallergenic, beeswax-buffed, sherry-cask-recycled, solid oak study station, the polished rim of his giant magnifying glass gleaming in the glow of the greenhouse-gas-neutral, yak-dung-powered, low-wattage lighting. A stone wish-holder at his side contains a yellow card bearing the slogan "*Pleased to help you! Write your request here or use the C-UP app!*"

I look around the library. I see no customers whatsoever.

I settle down next to the Professor on a chair upholstered in locally-sourced, hand-woven, soya-fed, individually-groomed silkworm strands, and begin typing on one of our specially commissioned ergonomic, hydro-damped silent keyboards.

'Quiet today.' As I type, the words appear on Professor Ahmet's screen. 'Any bookings later for your *Exclusive Mysteries of the Dead Sea Scrolls* silent lecture?'

The Professor's hands glide across his keyboard. 'To quote the Two Ronnies, *none whatsoever*,' he types. 'The place is deader than a turbot in butter sauce. The mysteries seem likely to remain exclusive for a while longer.'

'We are deploying a full-house strategy to attract to the hotel a wave of young and adventurous travellers, plus the sophisticated and intellectually bold,' I type. 'DaGurl has tweeted that your library is the best place to chillax on the planet.'

The Professor's forehead creases. 'An elderly gentleman was chillaxing in here last night,' he writes. 'I ejected him as his snoring might have disturbed the other guests, had any been present. I do not approve of chillaxing in the Alexandra Library.'

I leave the Professor to ponder his parchments.

At the Chrysalis Wellness Zone, dappled green lights spell out the words "Zen Secrets of the Billion-year-old Mountain" on the raw rock wall over the reception. Lamai, our chief therapist, spreads her full, red lips into a radiant smile of welcome.

'May I help you with a massage or a spa treatment, madam?'

'Do you have any vacancies, Lamai?'

I am trying to keep my face neutral as I ask this question. But the fullness of the dispenser offering our home-made, sugar-free, room-temperature, local-mountain-berry-based weight-loss-accelerator lemonade; the emptiness of the electronically-shielded, eco-damped waiting area; and the pristine state of the ethically-sourced hand-woven cushion covers on the sofas all tell their own story.

Lamai rolls her lower lip between her teeth and raises her perfect eyebrows. 'Yes madam. We have vacancies.'

I gaze at the reception area; and at Lamai, whose lips are now fuller and redder than ever. Could any hotel have a more welcoming Wellness Zone than this? What Reinhold is for half the world, Lamai surely is for the remainder. So why is the Caravanserai UP so empty?

'Make sure that DaGurl tweets out a picture of you when she visits,' I say to Lamai. 'And do that thing with your lips before she takes the photo.'

The story is the same in the Baykal Banya, where the Eagle's Nest Frigidarium is bare of flesh of any kind. In the Creativity Club, a mouth-watering cornucopia of complimentary snacks and beverages stands waiting for guests in a stimulating audio-visual environment which, unfortunately, not a single customer is present to enjoy. In neither the Moonrise Bar nor the Sunset Bar is a single chilled-out hedonist present to have their breath taken away by the spectacular views of the relic-covered plain, or their senses softened by the mind-numbingly high-alcohol UP-Tail cocktails which our bargirl Amanda has turned into an art-form.

Where is everybody?

It is as if Pablo's social media campaign with DaGurl, which has received thousands of responses, and which I have seen with my own eyes has turbo-charged our hotel's on-line presence, has achieved – nothing at all.

Parand sees me enter her office in the back of house. She rises to her feet, her grace and poise an oasis of comfort in the bleak wilderness of emptiness which my hotel has become.

'Tatiana,' she says. 'What is wrong?'

I can see that she is itching to make some guesses about what has upset me. But she remains silent. What might those wrong guesses be?

I tell her about our beautiful, guest-free hotel; and about Pablo; and about DaGurl.

Parand says nothing, but gazes at me with her dark eyes. Then she turns to her computer.

'You are right that the hotel is devoid of bookings,' she says. 'We have sixteen per cent occupancy. We have budgeted for seventy-five per cent. Our average rate per room tonight is two hundred and twelve dollars, when we have budgeted for seven hundred and four. This is killing us.'

'But we have the coolest, the most luxurious and the most ecological hotel on earth. DaGurl is writing on her Facebook page that the Alexandria Library is a perfect place to chillax. Our Facebook followers have doubled in a day. It is impossible for the Caravanserai UP to have only sixteen per cent occupancy.'

Parand looks at her screen. Again, I sense that she is deciding what to tell me. 'Publicity takes time,' she says at last, 'and social media is unpredictable. Look at this.' She swings round her screen so I can see it. 'The biggest new on-line site for hotel rankings is Supadiggs. It is especially popular with alternative travellers, adventure-seekers and trend-setters.'

'This is our target group,' I say.

'Yes. But on the Supadiggs ranking site, the scores of our hotel are below average. In fact, they are diabolical.'

Parand clicks again and I see an unfamiliar logo. 'But this site is not in our business plan,' I say. 'The Caravanserai UP has no target for it. I did not even know it existed. Why did you not tell me?'

'I should have thought there were other people in the hotel, perhaps including some so-called social media experts, who could have told you about Supadiggs before me.'

She clicks again and I am looking at a screen full of reviews of my beloved hotel, the Caravanserai UP.

The first hotel of which I have ever been General Manager. The hotel of which I am proudest in all the world.

It is as if these customers have been staying in a different hotel altogether.

The newest reviewer has given my beloved Caravanserai UP one star out of five. This is the minimum possible. The review is titled: *Computer Stolen* and explains how the guest had a laptop disappear from a public area in the hotel but could not interest any member of staff in this problem.

'Why did reception not inform security?' I say. 'Why did no-one tell me?'

The next review is headed: *Flea-bitten. Literally. Unbelievable.* This visitor says that she was offered a hypoallergenic locally-sourced hand-combed mohair blanket on an evening visit to the Apres-Scare bar. Within one hour her shoulders, neck, waist and legs were bitten sixty-six times by what she says were fleas. She has even posted a video. It shows the torso and lower body of a woman as she turns to display her front and her back. She is wearing only a tiny and rather pretty black undergarment. In fact, from the back, the undergarment is more or less invisible. The pale skin of her thighs, breasts, buttocks and lower waist is punctuated by dozens of angry red spots. Her face is hidden.

'She has a beautiful body,' I say, 'except for the flea-bites. It is so beautiful that I am even wondering if perhaps she is someone famous.'

'Yes,' Parand says. 'Maybe it is because her figure is exceptional that more than three million people have clicked on this review. Despite the flea bites, which I do not think are flattering.'

'Three million people think our hotel has fleas? How is this possible? We have no fleas at the Caravanserai UP.'

But when I look at the video of the nearly naked woman, I can understand why many people are wanting to click on it.

I scan other reviews. Titles range from the lewd: "*Hand froze painfully to iron railing at Eagle's Nest Frigidarium. Lucky it was only my hand!"*; to the revolting: *"Brown stains on sheets – dirty feet or worse?"* Several involve thefts: *"Gold necklace vanished while I ate breakfast"*, or *"Do not trust room safe"*.

In fact, more than half the customers who have visited the Caravanserai UP in the past three months and have posted reviews on the Supadiggs web-site have hated my precious, lovely hotel.

As an experiment, I click on the Supadiggs entry for The Happy Yak, our no-star competitor in the village nearby. It has rather few reviews, perhaps because The Happy Yak has rather few rooms, or guests. But most are positive. The most recent guest has described it as *"the epitome of cheap as chips"* and given it three stars.

My Caravanserai Ultra Platinum is being beaten in customer rankings by The Happy Yak. My hotel is empty, except – people believe – for fleas. I can see only blackness.

I shake my head. 'Where is Pablo?'

'Madam. Do you think Pablo can help?'

I want him to hold me in his strong arms, I think. But I say: 'he is my digital media guru. He will know what to do.'

'Maybe you need a different kind of help,' Parand says.

'You mean – Ms N? But – ' I try to think why I do not want to call for help from my friend; my mentor; and perhaps the most brilliant hotelier in the entire world. 'She is so busy.'

Parand says nothing.

'Someday I want to be like Ms N. But how can this happen if I keep asking her to solve my problems?'

Parand smiles. Then she flicks her computer screen so that the pages of negative Supadiggs reviews scroll down, screen after screen after screen. 'I think,' she says, 'that Ms N is good at solving problems. You should call her.'

THE NEXT MORNING DaGurl arrives at the Caravanserai UP. We have of course provided two limousines from the airport to transport DaGurl and her publicist and her manager and her social media technician and her curator, as well as a van to transport their luggage, which comes to a total of thirty-three pieces.

I am wondering whether the transportation of these thirty-three pieces of luggage is included in the thirty thousand dollars we are paying to bring DaGurl here, but Pablo tells me not to worry.

'She is DaGurl!' he says. 'She is travelling here on three separate but perhaps not entirely modern or safe airlines! Already her story of this journey is not only viral, it is...' he hesitates, then beams. 'It is contagious! Infectious! Out of control! Her luggage includes the Three Heads! Soon the Caravanserai UP will be not only the coolest, the most luxurious and the most ecological hotel on the planet, but also the most famous.'

As Pablo is saying this he puts his arm around me for a second and gives me a big squeeze, which although it is inappropriate makes me feel so wonderful that I am wondering if Parand is right to say that our hotel has problems Pablo cannot fix. In fact, when I feel Pablo's arm squeezing me I feel sure that he, DaGurl and the Three Heads are about to solve all our problems forever.

When I step forward at the front door to welcome DaGurl from her, or actually my, limousine, I am surprised. Instead of the most famous music and fashion and glamour icon on earth, I see a short girl in jeans and a black leather jacket whose face is looking as if she is perhaps the most fed-up person on the planet.

'Is this it?' she says. 'Thank God.'

'Welcome to our hotel,' I say, stepping forward. 'Good choice. I am the General Manager, Tatiana.'

DaGurl turns to me and reaches out her tiny hand. She stands up tall on her high heels and pushes back her shoulders so that her petite bosom rises to meet me. Her pink lips, which I now see have a subtle hint of make-up, part in a smile. When she shakes her head, her long, dark hair cascades across her shoulders as if she is perhaps exiting an exclusive hairdresser rather than completing a sixteen-hour journey on three separate and perhaps not entirely modern or safe airlines.

'Tatiana – may I call you Tatiana? Thank you so much for inviting me to your fabulous hotel! I can't wait to see the Alexandria Library and the Moonlight Serenade!' She presses my hand and I see flashes going off around us. 'And you must be Pablo – I hear you're *so* brilliant!'

DaGurl embraces Pablo, who is standing next to me. She presses her cheek against his and turns her face towards the cameras, which flash again. In fact, DaGurl holds this pose so long I feel a pang of jealousy and find myself thinking that if Pablo is so brilliant, perhaps he should have alerted me to the problems on the Supadiggs website before Parand. But when DaGurl enters the shady arbour which is the lobby of the Caravanserai UP and settles down on an unbleached natural-woven kapok-stuffed sofa for a complimentary foot-wash and massage, I begin to relax. As my best Balinese masseuse soaks DaGurl's feet with precisely-room-temperature water from a pitcher crafted by local artisans from billion-year-old clays, and I see more cameras flashing, and I hear DaGurl sighing and saying this is the best hotel she has ever visited, I forget my stupid jealousy and begin to think that DaGurl is 100% right to say that Pablo is *so* brilliant and that the problems of the Caravanserai Ultra Platinum will soon be over.

After DaGurl's feet have been soaked and pampered and massaged and encased in complimentary locally-sourced hand-woven mohair moccasins, I accompany DaGurl and a fleet of photographers and camera crews to the Jade Emperor Suite, which she declares is the most divine hotel room she has ever seen.

Things are going well.

I leave DaGurl to settle in. Pablo goes to help her curator, a stocky man named Yuri who dresses entirely in black and who is setting up the Three Heads in the Creativity Club. Pablo says this will take time, because the installation includes podiums, lighting, a banner promoting the Caravanserai UP and a complex hoist system to make the unveiling of the Three Heads as dramatic an event as possible.

If I am honest I am looking forward to seeing the Three Heads even more than I am looking forward to DaGurl's social media campaign, although I do not tell her this. But during the afternoon I am pleased by the professionalism of DaGurl as she enjoys the facilities of our wonderful hotel.

When DaGurl displays her tanned body in a minuscule bikini beneath the stalactite-studded void of the cavern at the heart of the mountain next to the gold-ionized waters of the Cavern Eco-Pool, I see that the Instagram video receives two hundred thousand "likes" in less than five minutes. The Twitter picture of her clutching the smallest size of our improbably fluffy, Egyptian cotton, acid-free Caravanserai UP-branded towels around herself on the terrace of our Eagle's Nest Frigidarium as she gazes out across the sun-drenched, relic-covered plain below is retweeted and liked half a million times.

In fact, when I am looking at DaGurl and then at the picture on DaGurl's Twitter feed, I am even wondering if perhaps DaGurl's publicist or her social media technician is making use of some digital enhancement to make those parts of DaGurl's anatomy which are protruding at the top and bottom of the towel a little more curvaceous than they actually are.

But when a video of the wild-haired Professor Ahmet showing DaGurl his most ancient Aramaic parchment in the Alexandria Library, together with a #CaravanseraiUP hashtag, is retweeted over a million times, I decide I do not care if her team are digitally enhancing her attributes. DaGurl's thirty items of baggage seem to contain an almost limitless selection of outfits. The image of her wearing big, black-framed reading glasses and a black tailored jacket next to the wild-haired Professor is, if you ask me, even sexier than the pictures taken in the Eco-Pool or the Frigidarium.

'That is correct, my angel,' Pablo says. 'Her media team are creating a series of interventions which will climax in the unveiling of the Three Heads in the Creativity Club at six p.m. By that stage, each new post will receive between one and two million interactions; and every news outlet in Europe, America and the Far East will find the time-window in which the unveiling takes place perfect either for their evening, morning or mid-day news bulletins and digital media summaries.' He pulls out his phone. 'Our Facebook page has gone from four thousand to twenty-six thousand fans in the six hours since DaGurl arrived at our front door. This is more than any other hotel in our chain, even the new Ultra Platinum-branded super-deluxe London Heart of Mayfair Experience where your old friend Ms N is now General Manager. In fact, we have three times more Facebook fans than her.'

If I am honest, I do not like the way in which Pablo is talking about Ms N, who I know is ten times as great a hotelier as I will ever be no matter how many fans our Facebook page may have. For a moment, I wonder whether I should tell Pablo to button his mouth and that I have asked Ms N for any ideas on what the hell is wrong with my hotel and why our guests are all moaning on the Supadiggs website. But I do not tell Pablo this because he is always telling me that I am wonderful and that I do not need help from anyone except, perhaps, Pablo himself; and I know I should be grateful to him for bringing to our hotel the social media phenomenon which is DaGurl and her Three Heads.

Before the grand unveiling in the Creativity Club, I visit Parand in her office.

'You see,' I say, 'the visit of DaGurl is a triumph. We have the largest number of Facebook fans of any hotel in our chain.'

'Yes.' Parand does not seem excited by this news. 'But it seems that these fans are not yet visiting us. We have not had a single new booking today.'

'How is this possible, when we have more than twenty thousand new Facebook fans?'

'I do not know. Nor do I know how it is possible, when we have only sixteen percent occupancy, for someone to write another bad review on Supadiggs.' She points to her screen. 'Another customer complaining about a theft. This time they have lost an item of luggage.'

I read the post, which is titled: *"Crooked hotel – avoid."* 'Anyone would think we were having a crime wave. But I am not aware of a single complaint.'

'No. I have checked with security, who say they have no record of any thefts in the past three months. Of course, not every guest will complain to the management. They may not even realise they have lost something until they return home. But to find so many complaints, and so few good reviews, is unusual.'

'It seems these people have had genuinely bad experiences,' I say. 'For example, it is true that we offer hypoallergenic locally-sourced hand-combed mohair blankets to our evening visitors to the Apres-Scare bar, particularly if they are soaked in the sweat of fear following a night walk on the Moonlight Serenade. But these blankets have never seen or even heard of a flea.'

Parand nods. 'Did your friend Ms N have any ideas?'

'No. I think she must be busy, or perhaps the time difference means she will reply later.' I do not say how disappointed, and indeed astonished, I am that Ms N has not replied, because usually she is fantastically organised and has always taken time to help me. But perhaps she is dealing with a crisis in her own hotel. 'Maybe the climax of our social media campaign, when we unveil the Three Heads, will unblock the bookings.'

'Yes,' Parand says. 'Maybe it will.'

NORMALLY, I AM thinking that I am a calm kind of person. Of course I did not enjoy it when Ms N asked me to balance in a steel construction cage when I was wearing my white blouse in the country of C —. I was nervous when I had to negotiate with some handsome Scottish gentlemen who might or might not have been wearing britches in the first hotel where Ms N and I worked together. I was anxious when Ms N suggested that we visit a so-called Gentleman's Club in Florida. But on none of these occasions was I so anxious as I am now, as I wait to see whether the unveiling of the Three Heads will save my beloved Caravanserai.

What would Ms N be doing now? In fact, what is she doing now? I check my e-mails. Messenger. Whatsapp. Facebook. SMS. Twitter direct messages. Could I have missed something?

It seems that it will be up to me to solve this problem on my own.

Or maybe it is up to me and the Three Heads.

I arrive in the Creativity Club at 17.45. DaGurl's publicist and manager and social media technician are at the front of the room, by the row of three plinths shrouded in a black cloth hung from the ceiling.

At least a dozen TV cameras and journalists are in the room, along with nearly all the guests we are having in the hotel. I am impressed that Pablo, or perhaps DaGurl's team, have managed to assemble so many media people, since this remotest, wildest and ruggedest corner of our beautiful but still economically backward country is not exactly full of TV stations or social media gurus. Maybe it is true that the media reports each time DaGurl farts, and the thirty thousand dollars is a good investment after all.

I am wondering also whether the hotel guests are here to see the Three Heads, or whether they have come to enjoy the complimentary food-based artwork which our executive chef Massimo san Giulio has created – in this case an array of pies, pastries, sausages and pheasant based on Pieter Breughel the Elder's *"Land of Cockaigne"*. At first I am not sure that a painting about gluttony and sloth is a suitable subject for the banqueting room of a luxury hotel. But on reflection, and seeing how guests are tucking into the buffet, I think that Giulio understands his business perfectly.

Looking around, I am pleased to see that our elegantly-muscled, tastefully tattooed and ultra-reliable Austrian mountain guide Reinhold is present. Our bargirl Amanda is here, together with our red-lipped wellness therapist Lamai who, because we are cutting staff to stem our losses during the hotel's occupancy crisis, has volunteered to help out as a waitress. Amanda has mixed several tall earthenware pitchers of a newly-created, mind-numbingly high-alcohol UP-Tail cocktail which she has called the Three Heads, served in our exclusive Ultra Platinum branded hand-blown English crystal balloon glasses and containing three different brands of gin, three of vodka, three of rum, and certain other ingredients which I am not at liberty to reveal. Amanda is guaranteeing that after one drink everyone will see three heads, and after two drinks they will feel as if they themselves have three. Lamai's task is to ensure that everyone present drinks as many cocktails as possible.

Our guests seem to enjoy the Three Heads UP-Tail cocktails, which like everything else in the Creativity Club are complimentary, and I hear much good-natured banter about how many heads everyone is seeing or feeling.

'Hello, gorgeous.' Pablo is standing at the side of the room with a glass of whisky and a plate loaded with food. 'DaGurl's team have done us proud, I believe. Our Facebook page now has fifty thousand fans. DaGurl's last Tweet, promising to appear with Three Heads from the #CaravanseraiUP at 1800 local, has been re-tweeted seven million times. The unveiling will be carried on over two hundred live-streaming services. Our Caravanserai is about to become the most famous hotel on the planet.'

'It is also the emptiest hotel on the planet.'

'Lambkin! Don't be miserable. These things take time.' Pablo frowns. 'I find it disappointing that you are so negative, when we are on the verge of such a huge success. Do you doubt my strategy? Or is it me?'

'No, Pablo! I love you. I would never doubt you. It is only – I will be worried until the hotel is profitable again.'

Pablo gives me a quick squeeze, which although it is inappropriate I do not mind because his arms are so strong and because the cameras are focused on the three shrouded plinths. 'Tootsie-pie,' Pablo says, 'half an hour from now, I guarantee you that the Caravanserai UP will be world-famous. Look – here comes DaGurl.'

DaGurl enters the room to a background beat of the chorus to her latest hit, *"Look at me I'm DaGurl"*. She is wearing the black-framed reading glasses and black jacket from the Alexandria Library with an ultra-short skirt and ultra-high heels, an outfit which I am thinking makes her look both serious and sexy, as if she is seeking to appeal to all types of potential customer. She dances through the door with so much energy that for a moment I am forgetting my empty rooms and am admiring the power she is putting into promoting the hotel. She moves in front of the shrouded plinths and the music dies down.

'Watch this,' Pablo says.

DaGurl's curator, Yuri, is crouched over a mixing console at the side of the room. I see him move some controls as a musical fanfare bursts out and spotlights illuminate a display showing the name, logo and website of my very own Caravanserai UP, directly behind the plinths. The display is so beautiful and perfectly positioned that I reach out and squeeze Pablo's hand.

When I am doing this I am feeling guilty, because he is right that I have sometimes doubted him and the wisdom of his campaign. But when I see how he has arranged the Three Heads and the display to ensure maximum publicity for us, I want to kiss him.

DaGurl steps forward. Her spectacles gleam in the spotlights. 'Ladies and gentlemen,' she says. 'I wish to present, from my personal collection of world-famous artworks, my three Messerschmidt heads. Here, exclusive and live from the Caravanserai UP, the coolest and most ecological as well as the most luxurious hotel on earth, I give you: The Vexed Man. The Yawner. And The Hanged Man.'

At the side of the room, Yuri the curator is hard at work on his console. A count-down starts: *"Ten. Nine. Eight…"*

Everyone in the room is leaning forward, watching and holding up phones to film as DaGurl seizes hold of the rope which will lift the black cloth from the world-famous Messerschmidt heads.

"*Six. Five. Four.*"

The sense of anticipation in the room is immense, although if I am honest I am not sure if this is caused by the imminent unveiling of the Three Heads, or by the effect of Amanda's mind-numbingly high-alcohol UP-Tail Three Heads cocktail, which she and Lamai are sloshing into balloon glasses from the mighty earthenware pitchers. Even our wild-haired librarian, Professor Ahmet, is watching from the shadows. I can barely resist squeaking with excitement. If only Ms N were here to witness this moment of triumph!

"*Three. Two. One. Zero.*"

DaGurl pulls down on the rope. A further fanfare blasts out. The black cloth is whisked into the air. The three plinths are exposed. On the first, the shining white bust of a man with his face screwed up as if he has smelled something awful. This, I know, is "The Vexed Man". On the next plinth I see the dramatic silver bust of a man who, if I am honest, looks as if he is screaming rather than yawning. On the third plinth –

I stare.

The third plinth is empty.

Around me I hear a gasp of surprise from the onlookers.

The silence is broken by a hotel guest, who has perhaps had more than one mind-numbingly high-alcohol UP-Tail Three Heads cocktail, who says in a clear, high voice: '*I want my money back. I can still only see two heads.*'

He is drowned out by a sound from the front of the room.

DaGurl, who is standing in front of the empty plinth, has opened her delicately made-up mouth further than I should have thought possible, and is screaming – a long, high, almost beautiful cry of loss. Every camera, every phone in the room is turned towards her. The scream seems to go on for ever.

At last DaGurl stops screaming and waves her arm towards the empty plinth. 'The Hanged Man. The most valuable Messerschmidt head of all. It has been stolen!'

I stare at the empty plinth, and think of the allegations of theft on the Supadiggs website. Then I see DaGurl slowly sink to the floor, tears running down her beautiful cheeks, in the centre of a circle of cameras filming everything and transmitting it live around the entire world. In the darkness on the edge of the room, something moves and I turn my despairing gaze towards it.

Ms N is standing there. Her face has an inquisitive expression with a hint of mischief, as if she is figuring out how to solve some problem.

FOR A MOMENT, silence fills the room, except for the clicking of electronic camera shutters. Then everyone starts shouting. DaGurl's curator Yuri steps forward, raises his arms, and yells that no-one should leave the room. Pablo walks over to where DaGurl is crouching on the floor with her arms wrapped around her body and helps her to rise to her feet, holding her by her shoulders in a way which, although I know that Pablo is only trying to comfort our guest of honour, again arouses in me an unworthy pang of jealousy. DaGurl's manager is shouting something into his telephone. Two young women with microphones and camera crews are approaching DaGurl.

Ms N is doing nothing. I look at her and raise my hands helplessly.

Ms N raises her eyebrows. *This is your hotel,* she is saying. *But I am here if you need me.*

I step forward. 'Wait,' I say. 'I am the General Manager of the hotel and I wish to say – ' what do I wish to say? I remember an incident at the first hotel in which I worked, involving an elevator full of blood ' – that I wish to sort this out quickly and fairly, before the police get here.'

DaGurl's curator frowns and shakes his head. DaGurl herself is wiping her eyes with a tissue Pablo has given her. Reinhold, our elegantly-muscled and ultra-reliable Austrian mountain guide, has moved to the doorway and is standing there like a glacier, to prevent anyone leaving.

I realise that he is not following my instructions – I have not given any – but those of Yuri, DaGurl's curator.

Yuri himself comes over and stands so close to me I can smell his minty breath. 'I hope you have a good lawyer,' he says. 'Those heads are insured for one hundred and fifty million bucks each. I hear you have had a spate of thefts at this hotel.'

I stare at him. *He knows about Supadiggs.* How is that possible?

DaGurl has started to give an interview. She is standing in front of the empty plinth and the illuminated panel advertising my hotel. TV crews cluster around her.

Pablo was right. The Caravanserai UP is about to become the most famous hotel on earth.

It will become famous as the theft-plagued hotel where DaGurl's $150m artwork was stolen live in front of one of the biggest audiences ever assembled on social media, TV or anywhere else.

Is this the end of me, my hotel, and my career?

Or can I turn this around somehow?

Something looms up in front of me. It is Ms N. She kisses me on each cheek and gives me a hug.

'Tatiana. How are you?' she says. 'I am sorry I could not get here sooner. When I received your email, I set off at once; but of course I had to travel on three separate and perhaps not entirely modern or safe airlines to get here. I do not wish to butt in, but – '

'Oh, Ms N!' I say. Of course I use Ms N's given name, but I have removed it here because Ms N is a modest person who does not like me to publicise her fabulous qualities. 'Please help me! Everything is going wrong.'

Ms N nods slowly and looks around the room. She examines the bank of guests filming proceedings on their mobile phones; DaGurl, giving her interview; DaGurl's manager, still shouting into his telephone; the empty plinth; and DaGurl's curator Yuri, who is staring at the plinth as if perhaps he is thinking that The Hanged Man might suddenly reappear.

'On the contrary,' Ms N says, 'most things are going right. You are GM of the coolest, most luxurious and most eco-friendly hotel in the world, for which DaGurl has just secured you some awesome publicity. After this, every art lover, conspiracy theorist, social media freak and journalist on the planet will want to come and stay in your hotel, quite apart from DaGurl's millions of fans. I predict a tsunami of bookings. But first, we must find out what has happened to The Hanged Man.'

'He is stolen.' I think of the accusation by DaGurl's curator. 'We have had a series of thefts.'

'Well, let us start there,' Ms N says. She picks up two empty glasses from the buffet and taps them gently together. The room falls silent.

But the first person to speak is not Ms N.

'So... who the hell are you?'

To my surprise it is DaGurl herself who is asking this question. Although she is using language which is not appropriate for a five-star hotel, she is speaking in a friendly way and I realise that DaGurl more than anyone is conscious that every word we are saying is being transmitted to a global audience by over two hundred live-streaming channels.

'Thank you for your question,' Ms N says. 'And you are correct to ask what gives me the right to investigate this matter. My status, if indeed I have any, is that I am an old friend of Tatiana, the rather wonderful General Manager of this hotel. Tatiana has asked me to help her sort out a rather curious digital problem, which has caused the hotel difficulties. But I suspect the root of the problem is not digital at all. It is probably, like nearly all other problems, caused by people.'

'Yes,' I say. 'I have asked her for help.'

Ms N smiles as if this is exactly the support she has been waiting for. 'Perhaps,' she says, 'although people are at the root of all this, the digital issues to which Tatiana has referred may offer us some clues as to who is responsible. It seems to me that we should examine four things more closely. First of all, Yuri.' She turns to DaGurl's curator. 'Both you and Tatiana have mentioned a spate of thefts at this hotel. I can understand that the hotel's General Manager might know about such a problem. But where did you learn about it?'

'I saw the thefts on the Supadiggs website,' Yuri says. 'Before we came out here. I took a look at the hotel.'

'Thank you. And let me guess. The hotel itself has no record of the thefts which the Supadiggs website records as taking place.'

'No,' I say. 'But it may be that the customers chose not to raise them with the hotel.'

'Is that typical? That a customer loses something in a hotel but does not mention it to the management?' Ms N is wearing her inquisitive expression for the cameras, as if she has no idea of what the answer to her question might be, although her hint of a smile tells me that she knows full well.

'No,' I say. 'Usually it is the other way around. Customers raise with us every little thing they believe has been stolen. We then help them to find the item down the back of the sofa, under the bed, in a zip pocket of their suitcase or in their husband's jacket pocket.'

'But in this case, by contrast, we have numerous hotel reviews mentioning thefts, but no complaints from customers,' Ms N says. 'An improbable combination.' She turns to the room. 'Have any of the guests here suffered any thefts during their stay, leaving aside the missing head?'

All around the room, people are murmuring "no," and shaking their heads. I am thinking that this sample is not necessarily significant, since we have only sixteen per cent occupancy and almost no guests are staying in the hotel. But the fact that the room is crowded with journalists, camera crews, DaGurl's team and numerous hotel staff as well as a sprinkling of guests makes the number of people responding to Ms N's question seem larger than it is. I sense that already people are beginning to be impressed by her line of argument; and that the idea that the hotel is plagued by crime is losing traction.

Ms N turns to Pablo. 'Second, let us examine the other digital aspect of the case. Congratulations on your social media campaign. I understand you have increased the Facebook fans of the Caravanserai UP from two thousand to fifty thousand in forty-eight hours by enrolling the help of DaGurl.'

Pablo seems to grow a few centimetres taller and I cannot help but feel proud of him. 'That is correct,' he says, glancing down at his phone. 'In fact, since the unveiling ceremony began at 1800, our Facebook fans have increased to over one hundred thousand. All messages on our Twitter and Instagram feeds are going viral. This has to be one of the most successful social media campaigns of all time. A textbook campaign. But the theft of The Hanged Man has ruined everything.'

'It is, indeed, a textbook case,' Ms N says. 'The question is, which textbook? Tell me, Tatiana. What has been the impact of the campaign so far on the occupancy of your hotel?'

I glance at Parand, who shrugs. Why is Ms N raising the delicate question of occupancy? 'So far, the campaign has brought us no extra bookings,' I say. 'But maybe it is only a matter of time.'

'Yes,' Ms N says. 'Again, I believe it may be constructive to examine whether that outcome is typical.' She turns to DaGurl. 'Do you often run campaigns which do not achieve their objectives? More downloads, more merchandise, more franchising, more column inches, whatever your target is?'

'Since you mention it, no.' DaGurl is still smiling as if she wants to be friends with Ms N. 'Usually, we are fortunate in that everything we touch turns to gold, social-media-wise. But then, we only got cracking with this campaign today.'

'Your social media skills do indeed seem remarkable,' Ms N says. 'But it is the connection between your digital genius and the third, curious, analogue aspect of this case which has me most puzzled. This analogue angle is the Three Heads themselves. It seems to me that you could have promoted the Caravanserai UP quite satisfactorily by coming here without any additional heads at all. It is your presence and personality, rather than your art collection, that drives your fans into a frenzy. I am guessing that these heads do not feature in most of your promotional activities. Did you take them to the Maldives, for instance?'

'No.' DaGurl says. 'This is the first time we have shown the heads on a promotional visit. But I thought it was a neat idea to bring them here. To show three sculptures in a hotel carved in the heart of a remote mountain – how cool is that?'

'It is indeed an idea almost as cool as this hotel's famous Eagle's Nest Frigidarium at midnight on New Year's Eve,' Ms N says. 'An unforgettable experience, by the way, for anyone contemplating an early reservation at the Caravanserai UP.' Ms N glances at me. 'Now, let us consider my fourth question about this case. This is: can it be a coincidence that, at the same time as a social media site carries uncorroborated reports of numerous thefts at a previously safe luxury hotel, a priceless artefact – the so-called Hanged Man – is brought here, and is promptly half-inched – stolen?'

'Now you put it like that, it does seem kind of weird.' DaGurl has been paying close attention throughout. She leans in towards Ms N as though she is frightened of missing a single word.

'Oh,' Parand says, looking at her telephone. 'We have a new booking.'

Ms N blinks at Parand and smiles faintly, as if she has been expecting this. 'I agree that if it is a coincidence, it is a strange one,' she continues. 'And congratulations on the booking. But before I draw conclusions, let us consider the Three Heads themselves. I have read that the names by which the heads are now known were added only when they were first exhibited, ten years after Messerschmidt's death. In fact, "The Yawner" is not yawning, but screaming. "The Vexed Man" is not vexed, but undergoing electrical shock treatment. And "The Hanged Man" is not hanged at all, but is tied around his body by ropes.

It turns out that the figures depicted by Messerschmidt were inspired by the patients of Dr Mesmer, the celebrated German physician who would tie his mentally ill subjects by cords to a magnetised tub in the belief that their ailments could be cured by influencing magnetic forces within their bodies affected by the planets – the so-called theory of animal magnetism.'

Ms N looks around her. Every face is baffled except for that of Professor Ahmet, who has been watching the voice recognition software on his tablet and now holds it up displaying the word: *"Correct"*.

Ms N smiles and turns to Pablo. 'Animal magnetism is perhaps a subject on which we have other experts in the room. I mention it because the heads, and Mesmer's theories, are a reminder that countless people over the years have believed in things which no rational analysis could justify. Such as today's belief in the magical power of social media. In this case, the most important question is: who first conceived of the idea of bringing the Three Heads to the Caravanserai UP? Was it you, Pablo?'

Pablo's face has turned white. He takes a step back. 'Yes. I mean, no. It seemed such a brilliant idea. Yuri supported it.'

If Pablo's face has become like chalk, Yuri's face is like pitch. 'Of course I supported this idea,' he says. 'I am the curator of the Three Heads. It is my task to ensure they are brought to the attention of the widest possible public. In this we have succeeded.' He gestures at the mass of TV cameras and phones around the room. 'But the idea came from him – ' he points at Pablo ' – and his woman.'

Suddenly everyone is looking at me. I stare at Pablo, and at Ms N. I see the red lights of the television cameras and the banks of telephones streaming my every action. How many people are watching me now?

'Hey! Another booking,' Parand says.

Ms N turns and winks at the cameras. 'Anyone watching this who wants to book a room at the Caravanserai UP had better get in fast,' she says; then turns back to me. 'But I am not sure you,

Tatiana, are the woman to whom Yuri is referring. Can anyone think of another woman connected with this affair? Perhaps with the campaign on the Supadiggs hotel review website?'

'Another booking came in. And another. OK. I'll shut up now.' Parand approaches me and whispers in my ear. 'I just raised our rate to five hundred dollars. Excuse me if I go to the reception. We need to make the most of this.'

I am pleased, as well as confused, to hear Parand say that suddenly our hotel is receiving the tidal wave of bookings which Ms N has earlier predicted. But I am trying to think of the answer to Ms N's question, which has reminded me of something.

'I saw one review with a video which a woman had posted. She said she had experienced – a problem.' Luckily, I am thinking quickly enough not to mention the alleged sixty-six flea-bites, or the hypoallergenic locally-sourced hand-combed mohair blanket, when my words are being carried live to audiences all over the world, even if I am confident the fleas never existed. 'I thought she looked familiar.'

'I should like to see this,' Ms N says. 'It is always important to pay close attention to complaints from guests. Could you show me?'

I take out my telephone and show Ms N the video of the nearly-naked woman, whose face we cannot see, on the Supadiggs website. Of course I am taking care to make sure that the images are not visible to the cameras which are recording us, first because the video is not suitable for family viewing; and second, because I am determined not to give publicity to the flea-bite story.

But Ms N glances at the video for only a moment.

'Of course I understand that neither you nor I has ever seen this person naked, Tatiana,' she says. 'But I once had this same woman attempt to draw my attention to the spectacular and, I should say, unmistakable juxtaposition of her bosom and her waist.'

Ms N takes a deep breath and stands up a little taller, although since she is what we in the hotel business call petite, this is not tall at all. 'If I am not mistaken, the video is displaying the most spectacular features of the body of your former guest services manager, Scarlett, who you fired after the incident with the hen party, the diamond boutique, and the devastatingly handsome young artist. And I think I can state with confidence that the person who made this video and placed it on the Supadiggs site, along with dozens of other fake negative reviews of your hotel, was your own head of sales and marketing, Pablo.'

Ms N turns to Pablo, whose face is so white that I am thinking he can have no blood left in his body at all. 'Would you like to tell us where you have hidden The Hanged Man, Pablo? Or shall I call the police and let them find it? Before you answer, I should remind you that the police in this beautiful but still economically not fully developed country are not yet one hundred percent reformed, accountable or cleansed of an atavistic tendency to deploy brutality, abuse and torture in the pursuit of what they consider justice.' She reaches up and gently holds his shoulder. 'There is also the small matter of putting on display at the Caravanserai UP the Three Heads together, as they belong. Otherwise the guests, and the TV viewers, and the hotel itself, will not get their money's worth.'

Every camera in the room is pointing at Pablo. For a long moment, he says nothing. Then he turns to me.

'I am sorry, precious,' he says. 'I let you down.'

'Let me down? You mean, you betrayed me, cheated me and lied to me morning, noon and night for months? Is this true?'

'Yes, cuddle-bear. I did all of those things.'

'I think you can stop the endearments, now.' I realise to my surprise that I am not sad, but angry. 'Why did you do it? I loved you. I was ready to give you everything.'

A sigh rises in the room, mainly from the lips of the women present.

'Yes. But Scarlett is persuasive. And one hundred and fifty million dollars is a lot of money.'

'Don't blame her, you idiot.' I prepare to slap him, but hold back as I remember the cameras. Then I slap him anyway. To my surprise, everyone in the room cheers. 'The only person you should be blaming is yourself. Where is the missing head?'

'Here,' Pablo says. 'She said to hide it in plain sight so we could smuggle it out in the confusion.' He points to the floor next to the buffet where Massimo san Giulio's *"Land of Cockaigne"* has become a wasteland of empty banqueting platters.

On the floor, hidden among a mass of other equipment and containers, is a squat black box bearing a sticker saying *"StreamShark"* and a strip of yellow tape on which someone has written in bold black marker *"Do not remove from Creativity Club"*.

Pablo picks up the box and hands it to me.

'I hope this helps a little bit, baby-cakes.'

'Don't call me that.' I turn to Ms N. 'Will you help me to open this?'

'Thank you, Tatiana. It would be my pleasure.'

I clear a space on the table and place the box on it. Everyone in the room crowds around, except for our elegantly-muscled and ultra-reliable Austrian mountain guide Reinhold, who is still guarding the door. Ms N and I open the latches; and the two sides of the lid fall open.

Inside, lying in profile in sculpted foam rubber, is the life-size stone head of a man. His face is screwed up; his head is bald; his nose is pointed and wrinkled; and his mouth is set in a grimace. Around his neck, apparently also carved in stone, is a tight noose of rope.

'I AM SORRY that this Scarlett person has harassed you.' Ms N sips her Dukes Vesper Martini, mixed by our bargirl Amanda to the recipe of Alessandro Palazzi at the eponymous Mayfair hotel, and gazes out of the panorama window at the moonlit wonders of the relic-covered plain far below. 'I sometimes wonder if I was wrong to book her into The Happy Yak, that night we threw her out of the hotel.'

'It was minus twenty degrees,' I say. My drink is the same as hers, in a spirit of celebration and solidarity. 'You are not a murderer.'

'No. I have never harmed anyone. But I cannot rule out that, on occasion, I have allowed people to do things which have led to them being harmed.'

'That is possible.' I am thinking of ultra-sharp Chroma knives; concrete; alligators; and an elevator full of blood.

'I think maybe we should have a word with the management of The Happy Yak and tell them that one of their employees has been posting fake hotel reviews. Perhaps they will decide that such a person is in need of new employment.'

'But how did you identify the link between Supadiggs and the planned theft of The Hanged Man?'

'The clue was in the brilliance of DaGurl,' Ms N says. 'It was clear to me that her ability to deliver results through targeted social media campaigns was extraordinary. I was certain, even before the theft of The Hanged Man, that DaGurl would fill your hotel. But the robbery and its resolution really stirred up a global media storm. So, in a way, Pablo and Scarlett did you a favour.'

'The hotel is fully booked for the next three months at an average room rate of over a thousand dollars. We will make several times what we paid DaGurl every night. No wonder this Vesper tastes so sweet.'

'By contrast, the campaign against your hotel on the Supadiggs website was amateur,' Ms N says. 'In particular, the focus on thefts, when none had been reported to the hotel management, suggested to me a potential link to an actual theft which the same people might be planning. The fatal mistake was for Scarlett herself to act as a model for the fake fleabites. I shall never forget her going off-script when she washed my feet in the hotel lobby, the first time I came here. She always was proud of her figure.'

'Why would she take that risk?'

'I guess she was seduced by the power of the Internet. Who

isn't? She will have guessed – rightly – that a sexy video would get her a lot of hits. She must have thought she was hot property when her fake flea-bites were viewed by three million people. Plus, she probably thought a story about your hotel being flea-ridden would get under your skin.'

'She was right. I was in despair.'

'Scarlett will be the one in despair, when she is ejected from the Happy Yak, or when Pablo comes to join her without a priceless artwork under his arm. I am not aware of any other hotels in which she is likely to find employment within five hundred kilometres of the Caravanserai UP.'

'She could have kept her head down. As it were.'

Ms N shakes her head. 'I hope you will forgive me if I say I admire how much your English has improved since we met in the Dionysus Bar at your first hotel. Why did you decide not to turn Pablo over the police?'

'He has suffered enough. I dumped him – after that, any punishment would seem trivial.' I smile. 'Also, he has saved my hotel – even if it was by accident.'

'I hope my references to the brutality, abuse and torture deployed by your local police forces will not cause you any difficulty with them.'

'Quite the contrary: our police are so unreformed, they will see it as a compliment.'

Ms N gazes around the Moonrise Bar. 'I wonder if Reinhold has any new tattoos. Have you checked?'

'I believe DaGurl may have checked. She has booked to stay on a few days longer in the Ultra Platinum Jade Emperor Suite at her own expense – including Via Ferrata access. Reinhold is a marvellous mountain guide. Indeed, in many ways he is mountainous himself. But he is not really my taste.'

'Perhaps, then, you should come and visit our splendid Ultra Platinum branded super-deluxe London Heart of Mayfair Experience. I have been GM there for several years. I promise to look after you if you visit. Maybe I could even introduce you to some friends.'

'Thank you. I would like to do that.'

For a moment I look at the bar, which is packed with news crews, art critics, adventure junkies and other customers, many of them apparently enjoying bog-water-fed, floor-malted, oak-mashed, peat-kiln powered, quadruple-distilled, treble-oaked, 25-year-old Isle of Staffa "New Moon Harvest" single-malt ultra-Scotch at one hundred and seventy-five dollars a pop. I think of the empty bar I was sitting in only a few days ago with Pablo, as he drank my whisky for free and called me "sugar plum" and "honeybun".

Then I think of Pablo himself, and I think: "problem solved".

I turn to Ms N and I raise my glass to hers.

Ms N is good at solving problems. One day, I want to be like her.

A message from Leigh Turner

THANK YOU FOR reading the *Hotel Stories*. I hope you enjoyed them. If you did, I would love it if you would write a short review on Amazon. Reviews are gold-dust for writers.

The disclaimer: all the *Hotel Stories* are works of fiction. None of the hotel customers, alligators, tycoons, Lovely Lassies, royalty, ice-hockey players, border guards, Prime Ministers, FBI agents or other characters who appears in the works is based on anyone I've ever met, heard of, or seen on TV. Nor, by the way, are any of the police officers, journalists, diplomats, presidents, military types, terrorists, Janissaries, secret agents, people-traffickers or diamond merchants who people my novels.

If you would like to learn more about my writing, including my Berlin thriller *Blood Summit*, my speculative comedy thriller *Eternal Life*, my Istanbul thriller *Palladium* or my diplomatic handbook *The Hitch-Hiker's Guide To Diplomacy*, see my website **rleighturner.com**.

Thanks again for reading.

Leigh Turner
London and Amsterdam, 2022

DISCUSSION QUESTIONS

1. How would you summarise *Seven Hotel Stories*?

2. In many of the stories, men are punished for bad behaviour. Are their punishments justified?

3. Would you like to stay in a hotel run by Ms N?

4. Does *Seven Hotel Stories* make you think differently about hotels?

The Characters

5. Would you rather go on holiday with Ms N or Tatiana?

6. What country do you think Ms N comes from? What inspires her to take action against men who behave badly?

7. Tatiana received a poor education in her "small village far from the historic capital of our not yet fully-reformed country". How much does this hold her back?

8. How do you picture Ms N? What about Tatiana?

9. Minor characters include Kyoko the fiery-tempered Japanese chef, Ms Sofia the President's daughter, Susan the Engineering Manager, Nigel the Security Manager, elegantly-muscled, tastefully tattooed and ultra-reliable Austrian mountain guide Reinhold and Ms Gentle, the sex worker. Which is your favourite?

The Stories

10. Which hotel story do you like most? Which story lines would you like to see more of? Please let me know!

The *Hotel Stories* universe

11. Tatiana's "beautiful but not yet economically advanced country" with its "wholly uncensored newspapers and television channels" and "100% corruption-free but perhaps not yet entirely world-class police force" is imaginary. Does it remind you of anywhere? What about the corruption-plagued country of C—, the setting for *The White Blouse*?

12. In which of the hotels in *Seven Hotel Stories* – not forgetting the Happy Yak Motel – would you most like to stay?

Printed in Great Britain
by Amazon